To Lawson,
May God always
bless your journey!

SHIFT

ALSO BY ZACK MASON

Killing Halfbreed
Shift
Chase
Turn

SHIFT

Zack Mason

Dogwood Publishing
Lawrenceville, Georgia

Published by Dogwood Publishing
Copyright © 2011 by Zack Mason

Trade Paper

ISBN: 0-9787744-1-8
ISBN-13: 978-0-9787744-1-7

E-Book

ISBN: 0-9787744-2-6
ISBN-13: 978-0-9787744-2-4

Manufactured in the United States of America.

9 8 7 6 5 4 3 2 1

First Edition: December, 2011

Cover Design by Matt Smartt

This book is dedicated to
God,
the Creator of Time and source of all good inspiration

-and-

to Jack & Barbara Mason,
without whom my writing
would never have been possible.

Like Secret Codes?

The author has been given exclusive access
to ChronoShift's website while it is under construction.

1. Go to www.Chrono-Shift.com
2. Login: 09071890
3. Click on "Notes" to see if you can solve
   the code.

PROLOGUE

It was a great day.

Mark Carpen eyed the deep, azure sky as he drove. Its bold blue hues were such as can only be seen in full summer, the kind of sky that never fails to buoy the spirit. White, billowy clouds towered endlessly above the horizon, further enriching the panorama. It promised a beautiful end to what had already been a wonderful afternoon.

He was tempted to roll the window down, to feel the wind on his face and the burn of the sun on his arm, but the air outside would be hot, and the kids were still sweaty from play.

They were on their way home from McDonald's. He'd taken Daniel and Brittany out as a special treat since Kelly would be stuck in parent-teacher conferences until at least six o'clock, and they'd had a blast.

Brittany, his toddler princess, all of three years of age, had been adorable as always, jumping around the brightly-colored playset with ice-cream running down her chin, calling for him to come and see whatever she was doing every fifteen seconds. Daniel, two years her elder, wore himself out till his hair was a dripping mop. He'd thrown himself down the curling tube that served as a slide so many times he'd probably worn a new rut in it.

Both were quiet now, settling in for the ride home, but Mark could still hear their laughter echoing in his mind as he maneuvered through suburban traffic. *You'd think they'd never been to a McDonald's before*, he smiled.

He treasured moments like these, these simple pleasures he could still give them, which were too few and far between since he'd been laid off.

Prologue

Most days, the loss of his job weighed on his mind like an elephant on a rope bridge, but every now and then, there were afternoons like this, when the unbearable pressure lifted for a while, and he savored the relief.

Nevertheless, later tonight, after all were tucked in bed, he knew the feeling of failure would return to roost like a crooked vulture, hunched on its branch, biding its time until its prey gave up and died.

A man needs to be able to provide for his family. It's deeply ingrained in his DNA. Even more so in a former Marine. As the days ticked on, one barren rotation of the earth after the next, his frustration built. He was failing at Mission One: Provide.

Kelly had to return to teaching in an effort to plug some of the gaping leaks in their financial dam. In spite of her reassurances that she didn't mind, he knew she did. Any day of the week, she'd rather be at home with the kids, and that made the pressure all that much greater.

He wasn't one to sit around twiddling his thumbs playing Mr. Mom though. He'd known other men who'd lost their jobs and been content to stay at home throughout their job search, idle on the couch while their wives brought in lesser salaries. He'd watched as their families slid further and further into debt because the guy's ego was too big to accept a job he viewed as beneath him. Mark had no intention of laying that kind of burden on his family.

Instead of waiting for the improbable: Having his dream job handed to him on a platter, Mark wasted no time in seeking lesser work. Within days of being laid off, he began waiting tables at a local restaurant. Whenever Kelly wasn't working, he was serving food, which was every night and all weekend. It brought in about $450 to $500 a week, which wasn't insignificant, but it meant he rarely got to spend time with her or the kids.

Daniel had just begun kindergarten. Brittany was still too young for that, so while Kelly worked at the school, Mark stayed home with his little girl. The days she went to preschool, he did his best to scrounge up extra work doing handy man jobs around the neighborhood, but times were tight. Few had discretionary funds for home improvement projects.

The moment Kelly pulled in the garage, he'd take off for the restaurant, only to return late, exhausted and smelling of stale grease. Their lifestyle wasn't a pleasant one, but as long as the set-up remained temporary in their minds, they could tolerate it. For the most part, they'd managed to keep their heads above water.

"Daniel! What are you doing?"

He could see his son in the rear-view mirror, wiggling around much more than he should be able.

"Get your seatbelt back on! Now!"

In that instant, a sports coupe whipped out of a parking lot ahead of them like a mad demon bent on destruction. It somehow made the turn without spinning out of control and then inexplicably stopped short with only twenty feet of space between it and Mark's Camry.

There was no time. Nowhere to go.

Mark desperately stabbed at his brakes, but panic pushed his foot past the correct pedal. Reaction time being what it is, it wouldn't have made much difference anyway.

They plummeted into the back of the other car at full speed. The screech of tearing metal ripped the air like a rude buzz saw. Mark rocked violently forward and his face crashed into the steering wheel. The explosion of the impact threw Daniel from the back seat into the windshield.

To this day, Mark knew he'd remembered to check his son's seatbelt before they'd left, but as kids will do, Danny had unfastened it.

The image of his son's body striking the windshield conspired with the damage to the vehicle to make Mark lose control. They twisted sideways, clipped a telephone pole, and flipped. Later, he would learn that it was in that moment he lost his little angel, Brittany. Daniel was already gone.

The acrid smell of burning oil filled Mark's nostrils as he fell unconscious.

***

The other driver had been a sixteen year-old football star from the local high school named Stephen Chadwick. He'd been out drinking and carousing with some of his buddies after school and had decided to show off in his new hot rod. He'd never seen Mark coming.

The mass of Mark's vehicle had forced the teen's into a ditch. The impact snapped the jock's spinal cord in two places, effectively ending his football career forever.

It finally occurred to the police five hours later to order a blood test on the boy at the hospital. Even after so much time having passed, his blood-alcohol level was still 0.13. Why and how the young man had gotten so drunk by 4:30 in the afternoon no one understood.

Nor would it matter, for when the teen's day in court came to face the DUI charge, the records of his blood-alcohol level were mysteriously lost, forcing the judge to drop all charges.

As it happened, Chadwick turned out to be a nephew of the governor of the Great State of Georgia. The governor's brother, father of the paralyzed quarterback, began to publicly blame Mark as the real culprit in the accident. He sued Mark civilly for two million dollars in damages, which was much more than his homeowner's policy would cover.

Tonight, Mark watched the rain.

It was heavy enough he could hear the deep patter of it on their roof even through the asphalt shingles. Clear rivulets rolled relentlessly down the outside of the darkened panes in their meager kitchen, creating vertical tributaries whose lifespan lasted mere seconds before being wiped away by new ones.

Crumpled envelopes and unwanted bills littered the crowded desk at his fingertips. He was powerless to pay any of it.

He'd been unable to work at all since the accident. He was as paralyzed emotionally as the Governor's nephew was physically.

Now, the lawsuit. The weight of it all was too much.

He felt impotent to face his grief, much less overcome it. The grief was the real weight, sitting like a ton of iron upon his chest, crushing his heart, pressing the air from his lungs every time he thought he might actually breathe anew.

He blamed himself.

Everyone reassured him with endless platitudes about how it wasn't his fault, how he wasn't to blame, but guilt haunted him nevertheless, a growing specter tethered to his soul. Why hadn't he realized sooner Daniel's seatbelt was unfastened? Had he been going too fast? Maybe even just a *little* too fast?

These were the questions his friends asked themselves and muttered to others in hushed whispers when he was out of earshot. And why shouldn't they? He tormented himself mercilessly with the same ones.

Secretly, he knew Kelly blamed him too, though she would never say that outright. On the surface, she'd tried her best to feign support. Underneath, she was writhing in agony and fury. He'd been the one driving. That it could have just as easily happened to her didn't matter. *He'd* been driving.

Some part of her deep within didn't really believe his version of the accident. Mark had hit the other vehicle from behind. Wasn't that the bottom line? If Mark really had no blame, would the outcome have been so tragic?

Naturally, her hidden wrath fell his way, burning her up with an unvoiced desire to throttle him, even as her hand caressed his back in a strained effort to comfort.

He knew all this. Understood it even. But he was too empty to address it.

Their relationship deteriorated quickly. Neither's form of grief was conducive to the healing of the other. The hidden tension was like an industrial corrosive agent slowly eating through the fragile rope that was their marriage. Without the kids to unite them, it was only a matter of time before it unraveled.

Still, Mark hadn't realized how weak their bond actually had become until Kelly approached him one night with her plan.

She had timidly introduced the idea of a divorce. If they divorced, she said, she could sue to have all their possessions placed in her name, and thus they would be protected from the lawsuit. She said they would still be husband and wife in heart and could remarry later of course.

He rejected the idea outright and chastened her for suggesting it. That was the last thing they needed. Plus, he didn't know much about the legal system, but he doubted such a thing would work.

Regardless, she was out of her mind with grief and not thinking straight, so several months later, she went through with the plan on her own.

At that point, having lost his children and now abandoned by his wife, for the first time in Mark Carpen's life, he lost the will to fight. What did he care if he lost the house and everything in it? Let her have it all. What good were the wrecked ruins of their material lives without a family to rebuild them?

He made a half-hearted attempt to find a good attorney, but no lawyer with any reputation wanted to risk alienating the governor. For an attorney who crossed the wrong people, there could be consequences in the courtroom later, and those few who were bold enough to risk it, Mark couldn't afford.

He retained the best he could find who'd accept the little he could pay, but as predicted, Mark lost. He now owed the boy who'd killed his children a little over two million bucks.

Hitting bottom served as a wake-up call, kicking him into survival mode, though without the normal, accompanying enthusiasm one needed to get through such a morass. He jumped back into work at the restaurant, but the lawyers immediately garnished his wages — and heavily. At least most of his income was cash from tips, so they couldn't garnish that. There was a court order, however, for the seizure of his car, the only material possession Kelly had left him.

Without a vehicle, continuing to work would become impossible. He avoided giving it up for as long as he could, but its seizure was inevitable.

His last chance was to file for bankruptcy. As much as he hated the thought, it was now his only option. Once again, the governor's attorneys filed every motion they could dredge out of the book to delay his relief. Mark's own attorney began balking at continuing to work on his behalf when Mark couldn't afford to pay his rates.

Mark probably would have eventually made it had he fought a little harder to get through the bankruptcy, but the inner spark he needed for inspiration had been extinguished in the accident.

He just didn't care. Not anymore.

So, this is how people become homeless, he thought. There was nothing left to fight for. If everything he acquired could be seized, why work? His wages would be garnished for the rest of his life. His credit was ruined. His family had been whisked away like chaff on the wind.

Grief racked his soul from every front, yet nothing tore his heart like the loss of his kids. Nothing mattered without them, without Kelly.

So, Mark went to the library and began studying maps.

Chapter 1

*"To everything there is a season,
and a time to every purpose under the heaven:
A time to be born, and a time to die;
a time to plant, and a time to pluck up that which is planted."*

-Ecclesiastes 3:1-2

"What in the world...?"

The weather-beaten shed stood in the clearing like a weary sentinel ready to be discharged from duty. Normally, such a building wouldn't have captured Mark's attention, but this particular shack was in the middle of nowhere.

The shack was old, that much was sure. Greyed, roughly-hewn slats ran horizontally along its sides. Supporting its frame was a stacked stone foundation, which gave a hint as to its age. It was not large enough to be a barn, more like a work shed.

A single, oversized door occupied the center of its front wall. It was latched, but not locked. Two small, square windows flanked both sides of the entrance. Mark tried to peer through their dirty panes, cupping his hands to block the sunlight from obscuring his view, but the effort was futile. The wood siding smelled musty, old, but not of rot.

Since there were no houses around, he double-checked the clearing for signs of some other previously existing structure. The shack could have originally belonged to a house that had long since burned down or otherwise been erased by time. If that were the case, however, then one would think it too would have been re-conquered by nature long ago.

In fact, this shed looked cared for. While the siding was weathered and bereft of paint, there were no signs of leaning or caving in. One of the corners sported a fresh, new board, which had probably replaced a rotting one. The weeds and surrounding undergrowth that normally would have crept up, prying and eating away at the wood with its tendrils, appeared to have been cut back on a regular basis. The grass in the clearing was also trimmed and neat.

The shed was mysterious for the same reason that Mark was out here by himself: Nothing — and no one — should be anywhere around.

At a mere thirty-five years of age, Mark was broken, both financially and spiritually. All that he owned in this world, he carried in the forty pound pack on his back. He was dirty, tired, and stank of having not bathed for weeks. Thick beard growth testified as to how long it had been since he'd seen a civilized bathroom.

He'd grown up in a suburb just outside Atlanta, with normal parents and a normal family. Uncle Sam had subsidized his time at Georgia State University, so after finishing, he'd owed the United States Marines a stint. He'd liked the Marines so much he'd re-upped several times, serving in Force Recon, which was the Corps' Special Forces group. He'd eventually decided he'd had enough and received an honorable discharge.

GSU was where he'd met Kelly, who'd been an education major at the time. They had separated while he was in the Marines, but after his discharge, they'd reconnected and gotten married just a year later. Two years of nominal matrimonial bliss and then Daniel had arrived. Two more years after that, beautiful little Brittany had bounced into their world.

Time is a funny thing.

One minute, you're cruising through life, satisfied, content. The next, all is destroyed, reduced to wrecked ruins smoldering by the roadside. The crucial difference can be just a second. One single, destructive second.

It wasn't that long ago Mark had been a successful computer systems analyst. Now, he was a homeless hermit living in the North Georgia mountains, wandering from campsite to campsite.

After losing everything in the lawsuit, he'd made an unconventional decision. He'd driven to the remotest area he could find on a map, an area devoid of towns, buildings, or people and with plenty of empty, unused land and national forests. An area full of promise for a life in retreat.

He would disappear into the woods forever, he'd decided, and forget about society once and for all. He'd live off the land, alone with his grief and bitterness. It was radical — but oh, was it needed.

His car, his last tie to his former life, he'd abandoned on a mountainous highway with the doors unlocked and the keys in the ignition. *Hope it gets stolen,* he'd muttered as he walked away, thinking a photo of a popular obscene gesture left on the driver's seat would have made a nice greeting card for the lawyers.

The moment he'd turned his back on that beat up piece of junk was a moment of sublime satisfaction. Satisfaction which he hadn't felt for quite a while. He was finally taking control of his life again.

He'd been out here for a little over two months so far. Not that he was keeping track of the days very well. Time in the Marines and Force Recon had more than equipped him for long term survival on his own. The only possessions he would ever need were in his backpack and around his waist, and he didn't plan on going back any time soon.

He was alone. Blissfully alone. Solitude in nature had finally begun to bring the healing he'd so desperately needed for so long but could never quite seem to secure back home.

Yet today, he found himself in the middle of nowhere staring at this strange shed, its square frame rudely piercing his fantasy of a lonely oblivion.

The ambient clicking of southern cicadas seemed to mute as silence descended upon his mind like a thick blanket. The outbuilding drew his attention, focusing it like a laser.

There was no way to see inside. If curiosity was to be assuaged, the door would have to be opened. It felt like a violation of the primitive, peaceful state in which he'd been living to enter a civilized structure again.

The latch lifted easily enough — no lock to block him. He'd expected the hinges to squeal but was surprised to see they were well-oiled.

Inside, the aroma of new lumber floated lightly upon the still air. The floor had been swept recently, and no dust marred the window sills. Naturally stained wooden slats lined three walls and the floor. A matching wood-topped island occupied the center of the room, and cabinets covered the entire back wall. A deep window seat ran along the right hand side. It had a hinged lid, indicating it doubled as a storage chest.

On top of the lid, directly under the window, lay a pewter-colored wristwatch, which sat atop a single piece of paper. Being the only apparent items in the room, he crossed the small space and examined both more closely.

The device did indeed seem to be a watch of some kind, though it didn't have any of the decorative trappings one would normally expect in a watch. No brand name, no stylish flourishes. Its bland, smooth face was interrupted by two rectangular digital displays instead of one. Underneath the displays was a single large red button. A stopwatch, perhaps?

Both of the small screens displayed more numbers than normal. A lot more.

Several tiny buttons lined both sides of the face, but the oddest part by far was the wrist band, which appeared to be completely integral to the watch. The band was made of the same smooth gray metal as the watch's face, but there were no links, no breaks, and no crevices in it, not even where it met the watch head. The band and face appeared to be one single, continuous piece of metal with no way to unlatch or otherwise separate it from the watch.

The piece of paper was a brief set of instructions. They appeared to have been typed on an old-fashioned typewriter, and the paper felt like the bond paper they used in the old days, yet the sheet was crisp and fresh, not aged at all. The instructions bore no title, but simply read:

1. Insert wrist into band.
2. Using the three buttons on right side of face, set the bottom display to:

010000P-09071890

3. Press the red button.

That was it. Simple enough, but what was this thing, anyway? Surely, it wasn't a watch after all. Not with that many numbers. Maybe a GPS locator?

Mark glanced nervously back through the door. He'd been foolish to trespass like this. In spite of its remote location, somebody obviously still owned this shack and had been here recently. The last thing he needed was more trouble.

He briefly considered that it might be some kind of taser, or other electric shock device...but why would a person have something like that laying in their shed? There didn't appear to be any electrodes on its underside, so probably not.

Regardless, he wasn't about to stick his wrist through the band and push that big red button until he knew exactly what it was. He avoided getting on a first-name basis with Stupid whenever he could help it.

Curiosity already had him by the tail though. With some trial and error, he managed to use the smaller buttons on the side to change one of the digital displays to match the numbers on the piece of paper. Then, *without* slipping his wrist through the band, he pushed the red button.

The watch vanished from his grasp.

At first, he thought it had fallen. He scoured the floor and even got down on his hands and knees, but it wasn't anywhere to be found. Standing back up, he scratched his head, his heart racing a little. *What had just happened?*

He whipped around, searching for some unseen indicator that might explain what was going on, or maybe a red blinking light that would let him know he was on Candid Camera.

Nothing.

Where had it gone? This really didn't make any sense. Had it become *invisible*? That just wasn't possible. He groped the floor again, this time for bumpy things he couldn't see, but it was devoid of any objects, visible or otherwise. No invisible watch.

Plus, he hadn't heard it hit the floor. He'd felt the weight of it lift from his hand, as if it had evaporated.

Flabbergasted, he started to doubt whether there had even ever been a watch. Maybe he'd just imagined it. No — the piece of paper was still here.

Whatever the "watch" had been, it was gone now. Where it had gone, and how he could get it back, he had no idea.

Maybe he should have put his wrist through the band before pushing the button after all. No. Then, he might have disappeared too.

Or would the watch have done something completely different if he'd been wearing it? If he'd vanished with the watch, where would he have gone? Maybe it simply annihilated whoever was wearing it when activated. A kind of trick weapon? Maybe it had annihilated itself in the absence of another object. Didn't seem likely though. Who would go to all the trouble to invent such an odd device just to kill somebody? Guns were so much easier.

The instruction regarding the setting of the digital display had to mean something. As fantastic as it sounded, the numbers must represent some sort of coordinates, perhaps a destination for the watch? That would make it a teleportation device. Still, the numbers weren't typical GPS format.

Just an hour ago, he wouldn't have imagined he'd be considering the existence of such a thing, but he'd seen it disappear with his own eyes, and the human mind quickly adapts.

Had he inadvertently stumbled onto the outskirts of a covert military base? The U.S. military managed numerous "black" projects resulting in technological advances years beyond what the public thought was currently possible. Laser weapons, cloaks that could make soldiers invisible. These were things off the pages of science fiction novels that the Pentagon began development on decades ago and with which it had already achieved limited success. He knew because he'd seen a couple of these projects in action himself while enlisted. Inconspicuous places like this shed were sometimes preferred to a large, blatant army base for disguising covert operations.

He recalled reading a few years ago that some German scientists claimed to have successfully teleported a few atoms across a short distance. So, you never knew.

Still, if that were the case, would they really have left such a valuable device out in the open where just anybody could stumble upon it? And with instructions? Definitely not. Then again, maybe they weren't expecting someone like him to be walking this far out in the wild.

He stepped to the door and peered into the woods for a long time, examining every direction thoroughly. Nothing.

He retreated back inside and systematically searched every cabinet and drawer for some answers, but the shed truly was as a bare as it looked. Absolutely every compartment was empty. Except for the storage area under the window seat.

When he lifted the lid of the window seat, another silvery watch gleamed up at him, as if waiting patiently to be discovered. *Was it the same one?* Had it fallen from his hand and somehow gotten inside the window seat? There weren't any holes in the lid through which it could have passed.

A chill ran down his spine the moment his fingers touched it. This one's digital display was *not* set to the numbers he had entered. Had it reset itself, or was this a different "watch"? Had it teleported itself from his hand into the box?

This was insane.

Underneath this watch was a different note, a much simpler one.

This time, put it on.

He fled the shack, gripping the watch so tightly his knuckles turned white. He rushed from one edge of the clearing to the other, peering into the late summer foliage for evidence that someone was setting him up, but there was no one out there. He was alone.

A cool breeze blew in from the northwest. He sat down heavily under a nearby tree, staring at the watch peeking through his closed fist. Dare he put it on?

The contemplation and second-guessing went on for more than twenty minutes. Finally, with great trepidation, he slipped it over his wrist. After all, he had nowhere to go, nothing left to lose really. Except his life. But what was that worth at this point anyway?

As soon as he'd passed his hand through the watch's wristband, a strange whirring sound erupted from within. The band constricted around his wrist swiftly, halting once it was snug against his skin. Panicked, he jumped to his feet and ripped at it, frantically trying to get it off, but the metal was very strong. There was no seam, no screws to pry at. He punched buttons, but to no avail; the band would not loosen.

He was stuck. What an idiot he'd been. He should have tried a stick or something else first. Not his arm.

He calmed a bit once he realized the "watch" wasn't going to do anything else to him. He and it were at an apparent stalemate. He didn't dare push the red button now, not until he knew what this thing was — and what it would do to him.

He would just wait right here. The shack's owner had to show up at some point and they would be able to shed some light on the matter.

Chapter 2

He snacked on some berries and wild roots he found nearby, drank from a nearby stream, and ate the last piece of beef jerky he'd been saving for a special occasion. In short, he relaxed. He'd gotten good at waiting, at doing nothing over the past few months.

The day darkened to night, but no one came. The cicadas enlivened the crisp night air, loud enough to rival a moderate-sized orchestra. Stars twinkled, seemingly dancing to their rhythms, and soft breezes blew through the trees in spurts that sounded like the rising and falling of applause.

This was real life, he'd decided, the kind of life people only caught a glimpse of when they went camping. This was *his* life now.

He pondered his past. If given the chance, could he have done things differently? It was hard to say. For the most part, he'd done the best he knew how at every turn.

There was no doubt one thing he would change would be that trip to McDonald's. If he could undo anything, it would be that fateful day of course. Yet, this was his existence now, and he enjoyed it for what it was....second best.

Eventually, his body's needs overcame his mind. He fell asleep, propped against the trunk of an old oak tree.

When morning broke, he awoke to the sound of birds chirping cheerfully in the branches over his head. The cool smell of morning dew jolted his senses from slumber to alert. His clothing was damp from it.

The stupid metal band still clasped his wrist like some sort of futuristic handcuff.

He yawned and stood, stretching his arms to the sky. He really should have gotten his sleeping bag out instead of sleeping against that tree. His neck felt like an ice pick had been shoved between a couple of the vertebrae. He jumped into his morning calisthenics routine to get the juices flowing and to try to work out the kinks he felt in just about every muscle.

Yet, the device on his wrist kept drawing his attention like a moth to a bug zapper.

Decisions, decisions.

Should he push the button or just keep waiting?

Truthfully, he was out of patience. There was no telling how long it would be until someone returned. Walking away wasn't a solution either, not until he was rid of it.

He scowled at no one in particular. Pushing the cursed red button was his only real option. It could cost him his life, but when you really got down to brass tacks, so what? There wasn't much left of that.

Drumming up courage, he inhaled deeply, closed his eyes, and pressed the button. Immediately, a strange, twisting sensation wrenched his stomach. His feet gave out from under him a little. He stumbled and then....*nothing.*

He opened his eyes, surprised. What had just happened? He was still in the woods, so he hadn't been teleported. He looked at his hands, verifying he could still see himself, so it was no invisibility machine either. But what was with the twisting in his stomach and the stumbling?

It *felt* like he'd moved. Almost the way a roller coaster feels right when you go over the crest of a hill and begin to fall. He'd stumbled because it felt like the ground had dropped away a few inches. Yet, here he stood in the same spot.

Was it his imagination, or had the breeze picked up? It was pretty windy now.

The air's temperature grew warmer on his skin, as if it were mid-afternoon instead of early morning. He squinted up into the sunlight. The sun certainly seemed too high in the sky for it to be morning. What time was it anyway? Had he really slept that late? It had definitely not been this hot just a minute ago.

Wait.

The shed was gone.

Where was the shed?

Maybe he should be asking where *he* was? Did the watch move the shed — or had it moved him? He was completely disoriented.

He reached down for his backpack, but his fingers only brushed air. It too was gone. The oak tree where he had slept caught his eye — it was only half as wide as he remembered. It looked shorter as well. The oak tree wasn't gone, but the other things were. So had he moved, or not?

A strange desperation filled him then. He jerked his head back and forth, trying to get a grip on the truth. Reality had just twisted before his eyes, yet understanding evaded his mind. His finger inched back toward the red button, wanting to push it another time, but not sure if he should.

He did.

Same odd sensations.

The trees in the forest line flickered and jumped, shifting really, as if he'd turned his head. Yet, he hadn't. His feet stumbled again, but this time the ground shoved him upward, enough to throw him off balance, and he fell back hard onto his rump.

Both the shed and his pack were miraculously back in place. The oak tree had returned to its normal size.

He exhaled, deeply relieved. Was he dreaming? Hallucinating? Perhaps he'd only imagined the disappearing shack.

He pushed the button again. No shack, no backpack. There was the same shifting of trees, the same twisting in his gut, all of it topped off by the shrunken oak.

A fourth time, and everything returned to its place. He lost his balance, stumbled and fell again. Very odd. Very odd indeed.

Then, nausea overcame him in a rush. He dropped to his hands and knees and heaved up the remnants of yesterday's beef jerky and berries, mixed with a touch of bile of course. After a full minute of retching, he flopped onto his back, chest heaving, trying to catch his breath.

What *was* this thing? What was it doing to him? Was it disorienting him, maybe injecting him with some kind of drug? Every time he pushed that button it was as if every tree in the forest simultaneously shifted anywhere from a few inches to several feet, yet every one moved in a different direction. The difference wasn't enough to put your finger on, but it sure threw your mind off. Was that what had made him nauseous? Or was it something else?

Perhaps the device just *acted* like a mind-altering drug. Maybe it sent an electrical signal through the skin which disoriented and confused the visual cortex of the brain.

Mark withdrew his hunting knife and carved a rough question mark in the bark of the oak tree. Once he was satisfied as to its visibility, he stepped back, shouldered his backpack, glanced around and pushed the button once more.

The queasiness returned and it was all he could do to keep from resuming the heave-a-thon.

He clearly felt his feet drop this time, as if he'd been floating a half-inch above the ground. The shed was gone, but this time, his pack was still firmly slung across his back. *That* was different.

He examined the oak, but there was no question mark. At this point, he wasn't really sure if he'd expected that or not.

Just then, a glint of sunlight reflecting off metal caught Mark's eye. In the grass to his left lay a silver object. It was the missing watch, the one that had disappeared from his hands, and it lay right where the shack had been.

So, the watch couldn't be a mind-altering device. Such a mechanism could potentially distort what he was actually seeing, but it would be pretty hard to "add" something as specific as a watch to his imagination. No hallucination could be that real.

Now that he thought about it, a mind-altering device couldn't explain the first watch disappearing before his eyes because he hadn't even been wearing one yet.

No, as hard as it was to believe, this thing was sending him somewhere. The question was *where*?

Was it a teleporter after all? *Was he really considering such fantastic ideas?*

He returned to the oak and carved a cross deeply into its surface. Then, he pushed the button.

He stumbled, yet would have stayed on his feet this time except for the violent nausea that returned with a vengeance. It racked his gut and drove him to his knees. He lost control of his body while his vision swam. It was a good fifteen minutes before he could pull himself together.

When he was finally able to stand again, Mark staggered to the oak and searched the trunk for his carving. He saw no cross, but the question mark he'd originally carved was back.

Check that. He could just barely make out the faint form of a cross right below the question mark. It looked like the bark had swollen up and over the marking, almost completely covering it, *as if the cross had been carved decades ago.*

Suddenly, Mark struggled for control over his breathing. Had he been shifting back and forth between *times*? Was the watch a time machine? How could such a small device do such a thing? It wasn't possible.

He closely examined the digital displays. He'd only changed the lower one, and it read:

010000P-09071890

If you read that the right way, the numbers could represent 1:00 PM, September 7, 1890.

1890.

Impossible. Absolutely impossible.

Ridiculous.

The upper display read: 080347A-09072011. If he followed the same line of reasoning, it would be read: 8:03 AM (and 47 seconds), September 7, 2011.

That *could* be today's date. Honestly, he'd lost track. *Was it September already?* Mark had purposely not kept track of the days since he'd begun this long hike of his, but he had left "civilization" in July, and that had been about two months ago. It could easily be around 8:00 in the morning. In fact, he'd be surprised if it wasn't.

Time travel was impossible — yet here he was, witnessing strange things that had no other explanation.

There was no easy way to prove what was going on one way or the other, at least not while he was in the woods. Since there was no obvious means of ridding his wrist of his new adornment, he was apparently going to have more than ample opportunity to test his new theory, and there were a lot better places to experiment than the middle of a forest. A town of some sort, for example, would provide definitive proof.

Plus, he was going to have to wait longer between pushes of that button if this nausea were going to continue. He couldn't take much more of that.

For the first time in a long time, Mark felt intrigued and excited about something.

Chapter 3

What then is time? If no one asks me, I know what it is.
If I wish to explain it to him who asks, I do not know.

~ Saint Augustine

Mark wandered, not fully decided on what his next course of action should be. He was still grappling with the idea, this inconceivable possibility of time travel through something as small as the thing encircling his wrist.

He'd left the clearing and headed west through the woods, but he hadn't walked more than the length of a football field when the trees parted again unexpectedly. A simple, two-story house stood in the center of a much larger, second clearing. Its style was traditional American and an old-fashioned, wrap-around porch dressed its bottom floor, adding a flourish of character. The siding wasn't painted, but stained a golden oak color you might see on someone's back deck. He instantly liked it.

At least one mystery was solved. Whoever owned this home had to own the shed as well, although the shed did seem much older. This house couldn't be more than fifteen to twenty years old.

With luck, perhaps the owner would be at home and could start answering some questions — and Mark had a *lot* of questions. If the house was as empty as the shed, maybe he'd just give into temptation and get a good night's sleep for a change.

He climbed the porch and pulled the screened door outward, cringing as it moaned loudly.

He knocked. No answer. No movement from inside.

Well, he'd already broken into one building. Why not go exploring a second time?

The front door turned out to be unlocked, but unlike the screen, the smooth silence of well-oiled hinges accompanied Mark's push as he swung it inward.

"Helloooo?" he called, listening expectantly.

No answer. He called a second time with the same result.

The home was indeed simple, outside and in. The furniture was sparse and minimalist, yet modern, all of it neatly arranged and dust free. The faint smell of freshly cut lumber lingered in the air, just like the shed, yet this time mingling with a stronger scent of lemony Pine Sol. The place seemed lived in, but was spotlessly clean.

Finding no sign of life on the first floor (Nor, to his dismay, any food in the refrigerator), Mark ascended the stairs. He winced when the last step creaked awfully.

On the second floor, he found the home's apparent owner.

In the master bedroom, an old man lay on his back in a king-sized bed. His countenance was peaceful, his eyes shut and his hands at his sides. His suit looked pressed, giving him an eerie appearance, as if he'd been laid out for a funeral.

Mark crossed the room to feel for a pulse. The moment he picked up the man's wrist, his eyes fluttered open and he stared at Mark intensely with a look that pierced him through and through. It was as if the old man knew every inch of him, as if he could see into the very depths of his soul with that penetrating gaze. Yet, somehow, the old man also felt familiar to Mark.

The fragile face smiled. It was a weak smile, but warm, animated by an intensity that momentarily equaled the stare. The man gripped his wrist and squeezed, like he was holding on for dear life, never taking his eyes from Mark's. After a moment, his grip loosened and fell away, taking the brief smile with it. The man's eyes fluttered shut and a strange, rattling breath escaped his lungs. His whole body relaxed with that breath, as if sinking deeper into the large bed. Mark felt his pulse fade, and then it finally ceased.

He waited several minutes to be sure, but he knew the man had died. He recognized the death rattle, that strange last breath the dying make as they expire. He considered calling the police to report the death, but he couldn't find a telephone anywhere in the house and they were a long way from any town. The old man had obviously known he was dying and had wanted to die here. Mark would just leave him where he lay.

Mark's earlier impression of the house being "simply" furnished crystallized into clarity. With the exception of a few items like the refrigerator, there was not a single modern appliance or amenity to be found. No television set, no radios, no telephones.

Maybe Mark really had traveled through time and was still stuck in the past. No — the refrigerator was stainless steel, a newer model. Puzzled, he continued to search.

The closets were bare. There were no toiletries in the bathrooms, no sign of anyone having living here. Except for the body in the bed.

It reminded him of the apartment of an old college buddy who traveled all the time for work: Sterile like a hotel room. He'd asked his friend once how he could stand to live in such a bland environment. His friend had replied that the opposite was true. Being gone so much, the only way he could stay sane was to keep his apartment clutter free and as low-maintenance as possible.

Was the old man a traveler like his friend? Even more importantly, was he a *time* traveler?

Mark took a closer look at the dead man and saw his wrist bore a silver "watch" identical to his own.

Guess that answers that.

Gently, he lifted the man's arm, trying to get a better look at the device's settings. Upon his touch, the device began to whir softly. Its band loosened and slid from the dead man's wrist to the floor with a considerable thud.

Startled, Mark snatched it up, eyeing the body suspiciously for signs of trickery.

No movement. The guy was dead.

If Mark's theory was correct, then the bottom setting of the old man's watch was set to three weeks ago. The top setting matched today's date and the current time.

Wait a second. How could the top setting match the current time if the man had died a few minutes ago? Checking his own watch, Mark saw his top setting matched the current time as well. Perhaps the top setting was actually nothing more than a normal clock which acted as a reference point, an anchor of sorts for the time travel mechanism. That made sense. It would almost be a necessary feature.

The rest of the house was pretty bare, but he was curious to see what he would find if he "traveled" back to three weeks ago, the time on the dead man's watch.

He didn't dare put this newest watch on since it would probably lock onto him just like the first one had. One irremovable, time-traveling device stuck on his wrist was more than enough, thank you very much, and unless he wanted to start looking like some New York City jewelry hawker, he'd wait until he found a way to get the first one off before adding a second.

If he activated the dead man's watch, it would probably just disappear from his hand. So, instead, he set his own to match the same time three weeks prior. Then, he dropped the old man's watch into his backpack.

He now had a total of three devices. One on his wrist and two in his backpack. *How many of these things were there anyway?* He definitely needed to start paying more attention to people's wrists.

Mark pushed his red button and felt the now familiar, but still unsettling sensation in the pit of his stomach. The bedroom in general did not change, but the old man's body disappeared from the bed. In his place was a sheet of paper.

Your suspicions are correct.
The device you are wearing is a time traveling engine of sorts.
Follow your instincts.

These notes were really starting to freak him out. They had been expecting him. *Somebody* had been expecting him.

Frantically, he turned the house inside out searching for further clues as to what was going on but found nothing of interest.

The face of his watch was glowing red. He hit the button to go back, but nothing happened. Great. He'd broken it. Now what was he going to do?

He redoubled his search efforts and delved into every nook and cranny, but there was nothing in the house or the shed that would tell him more.

The note said to follow his instincts, and instinct told him to head back to civilization. So, he set off into the woods in the direction of the closest highway.

What exactly does one do with *three* time-travel machines?

Had somebody specifically intended for Mark to find them, or were they left for whomever came along first?

He hiked the rest of the morning and most of the afternoon pondering these questions. In his imagination, time machines were big, bulky chambers, great unwieldy things with wires sticking out from all sides. How could something as small as a watch be so powerful?

From what little he knew of physics, time travel, if it were even possible, would require an immeasurable amount of energy. It was effectively unachievable.

This had to be some kind of elaborate hoax. If a person can mentally smack themselves on the forehead, Mark did so now. *Of course*, that was it. Traveling through time wasn't possible, and sure as heck nobody was going to find a tiny little watch in the north Georgia woods that could.

What about the nausea and the loss of balance though? Maybe that had been the result of some kind of electrical shock. Yet, the trees in the forest had shifted. The old man's body had disappeared from the bed before his eyes. The first watch had evaporated from his hand, and the cross carving had clearly aged. Were those just optical illusions?

He glanced down at the device. The red glow was gone. It was back to normal.

There was one way to settle this.

Stopping short in the middle of the trail, he flung his backpack to the ground and altered the second setting to match today's date, but twelve hours in the future. He punched the button.

Suddenly, he found himself shrouded in darkness. The sun was gone, stars twinkled overhead and the moon was out.

It *was* a time travel machine. He had just traveled twelve hours into the future.

Pushing the button again, he returned to the glaring heat of the midday sun. Along with a severe case of nausea of course.

He emptied the remaining contents of his stomach into some colorful shrubs which soon reeked of bile. Thankfully, he hadn't had much to eat since his last vomiting session and it wasn't long before the peaceful, post-regurgitation calm settled in. Then and there, Mark vowed to be more careful about how often he "shifted". Doing it too frequently was not much fun. He just hoped the effect wasn't cumulative.

The nausea was probably part of some kind of time-travel jet lag, he reasoned. A person could probably get a serious case of that, jumping around like he was.

A few hours later, Mark ran into Highway 129. He knew if he followed it to the left, he'd end up to North Carolina. To the right led down to Cleveland, Georgia. He turned right and started walking.

Curiosity was picking at him again. It had been several hours since he last used the watch. That had to be enough time to mitigate the nausea, right?

He twiddled with the buttons and set his target time back to the original 1890 date. He wanted to see what the road would look like back then.

Familiar stumble — a sense of falling about an inch.

The forest "shifted" as it had before.

Slight nausea.

The highway was now a dusty, dirt road, and it lay twenty feet to his right instead of under his feet. They must have changed its path when they paved it.

Besides the road jumping around, nothing else was different. Same Georgia woods, same sounds, same air and sky.

Kind of unsettling actually. In his mind, the late 1800's was life in brown sepia. Photos of the early 1900's were always in black and white, and those of the 1800's were brown. He knew those were just photos, but still, seeing 1890 in full color seemed weird.

The road was barren of movement. Just like a hundred years in the future. It was anti-climatic in a way. He wasn't sure what he'd expected to see, maybe a parade of people dressed in Victorian clothing, but there wasn't anything remarkable aside from the road. He poked around a little bit and then pushed the button to return.

A long, high-pitched tone sang out, and the display flashed to red again.

Dang!

It hadn't made that noise before. What did that mean? Frantically, he punched at the button over and over, but all it did was beep and flash.

The display had turned red before in the house, but it hadn't beeped then, and he'd only used it a couple of times since. He feared it might be breaking down on him. His breathing shortened. If he didn't even understand how the watch worked, how could he fix it? Its body felt warm against his skin. Maybe it had just overheated — or something. Would it reset itself again or was he marooned in 1890? He had no clue.

Broken or not, there was nothing he could do about it for now except to keep walking.

Beads of sweat broke out on his forehead as he continued down the dirt road that would one day be Highway 129.

Chapter 4

Time goes, you say? Ah no!
Alas, Time stays, we go.

~ Henry Austin Dobson

A few hours later, he arrived in what he guessed must be Cleveland, Georgia. The town was much smaller than the version of Cleveland he knew from his day. Its roads were a messy confluence of dirt and mud, and their configuration was also different from what he remembered.

Horses pulled wagons and buggies. Women walked about in cotton dresses and bonnets, and the kids had on outfits he'd only seen in the movies. Some were accompanied by men in rough-looking pants held up by suspenders. It was all so hard to believe....but there it was.

He suddenly realized he would stick out like a sore thumb in his 21st century clothing, so he decided not to go all the way into town, but instead retreated back into the woods to give himself time to think.

The watch was either broken, or it had overheated, or.....who knew? It could be anything. He hoped the problem was only temporary. He did *not* want to be stuck in 1890.

Well, now....wait a minute. Why *didn't* he want to be stuck in 1890? Why did he care? There was nothing left for him in the future. Hadn't he already given up on that life? Maybe he could get a fresh start here.

Yet, something about the idea bothered him. Perhaps he hadn't really cut all the emotional ties to his old life after all. Or maybe he just didn't like being stuck somewhere, regardless of where that place was. After all, any prison is a prison still.

Whatever the reason, the bottom line was: He didn't like it. Not that he could do much about it though.

He'd give it overnight. If the watch didn't start working again by morning, he'd assume it was broken and regroup then. For now, he wouldn't panic.

"Son, ya look loster than a frog in a desert!"

The voice came from behind.

Slowly, Mark turned. The voice belonged to a farmer wielding a shotgun. Thankfully, its barrels were pointed toward the ground. The man's crooked grin signaled a wary friendliness. His overalls were well-worn, patched in several places. Gray beard stubble lined his jaws.

"Them's gotta be the craziest lookin' citified duds I e'er seen. Where'd ya get 'em?"

Mark was still trying to recover and doing a poor job of it at that. He hadn't expected to speak to anybody. Psychologically, he'd woefully unprepared himself for the possibility. This world hadn't seemed quite real until now. This man was really here though, really speaking to him, and he'd probably died long before Mark was even born. It popped any lingering perception he'd had that this was somehow just one big, long dream. It wasn't.

"At...Atlanta." Mark stuttered, grasping for whatever story came to mind.

"Ya don' say. Ain't ne'er seen rags like that 'round here. What's this here world comin' to anyhow? Mays ah ask whatcha doin' on mah property?"

"Uh....Sorry. I didn't realize this land belonged to anyone. I was just hiking through the woods."

The man chuckled lightly, yet sincerely, the laugh lines around his eyes deepening in prominence as he did "Wall, ah'll be. Yeah, its mah farm, aw'right. Name's Johnson. Red Johnson."

"Pleasure to meet you, sir. Mark Carpen."

"Mark....like the Mark of the Bible?"

"Yes."

The man squinted, staring, as if he were sizing Mark up.

"Good name. Ya got the look of a famished bear 'bout ya, Mark." Red drawled his name as if it had two syllables. "How 'bout ya foller me on up to the house. The missus prob'ly's got a good spread set fer lunch."

***

Red's house was the typical farmer's house. Simple in style, white-washed boards covering the frame, a stone chimney running up its side. It was a fresh, well-kept version of one of those crumbling, old farm houses you might catch a glimpse of while driving by on the highway in modern times, wondering what life had been like there when it was still pretty. Now he could witness the answer to those wonderings first hand.

The warm aroma of freshly baked cornbread flooded his senses the moment he entered the Johnson home. Plates filled with salt pork, green beans, and other goodies covered the rough kitchen table.

Red's wife smiled meekly when she saw Mark and quietly set an extra place at the table for him. She did not seem at all bothered by his unexpected appearance. The way she acted, Red must bring strays like him home quite a bit, though he could tell part of it was she was shy.

Her floral stamped dress was modest and rustic, yet classically pretty. A well-used apron over her front displayed several fresh stains from today's cooking. Her long hair was pulled back and pinned up to keep it from interfering with her work, though a strand of it had fallen free and hung loose across the right side of her face. She was a brunette, but the color of her hair was a pallid brown. It did not have the same shine or silkiness as women's hair from....well....from his time.

It felt odd to distinguish things in terms of his time and the present. It was an unbelievable concept, the idea that his "home-time", once absolutely unified with his present, could now be separated from it.

Several barefoot, dirty-faced children scampered around the backyard, playing raucously. Red whistled and in the bat of an eye they'd run to the house, into the kitchen, and seated themselves obediently in their places.

"Yer just in time for Sabbath dinner. Leah can cook a mean meal when she sets her mind to it." He grinned from ear to ear, obviously proud of his wife. She blushed but seemed to appreciate the compliment.

"This here's Johnny, and that's Mickey. This little princess - that's mah Daisy"

"You certainly have a nice family, Mr. Johnson."

"Call me Red."

"Well, Red, thank you very much for having me to dinner." As if on cue, Mark's stomach rumbled loud enough to be heard by all.

Red threw his head back in laughter and the children joined in. Leah's smile grew, but she didn't allow herself a loss of composure. "You and yer stomach are both welcome here," Red assured him, "A man who cain't be hospitable, well he ain't got no right to 'spect no hosp'tality from the Man upstairs. That's what I say."

Mark did his best to not appear greedy as he shoveled the home-cooked food onto his plate, but he was famished and it'd been too long since he'd eaten decently.

"Whatcha doin' roun' these parts, Mark?"

"Passing through."

"Ya speak mighty refined, I must say, Mark. Don' sound like ya from Atlanta."

"No...uh, I'm from up....out west." He'd been about to say "up north" to cover his tracks, but then he'd remembered the year. He guessed Yankees probably still weren't being offered the welcome wagon very much in Georgia in 1890. It'd be another couple of generations before the animosity fully died down.

"Ya don' say. Where 'bouts?"

"California."

"What'd ya do out thar?"

"It was a long time ago." The last thing he needed was to trap himself in some elaborate lie and get tangled up in the details later. Best to keep it simple.

Rather than take offense, Red held up his hands, laughing, "No skin off mah nose. We kin be pow'rful curious 'round here, but a man's got a right to privacy. So, where ya headed?"

"Not sure."

"Ain't got no plans?" Red cocked his head, puzzled.

"Nope."

"Jes' a wanderin'?"

"I guess you could say that."

"Yup, did som' dat when I was younger mahself, that's fer sure. 'Till Leah tamed me that is. Figger to be in town fer a bit, or ya movin' on?"

"Don't know, sorry. Don't mean to be so vague. I'm just not sure what I'm going to do next."

Silence reigned.

"Well, Mark, ya surtainly seem to be an ed'cated cuss, but ah sure could use a hand 'round here if'n ya ain't got no plans. Ya lookin' fer work?"

Mark chewed on the offer. Even if he could get the watch working again and return home to 2011, how would he survive? He had no home to go to, no bank account, no driver's license, no nothing. He'd given it all up. How could he make it the modern world without any of those things? Regardless of the year, he was going to need some money. Maybe it would be easier to earn it here in 1890.

He nodded, slowly at first, then more decisively.

"Yeah, I could help out around here for a while if you need it."

Thus, Mark Carpen found a job 80 years before he was born.

Chapter 5

After Leah's wonderful feast, Red gave Mark a spare set of work clothes, which included a pair of overalls and a white cotton shirt, and helped him get settled in. Mark didn't wait to put them on. He was more than ready to get rid of the stinking rags he'd been washing over and over again for the past few months.

Red had a small bunkhouse in back of the main house where he put Mark up for the night. The mattress was a lumpy mess, but it had been months since Mark had slept in any kind of a bed at all, so his back groaned its thanks anyway as he laid down.

Yet, sleep evaded him. The night ticked on as he dwelt on the oddness of his predicament. He didn't want to be stuck in a year he didn't belong to. Then again, why would he want to go home to his own time when modern society had rejected him?

There was also the fact that he was penniless in both worlds. At least in 1890, his wages couldn't be garnished. Plus, no income tax. That was definitely a bonus.

If he were honest with himself, he'd grown tired of living alone in the wild. He was glad he'd done it though. There was something sublimely cathartic about surviving off the land. More importantly, it had given him time to heal.

Now that he was back around people, however, he realized just how much he'd missed the company of others. Maybe the life of a hermit wasn't really his cup of tea after all.

He just wished he could be around people from his own time. It was hard to explain, but in a way he felt like these people were already dead, like he was walking around with ghosts. Every single person he met in this time would be dead by 2011. Unless he met a baby who lived to be a hundred and twenty years old.

It was a weird mental hang up that he would have to get past. They weren't the walking dead. They were real people, flesh and blood. They were vibrant, full of life, and waiting on life still to be lived. Alive.

Mark took a look at his watch. He'd figured out that one of the tiny side buttons was just a light that illuminated the displays so they could be read in the dark.

5:07 AM.

It was amazing how the device kept pace with the movement of time in whichever "time" he was in, just like a regular watch.

The displays weren't glowing red anymore.

That meant he could get out of here.

A sudden, hard knocking at the bunkhouse door startled him.

"Up an at'em, Carpen! We got work to do."

It was Red. Spontaneously, Mark pressed the red button.

No flashing or beeping this time, just the now familiar feeling of shifting accompanied by a new and curious sliding sensation.

He was still in the bunkhouse, but now he stood several feet to the left of where he'd been a second ago. A ruined chest-of-drawers occupied his previous position.

Was the watch smart enough to know to shift his physical position so he wouldn't appear in the middle of a piece of furniture? He hadn't even considered the possibility that the space you were going to occupy in another time might already be occupied by something else. It was potentially a very fatal, and thus disconcerting, risk. Could this device be so well-designed that it took into account things like that? That would mean the watch had to know with great specificity the size and shape of his body. For that matter, he hadn't really thought about it till now, but it always brought his clothes along with him, which was a feature he was very thankful for.

It was able to see into the target time before he arrived and detect if there was an object in the way and then adjust his landing accordingly. Amazing. *Who* had designed this thing anyway?

Red's bunkhouse was clearly much older now. It looked like no one had been in here for at least 20 to 30 years. The walls were full of dry-rot, and the floor was gone. Junk and worn-out furniture was piled throughout. It smelled of ancient must. The roof had partially caved in and spider webs were the only adornment. It was flat-out depressing.

Yet, joy surged at the knowledge that the watch was indeed working again. Either he'd jiggled something back into place, or it could only perform a certain number of times before overheating.

Battling his way through the sticky webs and pieces of furniture that even Goodwill wouldn't take, Mark climbed his way to the rickety door and got out. Tall weeds and bushes surrounded the building. He only thought of it as a building because just a few moments before it had been a nice little bunkhouse with a comfortable bed inside it. In 2011, it looked like a trash heap.

He turned to face the main house. Unlike the bunkhouse, it didn't appear abandoned, but was definitely in bad need of paint and repair. A screened-in porch in the back and another full room on the left side had been added by somebody over the years. Trees took up most of the property now and grew thick on what had been cleared farmland just a few minutes ago.

He moved to the front of the house. The dirt road was now a paved highway again. It had been widened, moved, and now took up most of what had been Red's front yard.

It was mid-morning and just because he was curious, Mark knocked on the front door. He wanted to see if the people here knew about the Johnsons.

For a long time, there was no answer. He was about to give up when the door finally cracked ajar. An elderly woman peeked through.

"Can I he'p you," she croaked.

"Uh, yes, ma'am. I'm seeking information on a family that owned this house a long time ago. Would you know anything about them?"

She squinted terribly, trying to process his request. "No, my family has owned this house for over a hundred years," she replied, "Nobody else has ever lived here, young man."

He got excited. Could she be Red's daughter? No, this woman was probably in her 80's and would have been born around 1920. Too late to have been the young girl he'd met, but maybe a granddaughter?

"Is your name Johnson?"

"Name's Burgess...Mary Burgess. I'm sorry."

He was taken aback a bit. "Perhaps, there is a Johnson in your family history, somebody's maiden name?"

She opened the door a little wider and shook her head sadly. She could sense his disappointment.

"Nope. Sorry I can't be of more he'p. This here prop'rty belonged to by father's father, and his name was Burgess. I come from a long line of Burgesses."

"Ma'am, I'm sorry to be asking you all these questions out of the blue, but do you know what year your grandfather purchased this house."

"Well, not off hand, no....but I might be able to look through some of my things and see...." She scrutinized him, but the loneliness that pervades the lives of the elderly won out over caution for a stranger. Anything for company. "Come on in. I'll make you some tea and look through my papers."

He stepped inside. The difference in the interior decor was stark. Leah had kept her home bright and cheery and clean. Since then, it had obviously been redecorated many times and the current wall-paper was depressingly dark and faded, curling at some of its edges. Mary apparently hadn't been able to clean much for a while as dust covered most surfaces in these front two rooms. Newspapers were piled on the stairs and in the floors.

She sat him down on a sagging, dusty couch. A slender brown cat rubbed against his legs as she made the tea. She brought him a cup of it on a little white saucer and then went upstairs and rustled around for a few minutes. The hot tea was surprisingly good.

She returned, holding up an old, yellowed document triumphantly.

"I found the original deed to the house," she rasped. "I've kept it in my safe all these years, since father died. Here's your Johnson family, young man. Grandpa Burgess bought this house from somebody named Johnson in March of 1891."

"Really, 1891? Was it Red Johnson who sold the house?"

"Nope."

Mark set his teacup down.

"It was a woman. A Leah."

"Leah Johnson?"

"Yep."

Gently, he took the document from her and examined it himself. It said exactly what she said it did, and he didn't like what that implied.

***

As fortune would have it, the White County courthouse was located just a few blocks away. A short walk would hopefully reveal a little more about the sale of the Johnson home.

The historic courthouse was a square brick building standing two stories tall in the middle of a large, rounded median in the center of the town square. Its facades were punctuated by four chimneys, one at each corner of the roof, and a number of white window frames resting on grey stone sills. The city had surrounded the grounds with vibrant flowerbeds. He was chagrined to discover it had been declared an historical landmark at some point and turned into a museum.

He supposed he could go back in time and visit the old courthouse when it was younger and still in use.

He grinned. *What a novelty.* As a lover of history and historical places, the possibilities fascinated him.

Suspecting the watch could overheat with too much use, however, meant he needed to limit the number of times he employed it for the time being. He passed the old building by and continued a block further to the modern courthouse. Its walls were muted with stacks of thin, whitish-grey bricks and looked to have been built in the 1960's or 70's. The clerk who managed property records and other such items was thin, young and quiet. His hair was a greasy dark brown, and Mark sincerely hoped the oil was from some kind of hair gel.

"1891? Not too may records left from that time. Whatever's left would be over at the historical society." The clerk pushed his glasses back up the ridge of his nose, eyeing Mark and his clothing warily.

Uh-oh. His clothing. He was back in 2011, but now his attire was hopelessly antiquated.

Mark winced at the oversight. There were more tricks to time travel than met the eye.

The man wrinkled his nose a little. Mark realized he must stink as well, and here he'd been judging the clerk's hygiene.

"What kind of records were you needing exactly?" The clerk asked.

"I'm not really sure....any kind of documents that might deal with the transfer of a piece of land."

"There wouldn't have been much in the way of documentation from that time anyway. Deeds were sometimes kept by families, so the county might not have records of it. Even if they had, like I said, the older stuff is gone for the most part."

"Okay, guess I'm out of luck. Thanks anyway."

"You know....now, that I think about it. We may have something after all. An old coot by the name of Bridges from the other side of town came in here a few years ago with boxes and boxes of newspapers he'd collected over the years. I think some of those papers might have gone back as far as that. We threw a lot of the later stuff away because the library already had it recorded on microfiche, but we did save the older papers. Do you want to take a look at those?"

It was a long shot, but why not? He nodded and followed the man down into the basement. Rows and rows of cardboard boxes and filing cabinets formed a maze in the dank, musty space. The young clerk directed him to a specific pile of boxes in a corner.

"They're organized by year?"

"Yup. Not sure what the guy thought was so important about the things, but he invested a lot of time in them."

"Thanks. I guess I'll start looking." The clerk abandoned him to the search, and he dove in. His hopes rose greatly when he saw there were newspapers as old as 1886. It was amazing they were still legible.

It wasn't very long before he found the ones he was looking for. He'd met Red on the 7th of September, so he retrieved the newspaper dating Sept. 6th of that year and also the next one from Sept. 13th. Nothing of interest appeared in the Sept. 6th issue, but there it was, plain as day, right on the front page of the Sept. 13th.

Red Johnson Killed Clearing Land

Apparently, five days after Mark met him, Red had been killed by a falling tree that toppled onto him while he was trying to cut it down. There was nothing more in the next few issues of the paper, but about two months later, the editor made a call on all "good Christians" in the community to extend a helping hand to the Johnson family who'd "so recently fallen on hard times". That was all he could find. There was no report of the house being sold, but that probably hadn't been a news item. Most likely, Leah had been forced to sell in 1891 since Red was no longer around to provide for her and the kids.

He did an internet search at the local library to try and scrounge up info about what had happened to the Johnsons. John Johnson and Michael Johnson were such generic names it proved impossible to find anything pertinent. However, when he tried Leah Johnson combined with Daisy, he stumbled on the genealogy website of a man from Santa Rosa, California. Little Johnny Johnson had been his grandfather, which made Red his great-grandfather.

What few biographical sketches the man had on the site told Mark that Leah had become destitute a few years after Red's death and moved up north to Chicago to try and find work. All three children had been placed in an orphanage after she died in 1896.

Chapter 6

He couldn't remember exactly what time he had shifted out of Red's bunkhouse.

It was a crucial matter. The idea of popping back to 1890 inside the bunkhouse and running into his former self gave Mark the willies. Something about the idea of meeting himself as a separate person made him queasy.

If he shifted back while outside the bunkhouse and got the time wrong, he might appear out of nowhere in front of Red. That would blow everything. Coming into too late, which would mean disappearing for a period of time, would probably deem him unreliable and unfit for work in Red's eyes. No, somehow he had to shift back at just the right moment to intercept Red before he discovered Mark was missing.

He strolled back to the Burgess / Johnson home and made a beeline for the back yard. Red had come knocking somewhere around 5:00 AM. So, to be safe, he gave himself an extra hour and set the device's target time to 4:00 AM of that same morning. He stood behind the rotting bunkhouse and pushed the button.

Darkness.

It was night again. Early morning actually. The bunkhouse once more looked fresh and crisp, no weeds choking its frame into oblivion.

He couldn't help but be awed by the time-travel process, the whole concept of it really. He resisted the temptation to peek in the bunkhouse window. It was an easy thing to resist. He had no desire to even *see* another version of himself. Who knew what kind of havoc or paradoxes it might wreak.

He ducked into the shadows and let time tick by. An hour passed and the sudden, overwhelming urge to pee came upon him. Did he have time? Dang it, what time had Red come anyway? He didn't want to have to start over.

He wasn't going to make it. He'd best just hurry. He ran off the path a short ways and emptied his bladder as fast as he could. He'd made it back to the bunkhouse lawn when he heard Red knocking on the door.

"Up an at'em, Carpen! We got work to do."

"Over here, Red. I'm up already."

"Dagnabit, boy! You scairt the dickens out of me!"

"Sorry, had to relieve myself."

"Well, let's get to it, Carpen. Lots of work to do, yessir, lots to do!"

Mark worked harder over the next few days than he had in years. His trim and toughened body grew firmer under the hot Georgia sun and thicker with Leah's generous cooking.

Red spared him no task. Milking cows, collecting eggs, harvesting corn, removing stumps, he did it all.

Finally, Sept. 12th arrived, the day of reckoning.

Red thought there might be some rich soil in a field he owned to the northwest of the farm, but they'd have to clear it of trees before it could be plowed the following spring. Red decided that would be the work for the day. Frankly, it would be enough work for several months.

The field was a twenty minute walk from the house. Upon arrival, the hair on Mark's arm stood on end, an odd foreboding running through him in shivers. He attributed it to his foreknowledge of the tragedy about to unfold.

"Hey, Carpen! Head on o'er to those sprouts yonder and start takin' 'em out ifn' yer don't mind."

"Why don't I stay up here and help you with these bigger ones?"

"Cause it'll take us twice as long that's why!"

Mark hesitated. He couldn't just leave Red by himself. That would be a fatal mistake....to Red. He could quit and just sit there, watching Red work until whatever was going to happen, happened. All kinds of problems with that plan though.

"What's the matter with ya Carpen? What's the problem?"

"I've got a funny feeling is all. I can't leave you alone up here. I don't know why, but when my gut says something, I follow my gut, no two ways about it."

Red grunted. "I ain't nobody to argue with nobody's gut, so if'n you insist, I guess that's how we'll do it."

They'd burnt through half the day when it happened.

Red was chopping away at a good-sized pine tree. He'd cut a little more than halfway through, not enough for it to fall under normal circumstances, but there must have been some weakened strands in the back side of the trunk. Red was walking away from the tree to get a feel for where it was going to fall when the trunk cracked like a gunshot.

The tree creaked and began a slow, heavy descent that accelerated quickly. Red whipped his head back and saw what was happening. He tried to jump out of the way, but his foot slipped on some wet leaves, and he went down on one knee. The falling tree wouldn't give him time to recover before it struck.

As ready as Mark had been for something to happen, he still wasn't sure he'd have enough time to intervene. Thankfully, instinct propelled his body into action while his mind was still processing. He launched himself into Red's body, striking him full force in the side and shoulder, and knocked him clear of the danger. The effort was not sufficient to save Mark's own ankle though, which lay trapped beneath the fallen trunk.

Red's expression displayed a mixture of disbelief, awe, and fear. He'd just come very close to dying and he knew it.

Quietly, he rose and set to work digging to free Mark's leg. Amazingly, it was not broken. While an ankle might survive such with only some bruising to show for it, a skull would have been a different story.

Red called it a day and they walked back to the house in silence.

Chapter 7

*Dost thou love life? Then do not squander time,
for that's the stuff life is made of.*

~ Benjamin Franklin

September 13th, 1890 – Cleveland, GA

The next morning, breakfast was bigger than the morning feast Leah normally prepared. She'd really outdone herself. The kids scrambled in and hastily sat down before Red said Grace.

Bowing their heads, Red led them in prayer as usual, but this morning, he seemed to take a little longer than normal in thanking his God.

"Quite a spread, Leah."

"It was Red's idea, said today we needed to celebrate. He's takin' a holiday from work too." She giggled softly. An intimate moment passed between the couple.

Mark looked at Red quizzically, "What are we celebrating, Red?"

Grinning, he slapped Mark on the shoulder, laughing, "Why, boy! You done saved my bacon, don't you realize that? If it weren't fer the likes of you, I'd be a corpse, sure enough. Figure that's a mighty fine cause fer celebration."

Mark grinned back. "I tend to agree". He bit into a biscuit loaded with strawberry jam.

"Carpen, I do truly thank ya fer what ya done out there yesterday."

Mark shrugged, "Wasn't nothing. You would have done the same."

"Maybe, but that ain't how it worked out."

"Really, it's nothing."

"If'n ya don't mind, I'd like to give you something."

Mark sat there, unsure of what was coming and not just a little embarrassed by the attention.

Red's smile widened. "I thought about it all night, and I'm going to give you that field we were clearing over there. That's the least a man can pay for his life!"

Mark couldn't believe what he was hearing.

"Red....seriously, that's not necessary. I did what anybody would have done. Plus, I work for you. It's my job to look out for you, right?"

"Ya don't work fer me no more, boy, ye'll be working yer own land!"

Red was dead serious too. There was nothing Mark could say to talk him out of it. The plot Red was giving him turned out to be about 40 acres. Red insisted they go over to the land office later that day and file the deed change. Mark considered bugging out to 2011, but hey....why not let the guy do what he wants, make him feel better.

After walking the property, they went to the land office and transferred the deed. Mark felt bad, as if he'd cheated in order to profit from Red somehow. He supposed giving away a piece of land was better than your life, and Red wouldn't be satisfied if Mark didn't accept it. Plus, in saving Red's life, Mark *had* risked his own as well.

What really amazed him was that he, Mark Carpen, had just changed history. Red Johnson had actually died in an old version of history. Now, because of Mark's intervention, Red would live out many more days with his family. His kids would never see an orphanage. The impact would probably affect Red's family tree for generations.

It occurred to him that this land Red had given him could be the start of a way out of the financial hole he was in.

A plan began to form in his mind. He could beat all the lawyers and corrupt politicians at their own game.

Mark began to get excited.

He bid the Johnson's farewell and went on his way. If this plan worked, he was going to be very busy. There wouldn't be much time to come back and visit.

September 13th, 2011 – Cleveland, GA

Shifting forward to 2011, Mark was anxious to find out what his property was now worth. He could only imagine the inflation in price on 40 acres over a period of 120 years. Surely he could sell it for at least $2,000 - $3,000 per acre now.

He was headed to the Citgo to call information to find an appraisal company when he realized he didn't even have a quarter to use a public telephone. He would have to borrow a few dollars from someone to get started. No way around it.

Mark cursed. He was officially going to become a beggar. He hated the idea.

Then, it occurred to him that if he asked the appraisal company to come out, their fee would be at least several hundred dollars, and he didn't have the money to pay that either. He now owned a property that was potentially worth a decent amount of money, but the key word was *potentially*. He couldn't buy a Coke right now, much less pay for an appraisal.

Maybe he could just check with the county land registry and look up the land lot there. They would have it assessed at a certain value for tax purposes, and that would give him an idea of what it was really worth. The assessments were usually low....

Taxes! Property taxes would not have been paid for 118 years. His property would have been seized by the government long before 2011. Probably around 1895 or thereabouts. When it came to collecting its money, the government had a way of being on top of things. The acreage would not have been in his name for a long time.

This was going to be a lot more complicated than he'd anticipated.

He needed cash. Somehow, he had to get some. He needed to get back to Lawrenceville. Once he got home, he could redeem himself.

September 15th, 1890 – Cleveland, GA

"Carpen! I didn' 'spect to see ya ag'in so soon. Ya seemed mighty sure ya'd be gone a good spell, but, it's good to see ya, 'gardless."

"Red, I hate to say it, but I need to sell the field you gave me. Do you know anybody in a position to buy it?"

Leah stood behind Red, washing dishes. Her face fell. She looked rattled, but not for the reason Mark thought.

"Sorry, but I ain't got the cash to do it, friend, or I would," Red answered.

"No, no, I didn't expect you to," Mark said.

"Ya cain't sell it to that horsewhippin' Lancaster!" Leah blurted, "You just cain't!" Her outburst was completely out of character.

"Leah, hush up, dagnabit!"

"Who's Lancaster?"

"Dagnabit, woman! Sorry, Carpen. I didn' want to tell yer about him, not that I mind yer sellin' to somebody's else or makin' a profit, surely not. It's jes', well, there's this gentleman...."

"Ain't no gentleman!"

"....who's been after me to buy them acres for some time. I ne'er did aim to sell to him. Didn' take to him, if'n yer know what I mean. Seemed shifty, like som'tin else were behind it. Feel free to sell to 'im if'n ya got a mind to though."

Mark seated himself at the table and thought. "Red, if you don't like the man, then I probably wouldn't either. Is there anybody else?"

"Nope." The farmer shook his head slowly.

"Well, how about a trade then? Are you willing to trade me for my land?"

"What yer got in mind?"

"Would you give me a horse for it?"

Red's face lit up, his grin spreading from ear to ear.

"How about some fresh made biscuits with strawberry jam to go with it," Leah smiled.

Chapter 8

September 16th, 1890 – Lawrenceville, GA

It was an experience Mark had never imagined would be a part of his life. Riding a horse down a dirt highway *in the 1800's.* It was surreal to see his hometown as it existed back then. Dirt roads ran this way and that, their pattern roughly mimicking the grid of his modern city, yet not quite the same. Men, women, and children — all wore dated clothing. Horses and buggies filled the streets rather than automobiles. Instead of car emissions, the town square smelled of dust and horse manure.

The land Red had given him would have been very valuable, but there were a lot of complications to overcome in order to hold such a property for so long. To keep it, he'd have needed to find a reliable law firm or agency that could manage the property over the next century or so, pay the taxes, etc, and that would not have been easy. It would have to have been a law firm that would stick around for at least a century.

Or would it? He could travel to any year he wanted. He could transfer the management of anything from one firm to another at any time during the coming hundred years.

As with anything, the hard work was in the details. From the center of town, Mark steered his horse down what would one day be Georgia Highway 20 toward Loganville. After a few miles, he veered off the road into a field, guessing he was about where his subdivision would be in the future.

What he was about to do was gutsy, to say the least, but it was the easiest solution.

He shifted forward to June of 2010.

He'd had an early morning job that entire month and Kelly had always gone to work after him. He didn't want to try an earlier period, for many logistical reasons, and one emotional one. He didn't want to see his kids alive. The thought of it nearly wrecked him inside.

5:00 AM seemed like a good hour. He'd been off on the distance though. He showed up in somebody's backyard and had to walk another 500 yards to get to his own house. He snuck around to the back of it and waited out of sight.

At about 5:30, his old car pulled out of the driveway. Mark turned his head away. He still didn't want to see himself.

Kelly would be getting into the shower about 6:00. As soon as he heard the water turn on, he went to the back door and rattled it. If you jiggled it just the right way, he knew the dead bolt would slip out of its slot. *He should have fixed that back when Kelly had asked him to.*

Sneaking into your own house in the early hours of the morning seemed oddly criminal. He slipped into the family room, crossed it to the master bedroom, and then went to the closet. The water was still running in the shower. She'd be at least another ten minutes; she liked long showers.

He would need a larger backpack in the near future, so he pulled one down from the closet shelf. He remembered he hadn't been able to find this pack when he'd left this house for the last time a few months ago, but here it was now. It was much more spacious than the small thing he'd been dealing with for the past few months. He transferred all his stuff to it.

Next, he stripped to his boxers and stuffed his antique clothing into the pack as well. He would need some modern jeans and a shirt.

He returned to the bedroom. That water sounded *really* good. A steaming hot shower would do him wonders. His muscles almost ached at the thought. That bed looked awfully good too.

Hurriedly, he pulled an outfit from his chest-of-drawers to throw it on, but he wasn't quick enough.

Steam poured from the bathroom as Kelly opened the door. He froze, stiff as a plank. She let out a startled yelp.

"Mark! You scared me. I thought you'd already left for work."

"I....uh....I forgot something."

"Oh....what?"

"Uh...I...uh, spilled some coffee in the car and got it all over my shirt. Had to come home to change."

"Oh...okay. Are you all right, honey?"

"Yeah, I'm fine." He breathed easier. She believed it was him. Well, why shouldn't she? It *was* him, just not the right him. This was weird.

"Well, I'm going to finish getting ready."

"Okay, Sweetie." How awkward to call your wife "sweetie" after she'd abandoned you. But this Kelly had not abandoned him yet. But she would. She closed the bathroom door behind her.

He sniffed the new clothes deeply, enjoying the fresh scent of Tide on the recently laundered shirt. He put them on. Felt good, felt clean.

He stole over to her dresser where she always left her wallet. This was why he'd had to come at this time of day. He'd never be able to get at his own wallet, because it would always be on his former self regardless of the time, except at night, and a night-time break in was not very appealing. He owned several guns. Wouldn't that be the ultimate fulfillment of Murphy's Law, getting shot by yourself for breaking into your own house.

Mark slipped her debit card from her wallet, stuffed his feet back into his shoes, and left home through the same back door he'd come in. Well, his former home that was.

It was awfully tempting to stay. But how could he? Impossible.

He kept moving, circling back to the approximate place he'd left his horse in 1890. When Kelly came out of the bathroom, she'd just think he'd gone on to work.

***

September 16th, 1890 – Lawrenceville, GA

The next step would be tricky to accurately guess. He needed to gauge the distance well so he wouldn't pop up in the wrong place. He walked southeast, away from the county courthouse in the town square, down Clayton Street until he reached the old female seminary building, though it wasn't so old right now. That was one landmark he knew wouldn't change over the next century and it was right across the street from his target in the future. Now, he had to imagine the modern scene in his mind to see how far he needed to walk

Doing some major guesstimations in his head, Mark decided to walk another four hundred paces angled 30 degrees to the left of the Seminary building. The father and mother of a family passing by shot him a funny look as he wandered across the street into the yards of some homes there. He knew he looked suspicious, yet it couldn't be helped.

The surrounding field looked nothing like it would in the future, but it had to be the same place. It was the right orientation from the seminary. When he felt like he was at the right distance, he stopped and set his watch to:

010000P - 05312010

May 31, 2010 was a date after his children had been killed, but before he'd really been embroiled in the lawsuits that ended up costing him everything.

He pushed the button and felt his body forced to one side as he shifted. He must have tried to materialize in the middle of some object again.

"Hijo de mi alma!"

Mark found himself in what appeared to be the back stockroom of some business, apparently a music CD store. A young Hispanic woman screamed at the top of her lungs, eyes wide with fear. She fled the storeroom in a panic, yelling for help.

"Manuel! Manuel! Venga rapido! Apareció un tipo ahi atras! Socale, socale!"

Crap. He needed to get out of here.

He shifted back to 1890. That must have been *Discolandia*, which was an Hispanic music store located in the shopping center next to his target.

Mark retreated about a hundred feet toward the seminary and set the dial for a day earlier, May 30. No sense in trying the same day. Who knew if the girl would call the cops or not? This time when he shifted, his body slid upwards, and he was forced into a sitting position. Awkwardly, he fell back into a seat and realized he was now sitting in the passenger side of a vehicle in the shopping center's parking lot.

Man alive. Why did this have to be so difficult? Hunkering down, he slipped out of the car and moved away as fast as possible. Ever his luck though, the car's owner just happened to be returning to their vehicle at that very moment and they let out a yell, as any sane person would who'd just seen a stranger slip out of their car.

Great. Again, Mark shifted back to the empty field in 1890. Nausea came on strong and he vomited up what little food had been in his system. This was becoming entirely more difficult than it should be.

All right. Two strikes. This time he wouldn't take any chances. He walked back to the seminary building and, laying his hand on its bricks, shifted to May 29, 2010, another day earlier. The seminary was one building which would stay right where it was for the entire century, a safe reference point.

He was now safely in 2010, in the right clothing, and all he had to do was walk across the street to the shopping center and to his goal. Why hadn't he just done it this way this first time?

There it was, his objective in all its glory. The Bank of America ATM machine.

Using Kelly's ATM card, Mark withdrew $100 from his old checking account. He was glad he remembered her PIN number. It wasn't stealing if you took it from yourself, was it? It sure felt better having a little cash in his hand again.

All of a sudden, a memory came to him. A memory of a $100 missing from their checking account early that summer. $100 neither he nor Kelly could account for. She'd lost her debit card around that time too. They'd assumed she'd just lost it somewhere and somebody else had withdrawn the $100. The bank had sworn the correct PIN had been used though, and he vaguely remembered them thinking the withdrawal had been made before they'd lost the card.

Was he simply planting these memories in his mind after the fact? Was it some kind of effort on the part of his subconscious to reconcile conflicts between his past and his present, or was the memory real? Would he remember the missing $100 if he hadn't taken it now? Maybe taking the money actually altered the reality of his own past, or maybe his withdrawal simply triggered a memory of a forgotten event. How could he know for sure? The idea that his own memory might not be reliable was a concept he couldn't allow himself to entertain.

Those were impossible questions and they'd have to keep for another day. For now, he would stay the course as planned.

He returned to the seminary building and changed the watch setting to shift him back from 2010 to 1970. However, pushing the button this time did not produce the all-too-familiar-yet-still-unsettling queasiness in his stomach. Instead, the watch just beeped and flashed like it had back in the woods. It had shut down again.

There must be a limit on how many times he could shift in quick succession. Mentally, he counted back, recalling each shift. He'd shifted six or seven times in the past eight hours. He'd have to keep better track of that and figure out exactly what was going on.

So, for now he was stuck in 2010, which certainly felt a lot better than being stuck in 1890. He was going to need a place to bed down for at least 24 hours until the watch cooled off or did whatever it did to reset itself.

He crossed town to the Lawrenceville Motor Inn and spent $30 on a room for the night. Another $5 went to a meal at McDonald's, which left him $65 for the next day. At least, he'd gotten some food and a good night's sleep. That motel bed felt like heaven compared with Red's bunkhouse. He was getting downright spoiled.

***

Mark let a full 36 hours pass before making his next move. If he was going to go around disappearing and re-appearing on a dime, doing it at night would make things a lot easier. Less witnesses.

At 1:00 in the morning, he sat himself on the historic courthouse steps in downtown Lawrenceville and set the watch to 4:00 AM, Oct. 17, 1970. In the darkness, no immediate differences jumped out at him after he pushed the button, but then he noticed all the old, ugly storefront facades around the square were back. The brick sidewalks were gone. Fowler's Jewelers was in business again. The building next to it which had burned down years ago stood once more without a lick of soot on it. The City of Lawrenceville had done a lot of restoration work to the downtown area in the 1990's, but for him, it was all undone now. Behind him, the brick courthouse walls were no longer their natural, rusty color, but were painted white, as they had been in 1970.

He bode his time for a few hours waiting for the town to wake up and then strolled to Edge's Café. He bought himself a hot breakfast for $2.00 and ate it slowly, thoroughly enjoying the southern flavors and giving the business world a chance to crank up for the day. Then, he walked to the small office building he'd been eyeing all morning.

Brett Harrington ran the investment office and served as the town's main stock broker and financial advisor. His eyes met Mark with wary appraisal. Once again, Mark had forgotten to pay attention to the differing styles of dress. His 2010 clothing might seem very futuristic, or maybe just plain odd, to a 1970's man.

"Can I help you, sir?" Harrington was still trying to assess Mark as a person.

"I would like to purchase some shares in a company, please."

"Have you ever traded with me before?"

"No, sorry. Sure haven't."

"Well, it's pretty simple actually. We'll just set up an account for you. Do you know the stock symbol of the company you want to purchase?"

"Uh, no."

"What company do you wish to buy shares in?"

"Wal-Mart."

"Is that a new company? Never heard of it."

"Oh, you will." He couldn't resist that.

The stock broker raised an eyebrow, eyeing Mark even more quizzically. "I don't mean to be rude, but those are some odd clothes you've got on."

"I'm a bit eccentric. Please excuse the attire." Mark was getting a little quicker with the off-the-cuff lies and hasty explanations, but it'd be better if he were prescient enough not to need them.

"Well, anyway, I'll look up the symbol for you. I charge a 5% commission. How many shares did you want?"

"About $60.00 worth."

He pulled three $20 bills from his pocket and handed them to Harrington. Harrington took them and then stared at the bills.

"Is this some kind of joke?" he said.

"I'm sorry."

"What kind of stunt are you trying to pull? Did somebody put you up to this?"

"What do you mean?"

"These bills. They aren't real, that's for sure, but it's the best job of counterfeiting I've ever seen, except for the fact that some idiot made Jackson too big and printed him off-center. Probably wouldn't have spotted it if it weren't for that."

Mark mentally slapped himself on the forehead. Of course, the $20 bills he'd gotten out of the ATM in 2010 would look different than currency in 1970.

"Uh, yeah. Tom put me up to it, but you caught me." Hastily, he snatched the bills from the broker and rushed out of the office. *Tom put me up to it?* Well, he figured the guy must know somebody named Tom. Mark ran back to the courthouse and ducked into an external stairwell at its back, where he shifted forward to 2010.

It took some effort, but after visiting a number of different shops, he was able to exchange the twenties for some beat-up $1 bills. The style of those had not changed over those forty years as the bigger bills had.   If the broker were suspicious and examined them closely enough, he'd probably notice the $1 bills had been printed in years after 1970. That is... *if* he were suspicious. Mark would shift to one month prior to his first meeting with Harrington to avoid suspicion.

He spent another $10 on food and an outfit from Goodwill which would fit in better with the styles of the 1970's.

This time, Harrington didn't bat an eye. Mark gave the broker only $40 this time, holding the last $10 for other unexpected expenses. Harrington took his information, and promised Mark the Wal-Mart shares would arrive in a couple of weeks if he wanted the physical copies. Mark did.

He shifted forward two weeks into the future and collected his shares from Harrington. Then, he walked across the street to Brand Bank, a bank he knew would still be around for decades to come. He opened a safe deposit box and left the shares inside.

Next, he opened a savings account, deposited his $10.00 with the teller, and then went outside. He slipped behind the building, away from the eyes of traffic, and shifted forward to September of 2011, his original present time.

Jumping around through the years could easily become disorienting. He needed an anchor, an unchanging reference point from which he could measure everything else. This time, right now, September of 2011, was his actual present. As he explored the labyrinth of time, he would need to come back here every now and then and just live his normal life. He would call this his home time.

Chapter 9

September 17th, 2011 – Lawrenceville, GA

One more glitch stared him in the face. A driver's license. He'd left his driver's license behind with everything else he'd abandoned earlier in the summer. Of course, he'd need that license to retrieve his possessions.

It took a bit of finagling, but he reported his license stolen and got a replacement. When he finally returned to the bank, he was twice disappointed. First, over the past forty years, his original $10.00 had only turned into $44.67. *Goes to show you what a savings account at a bank is worth*, he mused.

The second disappointment was that his safe deposit box had long been closed out and the contents confiscated for failure to pay the annual fee for the box. 40 years of payments was apparently a little over $1,600.

Good grief. Why did this have to be so difficult? *You'd think making money with a time machine would be easy.*

Instead of using the safe deposit box, Mark could have just shifted from 1970 to 2011 with his Wal-Mart shares in hand, but then they wouldn't appear to have aged at all and probably would have been treated as a forgery when he tried to cash them in. The Securities Exchange Commission might be suspicious of someone showing up with four original Wal-Mart stock certificates that looked like they'd just been printed.

Frustrated, Mark withdrew his $44.67 in 2011, shifted back to the day after he'd opened his savings account in 1970 and redeposited the money. When he returned to 2011, his account now had a balance of $244.18. Still not enough, but it was better.

He contemplated doing the savings account trick again, but that would mean he would have to deposit almost 250 one dollar bills at the bank back in 1970. Such a quantity would greatly increase the chances somebody would notice many of those bills were printed forty years after he was depositing them. It was very likely the federal bank which maintained the cash reserves for the community banks in the area would notice and they would trace the funny bills back to Brand Bank. It wouldn't take Brand Bank long at all to remember who had deposited so many one dollar bills into their account. Tellers had memories and that kind of thing stood out.

Nope, he had to think of something else, and he had an idea that might just work. Mark withdrew some of his savings and walked seven blocks to the closest Wal-Mart where he purchased a number of potentially very useful items.

Ironic. He was using Wal-Mart to make money off of Wal-Mart.

***

April 16th, 1918 – Lawrenceville, GA

Mark pushed the glass door to the drugstore open and went inside. A tiny bell tinkled overhead as he entered. To him, the drugstore looked old-fashioned, though it was truthfully quite contemporary for 1918. Rows and rows of antique-styled glass medicine bottles lined the shelves along one wall and behind the counter. Other shelves and tables displayed common household items made of glass and iron, which again looked dated to him, but were correct for the period. He guessed this pharmacy simultaneously served as a sort of convenient store.

The floor was real hardwood, the kind of thin-slatted floor only found in older buildings, but this wood was of course not aged, did not creak, and smelled faintly of the linseed oil used to preserve it. The style of the entire decor was early 20th century, but none of it showed the wear and tear age brings. Of course, this was exactly as it should be, but Mark's mind was still assimilating the reality of the years he was traversing and the new, fresh feel of all the older-styled items still struck him as odd.

The ambiance evoked images right out of a Normal Rockwell painting. An elderly woman chatted with the pharmacist, who stood behind the counter. A teenage boy sat with two pretty girls close to the soda fountain sharing some milkshakes. It felt homey.

The pharmacist was neatly groomed, his hair peppered with even mix of black and gray, and he wore a white coat as a uniform. He paused his conversation with the woman long enough to greet Mark warmly. His smile implied he would be the kind of man who would be popular around town.

Mark took a stool at the counter and ordered a soda, listening carefully to the different conversations around the store. Before long, the youngsters left and two middle-aged women came in chatting about everybody and their dog's business. He'd only been here for a few minutes and already Mark was learning a good bit about social life of Lawrenceville in the 1910's.

Then, a lone mother in her early forties entered. Her face bore a look of desperation that seemed all too familiar with its lines, wrinkles that were as yet still faint, but surely weathered deeper each year by some great burden life had heaped upon her shoulders.

She asked the pharmacist for more of her son's pills — she'd run out. He retrieved a bottle from the shelf behind his head, and, with an air of panic in her movements, she paid and rushed out the door.

After she'd left, Mark inquired about her. In this age, the concept of privacy in medicine was non-existent and the pharmacist was more than happy to share his concerns for the poor woman and her family.

Her name was Lucy Henderson, the wife of one of Lawrenceville's most prominent and wealthy businessmen, Thomas Henderson. Their son Jeffrey had suffered from a lung disease since he was a young child, and it only seemed to get worse every year. They had tried all kinds of medicines and remedies, but nothing seemed to work. Young Jeffrey just kept getting worse.

It was worth looking into. Mark bought a few random glass medicine bottles from the pharmacist, paid for his soda, tipped his hat, and left.

***

"May I help you?"

Her beauty was not flirtatious, nor glaring, but a regal beauty as one would expect from the wife of a prominent businessman. Her auburn hair was swept into a bun, a couple of streaks of gray in it the only sign of her real age. If she used cosmetics, she used them modestly.

"Yes, ma'am. I heard that your son Jeffrey has some difficulty with his lungs. I don't mean to be presumptuous, but I think I may be able to help him."

She was taken off guard, which was understandable.

"I'm sorry, sir, but I don't understand. Are you a doctor? I don't know you."

"Of sorts. Please, I heard about your predicament. I am not sure if I can help, but if you will let me examine him, I may."

She was not sure what to do. She sized him up for several seconds.

"Wait here," she finally breathed. "Thomas!" She receded into the house. After a minute, she returned. "Please come in. My husband is waiting for you in the study."

He was a solid, sturdy looking man. As he and Mark shook hands, his no nonsense grip communicated an honesty one could respect.

"I'm Thomas Henderson," he introduced himself.

"Mark Carpen."

"Lucy says you're offering to help my son. What do you know about him?"

"Just that he's sick with a lung disease and no medicine has worked for him so far."

"And why you think you can help?"

"I won't know if I can until I examine him, but I wouldn't have come if I didn't think it were possible."

"What are your qualifications? Have you been to medical school?"

"My qualifications aren't important. I have some medicines that may help him. What do you have to lose?"

"Well, it occurs to me that you may be a quack out to make a quick buck preying on desperate families, sir."

"I won't ask you to pay me until you've seen the medicines work."

"What if these "medicines" hurt Jeffrey?"

Mark shrugged. Henderson stared him in the eye for a full minute weighing the man and his offer. In the end, he either decided to trust Mark or desperation just won out. They clearly believed their son was on the road to death if they didn't find a new treatment that worked.

"Come this way please."

He led Mark to a bedroom in the back of the house. Jeffrey looked to be about seven years old. He lay on his bed motionless, covered with blankets in spite of the heat of the day. His skin was pale, his breathing labored. He seemed very ill, and Mark understood why they thought he might die if his sickness was not remedied

After they explained the history of the boy's illness, Mark was relieved. For a moment, he'd worried the boy might actually have some serious disease for which Mark could not help, but he'd gambled that little Jeffrey might simply be suffering from some ordinary ailment that the medicines of 1918 just could not handle.

From the description of the symptoms, Mark believed the boy had asthma, which was probably allergy induced. Yet, since the asthma and the allergies had gone unabated for so long, heavy mucus dripping into Jeffrey's lungs had probably since turned it into a case of pneumonia.

In 2011, Mark had purchased a plethora of over-the-counter drugs while he was at Wal-Mart, rightly figuring that Extra Strength Tylenol might be a big hit in 1918. He'd stuffed his backpack with everything from Sudafed to Pepto Bismol. Before coming to the Henderson home, he'd emptied the old-fashioned, glass medicine bottles he'd bought at the drugstore, throwing the useless 1918 pills into the woods, and peeled off the labels. Then, he'd removed several of his Wal-Mart drugs from their aluminum packaging and poured those pills into the empty bottles so his modern medicines wouldn't appear futuristic to the people from this age.

He went to the boy and laid his hand on his forehead. He had a strong fever. Definitely an infection in the lungs. Mark pulled out a Primatine Mist asthma inhaler. He sat the boy up and told him to breathe out deeply. The poor boy didn't have much breath to give. Mark depressed the inhaler in the boy's mouth as he breathed back in. After a couple more times, the boy seemed to be breathing easier.

His parents stood astonished with their mouths agape. They hadn't expected any quick improvement. Mark handed them a bottle filled with antibiotics he'd had in his backpack since when he'd first gone to live off the mountains. They were strong ones and would likely handle this infection okay.

"Give him one of these pills three times a day, with food. He has an infection in his lungs. These will help with that." He handed them several packs of Primatine Mist tablets and several inhalers. "The inhalers will help when he has moderate trouble breathing. If he has serious trouble, give him the tablets, but try to limit how many you give him because they can be addictive."

They nodded.

"Do you have any cats or dogs?"

"Yes, we have several cats."

"You must keep the cats outside the house permanently. They must never come inside again. Then, take all your furniture, blankets, and pillows outside and bang the dust out of them until you don't see any more. After that, scrub the house from top to bottom and get rid of any dust you find.

"I also strongly recommend having cement poured underneath your home so it's not sitting over wet dirt. Your son may be allergic to mold spores too.

"Even if you do those things, he may still have trouble in the Spring and the Fall. If he does, just give him some of these." Mark handed them some Sudafed, Chlor-Trimeton, and Benadryl. "Try different ones to see which works better. Some will keep him awake, some will put him to sleep. These are not as strong as the other tablets I gave you, so use them accordingly. Any questions?"

Both Thomas and Lucy were dumbfounded by the assertive recommendations, so they just shook their heads. "Oh, by the way, if you have any feather pillows, get him some different ones — and keep horses and other animals away from the house too. I'll be back in a few months to check on you. You can pay me then if the medicines worked."

Chapter 10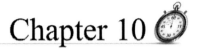

June 16th, 1918 – Lawrenceville, GA

The humidity was thick and choking. Mosquitos swarmed around Mark's head as he made his way up the block. He swatted at them sporadically but eventually gave up. He was going to have to remember to pick up some Deet spray next time he was at Wal-Mart.

Thomas and Lucy Henderson had seen him coming and were waiting for him on their front porch. Both were smiling from ear to ear.

He stopped at the bottom of their steps. "How is he?"

"See for yourself." Tom called out toward the back of the house, "Jeffrey!" Shortly, the boy who had been so sickly just a few months prior, now ran energetically to his father, perfectly healthy.

"Those medicines were wonderful, Mister. They're miracle drugs. Jeffrey's never felt so well. What are they?"

"Did you pour concrete under the house?"

"Yes, we followed all your instructions to the tee. Do we have to keep the cats outside and the horses away still?"

"Absolutely. I'm not sure what Jeffrey's allergic to, but there's a number of common culprits which could cause his breathing problems. If you bring those animals back, he could relapse and you would need even more medicine."

"Would you like to have dinner with us. It's about ready."

"Sure." Mark didn't make a habit of passing up free meals, especially home-cooked ones.

The dinner was piping hot and delicious. Mark enjoyed eating with a family again — it reminded him of being at Red's house. After dessert, Mr. Henderson offered him $100 for the medicines Mark had given them. It was the equivalent of two and half months of pay for a working man in 1918. He took it.

He found a few other things to sell around town. He sold several bottles of Pepto-Bismol and Tums to a lawyer for $5. He sold an old Walkman he got at a garage sale to an elderly gentleman for $10 along with several packs of batteries. The man was amazed he could walk around his yard listening to the radio with tiny speakers in his ears.

If one compared what he was being paid for these items with his original cost in 2011, it would appear to the layman that he was actually losing a little bit on each sale, but what he was really doing was converting his 2011 dollars to 1918 cash. $5 in 1918 would become $500 in 2011 after ninety years of compound interest.

These sums might seem paltry, but they were significant to these people who might only earn $30 to $40 per month. In the end, he collected a little under $200 total.

An added bonus was that Brand Bank already existed in the same location in 1918. In fact, the marble stone header above the door said 1905. He deposited his money in an account there and was confident it would carry through all the way to 2011.

He decided to check on his account every three to four years after 1980 (the computer age) so the bank wouldn't declare his account inactive and send his money to the State Treasurer's Office.

When he finally arrived in 2011 again, he now had $2,124 waiting for him in the Brand Bank savings account, more than enough to cover his safety deposit box fees. A few more shifts back and forth, and he'd worked out all the glitches in paying the fees before the contents were confiscated.

He was finally able to retrieve his Wal-Mart shares, all properly aged, and still had enough of a cash reserve to pay for a taxi to Atlanta.

***

In Atlanta, he located a securities firm that would help him cash in. The four original shares of Wal-Mart stock netted a cool $350,000. Not chump change by any degree.

It was all downhill from there. He was only limited by his own creativity in the different ways he could make money. However, there were lessons he'd learned from his forays back in time so far which he was careful not to neglect.

One of the first things he did upon reaching Atlanta was to do some research into finding a large, reputable law firm that had existed for at least 80 years. He needed a firm he could hire to manage his affairs over decades, a firm he could visit at any point in the last century and find out how his assets were doing at any given moment. They would need to be able to handle the sales of properties and stocks, pay income and property taxes, collect dividends, manage his bank accounts, etc., so it had to be somebody reliable.

At first glance, one would think it would be an easy task to find such a firm, but most law firms did not have such a long life. In the end, he chose one firm to manage his affairs from the 1920's to the 1950's, and a second firm to manage them from the 50's to the present. It was a simple matter to go back to 1953, the year the first firm would close its doors, and transfer everything into the hands of the other.

He also had to find a larger bank which would be intact for that same span of time. Finding enduring institutions to handle finances would be essential.

Once he'd nailed down many details such as those, Mark began to research in earnest. He became a regular at the public library. He bought all kinds of almanacs and yearbooks for different industries.

Before long, he was going back in time and buying key stocks at the right times. He made a killing in 1929 by selling short across the board.

He also tried his hand at gambling. Of course, he always won. He bet on World Series games, Super Bowls, horse races, boxing bouts, sailing cups, golf tournaments, you name it. He always bet on the long shots, though, the ones he knew from history had overcome the odds to win. Why waste time with penny ante stuff? Better just to go for the gold every time. He made a ton off of Seabiscuit's first winning race. The odds had been 70 to 1.

While at first glance it seemed possible to make an infinite amount of money jumping through time, the truth was, one had to be careful. For example, he would have loved to bet all $350,000 on Seabiscuit in that 70 to 1 race, but the idea posed two problems.

First, how do you move that much money back through time. He solved that problem by learning to convert his funds to physical gold and then transporting the gold back with him, but that could be cumbersome.

The second problem, however, could not be overcome. Placing a $350,000 bet on Seabiscuit would have netted him a theoretical $23.5 million, yet such an amount would have broken the track and put the owners in bankruptcy. They wouldn't have been able to pay his winnings, and it would have drawn unbelievable amounts of attention to him, which of course he did not want. It could have even drawn suspicion upon the owner of Seabiscuit as to somehow rigging the race.

No, Mark had to be content with medium-sized wins, which he then invested in long-lived and profitable stocks that he redeemed in 2011. He had to be careful how much of each stock he purchased too. If his percent ownership in any one company became too great, he could bankrupt them in the future when he cashed his shares in.

He bought lots of land in Buckhead, a suburb of Atlanta, while it was still rural and sold his properties for millions once it became the hot spot of Metro Atlanta. He did similar things out in Cobb, Gwinnett, and North Fulton counties, where he knew prices would go up and when.

He bought gold mines in California and oil wells in Texas long before anybody knew what would be found on those lands. He bought land all across the country in places he knew the U.S. government would be forced to pay him top dollar in order to pursue its highway projects.

He invested in Starbucks, Apple, Microsoft, and Home Depot long before they ever became famous.

In short, Mark Carpen went from broke to a billionaire in a matter of months.

Chapter 11

February 21st, 2012 – Atlanta, GA

Mark leaned back in his plush, black leather chair and let out a long awaited sigh. He hadn't allowed himself to fully relax until now. The specter of that million dollar lawsuit had haunted him from the shadows for too long.

This morning, however, when he'd opened his eyes, it had hit him — he truly was financially secure now, able to take on any horde of attorneys that wanted to mess with him. He felt like an abused puppy that had escaped its master and was just now realizing its freedom was real.

It was a new day. Spring was just around the corner, and he finally had no worries. He had managed to net almost $20.3 *billion* in just five months time, an amazing feat in of itself. Once he'd passed the half-billion mark, he'd begun to stash his accounts in various international banks around the world, from Switzerland to the Caribbean. No reason in particular other than he still preferred to avoid drawing much attention to himself.

His sudden wealth was not noticed by the modern world, for to them he had simply inherited funds which had been in bank accounts untouched for decades. He'd paid off the lawsuit damages he owed to the Governor's nephew in full, and what had once seemed an unbearable burden was suddenly off of his back.

His ex-wife Kelly had discovered his new found wealth, though she wasn't sure exactly how much he had, and sued, claiming he'd hidden funds from her during their marriage and was entitled to half. Technically she was right, but his old married self would have never known about the huge bank accounts available to him now.

He could have hired the best lawyers money could buy to rip her case to shreds, but he didn't have the heart. What did he care? He could get more. Besides, she was willing to settle for a couple hundred million, why not just give it to her and be done with it.

He considered trying to reconcile with her. Now that he had money, they had nothing to fear from the lawsuits which had ruined him before. Maybe their marriage would survive if they were without the financial strain.

The more he deliberated though, the more he realized they'd had no hope once the kids had been taken. The grief had been too much to handle together. Too much.

He longed for the way things used to be. He ached to see Daniel and Brittany. He wanted it to be the four of them again, living happily in their cozy, three-bedroom ranch. Saturday morning cartoons and frosted flakes. Family picnics in the park and snuggling on the couch at night.

He would trade all the wealth in the world for a chance to get his old life back. He could *travel* back in time, but he couldn't *turn* back time. He could go back a few years and see them at any age he wanted, but he couldn't be a part of their life again. You can't put the eggs back in the basket.

Money and grief are lonely partners, he was learning.

Epiphanies have a way of shining a piercing light into an abandoned area of our mind, a place full of cobwebs where we thought new ideas were impossible, and at the same time mentally slapping us upside the head for being so dense we hadn't considered a possibility before. The truth dawned on him.

He had a *time machine*. He'd saved Red from the falling tree — which had to mean he could *prevent the Accident.* Excitement and anticipation rushed into his veins like a narcotic. He was more than ready. He would be kicking himself for months to come for not having thought of it before.

This should have been the first thing he'd done. Then again, when he first found the shifter, he hadn't even had enough money to eat, much less provide for his kids. Now he could operate from a much stronger position to save them.

It was all moot anyway. At this point, he just needed to get busy.

***

Friday, May 23rd, 2009 3:17 P.M., Lawrenceville, GA

Mark's nerves were humming. He sat in a rented sedan along GA State Hwy 124 in the parking lot of the Hair Cuttery. There were no customers this afternoon at the tiny hair salon, which was located in a quaint old, red train caboose behind him, and that was good. It made for fewer potential complications.

His plan was simple. Mark knew that he — his former alter ego that is — would be driving by in approximately five to ten minutes with his children in the back seat of the car, unaware of the fate awaiting them around the corner. His former self would turn right onto Hwy 20, and just as they were passing the old Belk's shopping center, the drunken football star would whip out in front of them, slam on his brakes, and the unbearable tragedy would begin.

Unless Mark could change it that is. All he had to do was watch for his Camry. When he saw it coming, he would pull out in front of "himself" and basically do everything in his power to slow the other car down. Hopefully, he would change the timing of events just enough for his family to be saved.

He looked at his hands. They were shaking. Changing history was a whole different matter when it was your own family at stake.

There it was. The Camry was coming. His heart leapt into his throat as he slowly pulled out into the lane in front of the vehicle bearing his children. He purposefully restrained his eyes from looking too closely at the other car. He did not want to see them yet. Not until he knew they were safe. Once they were safe, he would give them the biggest hug a father has ever given his children.

He accelerated to the speed of normal traffic, and then, as the car drew close, he stepped heavily on the brakes, shortening the gap between them. The blue Camry switched lanes to avoid him, but Mark had anticipated this and changed too. Another few seconds, and he would be affecting the Camry's speed.

The Camry moved to switch back to the right hand lane without slowing down, and Mark tried to counter but his foot slipped off the gas at the crucial moment, costing him his lead and his chance to stay ahead of the other car. It passed by smoothly and continued on its way.

He slammed his fist into the steering wheel, cursing as he watched the Camry turn right into oblivion.

Friday, May 23rd, 2009 3:08 P.M.

This time, Mark waited much earlier on the route he'd taken that fateful day, closer to the elementary school. He'd modified his plan. This time, he would pull out behind the Camry and, at the best possible moment, say at a red light or a stop sign, he would gently rear-end himself.

Once he'd caused an accident, Mark would shift forward to the future, abandoning his current vehicle. His old self would be forced to stop and get out. That would ensure a significant delay, and even a few seconds difference would save them. He laughed, imagining the look he'd probably have on his face when he saw it was a driverless car that had rear-ended him.

There the Camry was again. Mark deftly whipped his rental in behind it. It was just a matter of timing now. He stayed close on their tail, studying the situation, ready for any opportunity. If they just came to a stop somewhere, it would be so easy.

Suddenly, flashing blue lights filled his rear window.

You have got to be kidding me.

It couldn't be. Not here, not now. He was being pulled over. Could he ignore the officer and still put the plan into effect? He wasn't sure.

He could risk it, but instinct told Mark to try again in a different way. He decided to cut his losses.

He pulled off onto the shoulder and waited obediently for the officer to approach. The ticket was for following too close.

Chapter 12

It's a long trip alone over sand and stone
That lie along the road that we all must travel down

"Long Trip Alone"

~ Dierks Bentley

Friday, May 23rd, 2009 2:30 PM

The pizzeria was one of those buffet places where $3.99 would buy you all the pizza you could want in one sitting. It was decorated nicely enough for a budget restaurant, but definitely left no doubt as to its level in the gourmet chain.

The place was not very full, being well after the lunch hour, but there were several families with young kids enjoying a late afternoon meal together.

From the depositions taken during his trial, Mark knew that Stephen Chadwick, the 17 year old who would kill his children in a little less than an hour, had spent this afternoon at this pizzeria before the accident.

Mark's plan was, once again, simple. He would do whatever it took to stop or delay the Chadwick boy. He would wait until it was time for Chadwick to leave, and then he would pick a fight with him. One way or the other, he would make sure the boy was delayed from leaving the premises.

Bile rose in his throat as he watched from several tables away. When Chadwick entered the restaurant, he was already drunk. Mark endured the torment, seething as the brat stuffed his face full of greasy pizza. He was laughing it up with several of his friends, ignorant of the pain and travesty he was about to wreak. They'd snuck a couple of beers into the joint.

Apparently, the boys hadn't had enough yet. It would be a pleasure ripping Chadwick's face off. That was something he'd longed to do for quite a while. A preemptive strike for justice.

His blood pressure rose. His hands trembled slightly under the rush of adrenaline. This would work. He was finally going to save his kids, something he'd never even been able to do in his dreams.

Mind humming, he narrowed his eyes, focused on his prey. It was time. The young Chadwick stood up to go, guffawing at something that had been said. To Mark, it looked like a disgusting, mocking sneer. Mark rose from his chair and made a beeline for his target.

While Mark was still twenty feet away, another patron, who by all appearances was the very definition of the word redneck if there ever was one, stood to refill his Coke — right in Mark's path. The collision was brief and not too jarring, but the man took offense and spouted off an insult. Mark's eyes remained locked on Chadwick. Nothing would distract him from his purpose. The redneck was still in the path, so Mark pushed him aside, but the guy unexpectedly went down in a heap.

Mark bypassed his fallen form and pushed his way further toward Chadwick. Other patrons were noticing the commotion he'd caused with the redneck. Chadwick sensed something was going on and turned to face him. Mark leapt forward, snarling, striking for the boy's face, ready to tear into him like an animal. In a drunken panic, Chadwick turned and tried to dodge. He was aided by one of his sober friends who anticipated the swing and pushed at Mark's arm, deflecting the blow.

Mark would have to fight all of them. So be it. As long as he could stop or delay Stephen Chadwick, nothing else mattered.

He had just dropped into a fighting stance, ready for the enlarged battle, when something solid hit him hard in the base of the skull. Mark collapsed helplessly to the floor. It wasn't a crippling blow — he'd be fine in a minute — but he was stunned, taken completely off guard. A second later, the redneck had rolled him over and began punching him repeatedly in the face. A mad melee ensued with some customers yelling and others trying to pull the two of them apart.

Mark, however, was oblivious to the blows. He was watching his prey slip out the door, unimpeded.

Friday, May 23rd, 2009, 2:47 PM

He had a knife and he was through playing around. All Mark needed was one unobserved moment to slash a few of Chadwick's tires. *That* would do the trick.

Unfortunately, the vehicle parked right to the side of Chadwick's pulled out right when Mark had been set to move, forcing him to wait. Another car then pulled into the space in front of Chadwick's, and its driver sat for what seemed an eternity talking on a cell phone.

At last, when a casual observer might have thought frustrated smoke was about to begin billowing from Mark's ears, the man ended what had to be a needless conversation and finally left his vehicle.

With no hesitation, Mark strode to the sports coupe. A very satisfying hiss accompanied Mark's knife as it sank deep into the front tire. Twisting the blade, he gouged a wider hole to let the air out even faster. It was flat in no time.

A commotion arose behind him from the pizzeria. Chadwick was coming out. Quickly, Mark stabbed a second tire and then ran to the other side of the parking lot where he could watch to see if he'd finally succeeded.

Chadwick was so drunk he never noticed the flat tires. He got in the car and peeled out of his space. In no time, his tires would be ripped to shreds and he'd be riding on the rims.

Unfortunately, the end of the parking lot would come long before then.

Chadwick screamed onto the street Mark was working so hard to keep him off. Then came the assaulting screeching of tires, breaking glass, and a twisted Camry in the drainage ditch.

The bitter vomit rushing up his esophagus weakly symbolized the gut-wrenching grief ripping through his soul at the sight. He hadn't wanted to see it again. *He had* not *wanted to see it again.*

Friday, May 23rd, 2009, 2:43 PM

Mark called the police to report a drunk teenager who'd parked in a certain shopping center and was now eating at the pizzeria there.

They responded, but not until it was too late. Not until there was already an accident on the scene.

Friday, May 23rd, 2009, 2:03 PM

Mark reported the drunk driver again, but way ahead of schedule to compensate for their slow response time. This time they showed up too quickly. Chadwick hadn't even arrived yet.

Friday, May 23rd, 2009, 1:27 AM

Mark stood outside Chadwick's darkened home. Moonlight glinted off the teen's silvery Toyota Celica in the driveway.

Tonight, Mark brought his knife once more, but this time he'd also brought a Slim Jim to jimmy the door and a gallon of bleach. He approached the car.

He would make sure the car was completely inoperable this time. He would slash all four tires. He'd pop the hood,

remove the distributor cables, and take them with him. He'd
cut the battery cables, and drain the radiator. To make doubly
sure the car would stay immobile for quite a while, Mark
would pour bleach into the oil to lock the motor.

Many people thought adding sugar to a gas tank was the
way to destroy an engine, but Mark knew that was an urban
legend. Bleach in the oil was the way to go.

While he was jimmying the driver side door to get the
hood open, security lights suddenly blazed from the house. A
shout went up, and there was no time to wait. Mark dropped
his tools and took off down the street. He would have to find
another opportunity.

Friday, May 23rd, 2009, 1:47 PM

It was an hour and a half before the accident. Mark
strolled through his old neighborhood. His alter ego (former
self) would soon leave to pick up Daniel and Brittany from
school. For a short amount of time before then, the Camry
would be parked in Mark's driveway, unattended. If he
couldn't get to Chadwick's car, maybe he could paralyze his
own.

As soon as he reached the front of his house, however,
Mark muttered a curse under his breath. He'd miscalculated
the timing. The front door was opening, which meant his old
self was emerging to begin running errands. Mark whipped his
face away to keep from being recognized, and walked on.

Friday, May 23rd, 2009, 3:16 PM

Mark was determined to end it. This time, he was
perched on the roof of the shopping center with a high-powered
sniper rifle.

From the corner of his eye, he sensed movement around
Chadwick's vehicle below. He knew it had to be one of his
former selves slashing the tires, but it still gave him the heebie-

jeebies to even think about seeing himself outside a mirror, so he ignored the form.

A minute later, Chadwick exited the pizzeria. Mark centered the drunken teen's head in the crosshairs of his scope. This rifle was new to him, so he'd practiced for over a week at a local shooting range, fine-tuning his aim with it and the scope. A good sniper made sure he knew his weapon. It was now accurate to several miles, and Chadwick was only a hundred feet away.

The rifle rested on a tripod to hold it stable as he took the shot. The wind was virtually non-existent. He would not miss.

The revolting face bobbed in his sights, as if it were only a few feet away. He stayed his finger until the right moment. Slowly, then, he depressed the trigger, squeezing it gently without the slightest pull or jerk.

Click.

He pulled it again.

Click.

Jammed.

By all rights, the peaceful summer afternoon should have been shattered by an explosive rifle round tearing toward its target. Instead, the birds nearby kept chirping their tunes happily, undisturbed. The acrid smell of burnt gunpowder should be rewarding his nostrils, yet nothing but fresh air was to be had.

He tried several more times, but something inside the rifle was seriously jammed, and his hurried, frustrated fingers could not release the mechanism in time. He watched with angst as the jock jumped into his car for the millionth time.

Mark kicked the rifle with all his might and sent it skidding across the roof. He would not wait for the inevitable. Not again. He shifted forward to 2012 to escape the nightmare he was forcing himself to relive endlessly.

Chapter 13

May 23rd, 1959, Milledgeville, GA

There was more than one way to skin a cat, and Mark wasn't about to give up. It was time to get serious. Very serious.

It had taken a little research to find the right town, but he had done it. He now stood on a onion farm just outside of Milledgeville, GA in 1959, awaiting the right opportunity.

And he soon had it. From his observation post, Mark watched his subject packing empty wooden crates in the back of his truck and realized he would soon be going into town for something. Mark drove his car up the highway several miles and parked on the shoulder with the engine idling. When the truck drew near, Mark whipped his vehicle sideways into the middle of the road, completely blocking both lanes of the highway.

The truck's brakes whined to a stop. Throwing his vehicle into park, Mark leapt out, decisively aiming his rifle at the driver. He also had a couple of .45's hidden in holsters under his shirt, and a Bowie knife — just in case. No jammed gun would stop him this time.

The driver nervously stumbled from his pick-up, hands over his head, baffled by the unexpected threat. Mark ordered him to his knees in the dry road.

This was young 17 year-old Robert Chadwick, running some innocent errand for his father. He would grow up to become the father of Stephen Chadwick, the boy who would kill Mark's children.

Robert's wide eyes were full of fear, darting back and forth in search of some explanation or escape. He was completely unsure of himself. Some maniac had just stopped him with a gun and he had no idea why. His lower lip quivered, his hands visibly trembling.

Mark steeled himself. He would feel no remorse.

As an adult, Robert Chadwick would arrange to have his son's DUI records lost in order to protect him. In spite of knowing Stephen had been drunk, this man would file a lawsuit against Mark, further destroying Mark's family. This was the man who would someday choose family and greed over justice and righteousness. If he died, if he no longer existed, he could never father his son, and Mark's children would not die. It was that simple.

Mark took aim, steadying his arm until it felt like an iron beam, his bead centered right on the young man's forehead. Just a little pressure on the trigger and half the boy's head would disappear. The seconds ticked by. He tightened his finger.

He couldn't do it.

The hate and bitterness weren't strong enough to erase the sense of basic decency which resided somewhere deep within. He squeezed his eyes shut hard in forced concentration and tried to overcome it. He needed to kill this boy. It was the only way.

With all his might he tried to rip that decency out, roots and all. Vengeance was calling, and he wanted to give himself over to it.

Mark cursed and dropped his weapon into the dust. The boy, seeing his respite, leapt back into his truck and tore off toward his farm like a panicked madman.

Mark didn't wait around. He'd failed again.

May 22nd, 1959, Milledgeville, GA

The diner was a regular grease spoon, but was an obvious hit with the locals. Most of the tables were filled with the weekday lunch crowd.

Mark stared blankly at the order of scrambled eggs he was idly pushing around his plate. He'd just shifted back one day earlier to take a second try at Robert Chadwick, but now he was questioning that plan. He'd probably just freeze up again.

He was very disquieted by the fact that he hadn't been able to pull the trigger. Surely, any loving father would be able to kill in order to protect his children. Wouldn't he? It wasn't exactly killing though, was it? *More like murder.* Was his morality streak really so strong that it wouldn't let him kill a man, even if that man being alive meant his kids would die.

The more he deliberated, the more he realized just how dangerous these time travel watches were. If Mark wanted to, he could jump from time to time killing just about anybody he chose, or stealing anything he wanted, and simply shift to another time to avoid getting caught. *If these devices ever fell into the wrong hands....*

Mark reached down and grabbed for his backpack protectively. He unzipped it far enough to see that both the extra watches were still safely in his possession. He'd have to be more careful with them.

The truth was his frustration level was soaring. He'd tried just about every way he could imagine to save Daniel and Brittany. He did still have a few options. He could try to kill Robert again, or he could try to prevent Robert Chadwick from meeting his future wife, which would eliminate Stephen's conception. He could try to get Chadwick Jr. flunked out of school before he became a football star, or sabotage the Governor's campaign before he was elected. Why not just call a bomb threat into his children's school earlier that fateful day?

Did it matter? Everything he'd tried so far had failed. He could understand a glitch or two, but the obstacles he'd encountered were inexplicable. There was no reasonable way he could mess up so completely every time, unless he really was dumber than he thought, and he didn't think that was the case.

Maybe it was just impossible to change past events. Maybe there was some mysterious, cosmic force out there making sure nothing changed.

No, that couldn't be. He had definitely changed some things so far. Every time he went back in time to make an investment and returned to find his modern day bank balance higher, it proved he could change things. Plus, he'd saved Red Johnson from dying under that tree. He could clearly alter the past. *So, what was going on?*

"Give up yet?"

"Uh....what?" The voice shook Mark from his reverie.

"I asked if you'd given up yet." The speaker was a sandy-haired young man in his 30's, dressed in blue jeans and a short-sleeved button-down shirt typical of the 1950's. He looked very muscular and clean cut. Under any other circumstances, Mark would have sworn he was military.

"Given up on what?"

"You know what I mean. Given up on changing the past."

"I'm in the past....I ...er....I mean...what are you talking about?"

The man sat at a table across from Mark's. He was calm, sure of himself, and would not break his unnerving stare. He leaned back into his chair, the very image of a man relaxed, which was the complete opposite of Mark, who was bordering on a nervous breakdown.

"I'm talking about your children, Mark."

Taken aback, Mark suddenly leaned forward and hissed, *"Who are you?"*

None of the other diner patrons noticed the conversation.

"Hardy Phillips, pleased to meet you". He extended his hand.

Mark declined.

"Okay....Hardy, who are you and what do you want?"

The man merely grinned, tapping his wrist lightly, drawing Mark's attention to it.

Mark gasped. This man wore an identical time travel watch to his own. At least, it *looked* just like his.

Mark sat back with his arms crossed and waited for an explanation.

The man's grin only grew wider, which was irritating. He placed a scrap of paper on the table and slid it toward Mark. It was a sequence of numbers:

120000P06052012

Which was, of course, 12:00 noon, June 5, 2012.

"Meet me at that address, in your office. We'll talk then." Phillips stood and exited the diner. By the time Mark got outside, the stranger had disappeared. He'd probably shifted out.

He had a million questions to ask, and no one to answer them. Unless he kept this appointment that is. Not much choice in his book.

Chapter 14

If you get there before I do, don't give up on me.
I'll meet you when my chores are through.

"Love, Me"

~ Collin Raye

12:00 PM, June 5th, 2012, Atlanta, GA

"Welcome. Have a seat." Mark motioned for Phillips to take the chair in front of his desk.

"I wasn't quite sure if I *would* be welcome," his guest replied.

"Figure of speech. I'm not sure you are yet."

There was that irritating grin again.

"Mr. Phillips, you approached me, from out of the blue, frankly, and you mentioned my children. I want to know exactly what you know about them, and I want to know *now*."

"We'll get to that. First things first."

Mark glared.

"Mr. Carpen, we know a great deal about you...."

"Who's we?" Mark demanded.

"At the moment, that's not important. What I can tell you is that we know you have become aware of certain, shall we say, possibilities within the realm of physics of which most people are not."

"You mean time travel."

"Yes."

"And?"

"How do you feel about it?"

That was an odd question. He thought for a minute. "It's pretty amazing. Hard to believe, if you know what I mean."

"Yeah." Phillips stared at the desk. He picked up a pen and tapped it lightly on the walnut-stained wood. Silence.

"Mr. Carpen, I asked you a question before."

"You mean when you asked if I had given up yet?"

"Yes. Have you?"

"Speak clearly."

"Have you given up trying to save your children?"

"Of course not! I'll *never* give up on that." Mark felt a fury building within.

Phillips was nonplused. "Haven't you noticed some....how should I put it....a bit of frustration in your efforts?"

The angry flames in Mark's heart momentarily soothed. "Sure."

"Yet you experienced no similar frustration while building your wealth." He said it as if stating a well-known fact.

"How do you know all this?" Mark whispered harshly. "I had my frustrations building wealth too. Lots of little obstacles kept getting in my way. Just because the obstacles surrounding my kids have been bigger doesn't mean I can't save them. I just have to try harder. How dare you tell me to give up?"

"I admire your perseverance and optimism. I'd feel the same if they were mine. Still.... haven't you wondered if there might be something else at play here?"

Mark stared blankly.

"Why don't you just tell me what you have to say and stop playing games?"

"I'm honestly not trying to play games, Mark, I simply want to know your opinion — if you've noticed anything strange or not."

"Well, yes," He breathed, "No matter what I seem to try, nothing works. It's always the most innocuous little mishap too. It was just frustrating at first, but when my rifle jammed.....well, that just seemed *too* coincidental."

"And?"

"And I don't know! *You* tell *me* what it means."

"As to meaning, I've no idea, Mr. Carpen, but in my experience, there are some events in time which cannot be altered. The space-time continuum, or whatever you want to call it, simply does not allow it."

"That's a bunch of crap."

"Accepting or denying reality only affects the health of the one facing it, but reality cannot be changed by our belief about it."

Mark responded by staring at Phillips even harder, as if he could pierce the man's thoughts with his glare.

"I'm sorry, but I don't believe it's possible to save your children. I know that hurts, I'm sorry, but I believe it's the truth."

"Get out!"

Phillips shrugged his shoulders and sighed.

"As you wish."

Then, he disappeared. A static electric hum and the faint smell of something metallic burning hung in the air after he'd gone. *So, that's what it's like to witness a time-shift.*

Mark couldn't believe the gall of the guy, presuming to tell him his business with respect to Daniel and Brittany. They were his. His precious, beautiful children. He took up the photo he had of them on his desk and caressed their cheeks with a finger.

It was a picture of them playing in the park. Kelly had taken it one day when they'd gone on a family picnic. Danny had been four then, Brittany two. Their skin glowed healthily in the sun's rays. They looked so happy.

How could Phillips know if he would succeed or not? He couldn't. He was just a nay-sayer, a negative thinker. The world was full of them.

Who was he anyway? It didn't really matter. One way or the other, Mark was going to save his kids.

Friday, May 23rd, 2009 3:12 PM

This plan would work. It was the simplest of all his plans, so there would be no screw up.

Mark stationed himself on the shopping center's sidewalk, right outside the door to the pizzeria. The moment Stephen Chadwick emerged from the restaurant, Mark would tackle him and slam him to the ground, and he wouldn't stop beating Chadwick until he was sufficiently delayed or dead. He didn't care which. There'd be plenty of witnesses, but he didn't care. All he needed was a couple of seconds.

Nothing could interfere this time. There were no guns, nothing mechanical which could malfunction. It would go down too fast for a third party to get between them. He'd eliminated any chance for failure.

At long last, the door swung out. In his mind's eye, everything began moving in slow motion. Chadwick stepped onto the sidewalk. Now was the moment.

Move, move!

Something was wrong with the message his brain was sending to his feet, because they wouldn't budge. He felt paralyzed, as if he were fighting some incredible, invisible force which sapped all his strength. His arms were stuck too. Despite all effort, they hung limply at his sides.

He tried to scream in outrage and anguish, but when his mouth opened, nothing came out. His lips moved in desperate silence like a fish gasping for air. He continued to struggle with all his might, determined to overcome it, and he finally managed to shuffle his right foot a few inches forward, but that was all he could do. He was utterly helpless.

Chadwick was walking toward his car now. Frustrated tears rolled down Mark's cheeks, yet still he could not free himself from his invisible prison. The drunken teen got in his car, a horrifying moment he'd already relived far too many times.

Mark collapsed onto the concrete and curled into a fetal position.

"No! No! No!." Anguish, rage, grief — it all boiled inside in a terrible emotional stew. "Nooooooo!"

He wept freely when he heard the screeching tires. That sound would rip through the farthest reaches of his mind forever. Then, the sharp clap of metal striking metal followed by a dull thud as his Camry hit the ditch.

Never again, he vowed. *Never again will I come back here and hear those sounds.*

He needed to sit up before he vomited. When he did, a piece of paper fluttered off of his shoulder.

Chapter 15

You know a dream is like a river, ever changin' as it flows
And a dreamer's just a vessel that must follow where it goes

"River"

~ Garth Brooks

The slip of paper contained a simple two-line message. It could only have been left by the mysterious Hardy Phillips. He had shifted in and out while Mark had been incoherent with grief.

I am truly sorry for your loss.
013000A06072012 W. Monument

Hardy Phillips, whoever he might turn out to be, was somehow right. Mark had to admit it, despite the pain such a decision caused him. Something was wrong, something he did not understand. Some unseen force was preventing him from intervening in his own children's death. Could it simply be what people called "fate"? It didn't make sense.

Regardless, he had no intention of meeting Phillips anywhere, especially on his terms. For all he knew, Phillips was somehow controlling all of this. He could be the very one standing between Mark and his kids. He wanted nothing to do with the man, or anyone else for that matter. He felt the grief building again like a swell of water pressing against a weakened dam.

Mark returned to where he'd left off in 2012 and threw himself into what was now his life's lonely work: building and amassing wealth.

His accounts now stood at a sum total of over $20 million. It was distributed into numerous bank accounts around the world. He created a couple of foundations to hide much of it, not so much from the IRS, but from the public. He made sure the accountants paid all his taxes every year, but he didn't want it widely known how rich he actually was. That kind of attention was not needed.

He established a couple of dummy private corporations in the 1960's and through them purchased substantial numbers of shares in many businesses which he knew would skyrocket in value at some point in the next 40 years.

He bought more shares of Starbucks, Apple Computer and a few other well-known companies while they were still fledglings, but for the most part he stuck with high-performing but lesser known entities. Again, the reason was to maintain a low profile.

Another month of work and he had grown his assets to over $100 billion. *Surely that was enough.* What could a person possibly do with that much money? He calculated that if he spent $3 million dollars a day, it would take him 90 years to spend it all. Actually, he was earning $33 million dollars a day in interest, so if he wanted to deplete his money before he died, he'd have to spend over $50 million per day. Amazing. How far he'd come, and in such a short time.

Yet, there was no joy in it. The first $4 billion had been kind of fun, but now the work was just another routine. Use the time machine, make more money. For what? Who cared? He could buy anything there was to buy in this world. He could buy a hundred Caribbean islands if he wanted, but why would he?

There was only one thing he wanted. His kids. No amount of money would bring them back.

Life had become a drudgery. Not only had he lost any reason for joy, but nothing was a challenge any more. When life got too easy, it became boring. How ironic. You long for a life of ease your entire working life, but now he knew it was better for that fantasy to remain unrealized. Maybe it would be better if he had a family to share it with, but he didn't. He was lonely. Without purpose.

One day, late in July, he found himself buying a ticket for Washington, DC.

What the heck. Why not?

The paper Phillips had left was instructions to meet at the Washington Monument on June 7th. Mark had been adamant just a few months ago about not meeting with Phillips, so what had changed?

Mark had changed, that's what. He wanted answers now.

He planned to get them.

***

June 7th, 2012, 1:30 AM, Washington, DC

Blue moonlight washed the marble obelisk in a cold glow as it stood stoic guard over the sleeping city at its feet.

Phillips was there, of course.

This night, Mark would have his answers, one way or the other.

"Nice to see you, Mark."

Phillips straightened and leaned forward, offering his hand. This time, Mark took it.

Mark silently appraised the man anew, taking time to study his face before speaking. He seemed trustworthy, but appearances were so often deceiving.

"Who are you?"

"You can call me Hardy."

"No, I mean, who are you? Military, CIA, who?"

"I'm not at liberty to say much at this point. Just that I was sent to contact you."

"Who sent you?"

Hardy shrugged.

"What do you want?"

"I have a job for you."

"A job?" He was incredulous.

"Well, more like a mission."

This was sounding more suspicious by the minute.

"Why me, of all people?"

Hardy pointed at the device on Mark's wrist. "You've got a shifter."

"You've got one too."

He shrugged again.

"I didn't come here to play games," Mark said.

"You're right, I'm sorry. I know you've been through a lot. I also understand you don't know me from Adam and are rightly somewhat suspicious.

"In the last two years, you've lost your kids and your wife. You lost all financial stability only to regain it miraculously through some weird device that could have jumped off the pages of a sci-fi novel, allowing you to skip from time to time at will. Yet, the same device that allows you to build fantastic amounts of wealth, cruelly cannot provide for the return of your children.

"I know all this and I sympathize. Still, all I can reveal to you at this point is that I represent a company named ChronoShift. The company wishes to hire you as an employee — as a "time jumper", if you will."

Mark interrupted, "Who owns this company?"

He held Mark's gaze without wavering. "I am not authorized to reveal any further details regarding the company yet. For now, you will have to accept my proposal, or reject it, based solely on the description of the mission."

"I won't sign any kind of contract unless I know better who I'm dealing with."

"We're not asking you to."

"What's this mission you keep talking about?"

Phillips reached into his windbreaker and pulled out a newspaper article. Even in the dark, Mark could tell it was severely yellowed.

Boy, 12, Killed by Gang

Chicago, IL

Herbert Walker Jr., 12, of Chicago, was killed yesterday on the waterfront, the apparent victim of thieves. Witnesses on the scene informed the Tribune that pay had just been distributed earlier that evening at the factory where Walker worked. Walker and another boy had been on their way home when he was attacked by some thugs. His body had been searched and any monies had been removed by the time police arrived. As of this morning, police have no suspects and ask any citizen with information to contact the Chicago Police Department immediately. No surviving relatives are known.

The article was dated April 16, 1934.

"Who was this boy?"

"An unfortunate soul whose flame was snuffed out prematurely."

"You want me to go back and try to save him?"

Hardy smiled. It was a friendly smile, and a hard one to resist.

"How do we know he wouldn't be just like my kids? I mean, why would we be able to save him if I couldn't save my own?"

"We have strong reason to believe it wouldn't turn out that way."

"I'll think about it. How about that?"

Hardy smiled again and handed him the newspaper article. "When you get back, I'll be in touch."

Dang this Hardy Phillips and his smug assuredness.

Chapter 16

April 12th, 1934, Chicago, IL

"Herbie, wait up!"

A skinny red-headed kid ran to catch up to the slightly older boy. Freckles dotted his face and neck heavily.

"Hey, Chuck. What gives? I thought you had to work the night shift."

"Nah, skipped out."

"Man, the old man'll have your job *and* your neck for that."

"Aww, he can shove it. I'm tired of that ol' dirt bag anyhow. All he does is work ya to death for pennies."

"Ya gotta eat."

"Yeah, but I got enough fer today. That'll do. I can get me a job somewhere's else any time."

"Don' know 'bout that, jobs are scarcer than hen's teeth right now."

"Lay off, will ya, Herbie. Ya gonna hack my case all night or we gonna go eat."

Herbie laughed. "Let's go."

Mark eavesdropped on their conversation from across the walkway. Herbie was Herbert Walker Jr., the boy who would be murdered in a few days. Earlier today, Mark had asked for and gotten a job at the same factory where Herbie worked. While Herbie and others his age would work for a mere 30 cents an hour, grown men normally earned closer to 50 to 55 cents. Mark, however, had walked in off the street and offered to work for only 25 cents an hour. These were tough times and men were desperate.

The foreman, Rory O'Toole, was hot-tempered and mean. You could see it just by looking into his squinty eyes.

That he was a drinker was evidenced by his bulbous red nose and blotchy, vein-filled cheeks. He'd immediately jumped at the opportunity for cheaper labor and hired Mark, firing one of the other men to make room for him.

Mark hadn't wanted to get anybody fired, but he needed to stay close to Walker so he could learn his habits and be in a position to save the boy later.

He learned over the next few days that Herbie and his friends were more than familiar with hard work. They arrived at the plant every morning around 6 AM and worked until well into the evening, and it wasn't uncommon for O'Toole to ask one of them to work on through the night shift too.

Much of the time, Mark succeeded in positioning himself near the boy during their shifts. Anywhere that Herbie went, Mark was sure to go. He became his clandestine shadow, unseen and unnoticed, yet never more than twenty feet away, listening to conversations, identifying potential threats.

Mark learned a good bit about the boy. He was alone in Chicago, trying to earn enough money to keep room and board at a nearby shelter.

His parents had heard work was to be had out in California, and in these hard times, any chance of hope, even a mere rumor, was enough to make a family jump. They had begun a migration of the whole clan from Philadelphia out west, but the expenses of the trip proved to be too much of a burden. Every mouth to feed was one mouth too many, and Herbie was old enough to make it on his own. At least, they had desperately wanted to be believe he was. So, they'd left him to fend for himself in Chicago.

The Depression ripened young men and women into adults long before their time, and that early maturation often led to early rotting as well, though in Herbie's case, the morals his parents had impressed into him seemed to be enduring.

They'd promised to write, but he'd never gotten a letter, not that he didn't keep checking the local post office. No phone calls either. Chicago was a big city, Herbie reasoned.

Some day he'd save up enough money to follow them out to California. Then, they'd be together again.

Young Walker had been working at this factory for several months now, and by all accounts, he was a great employee. He excelled at whatever he did, and made an effort to go beyond the call of duty, even though he was never rewarded for his efforts. Instead, he lived under the constant threat of losing his job to someone who would work for less. Still, the boy plugged on, working toward some unknown goal he kept private inside his head.

***

Today was the 16th and the lunch whistle had just blown. Tonight was the night Herbie would be attacked and killed. Mark had already pieced together parts of an overall plan to intervene, but he still had to work out the details.

For now, all the men were pouring out of the factory, so Mark began following Walker and a few others out to the waterfront where they would snarf down their cold sandwiches before the whistle shrieked again, signaling the end of the very short break.

"Hey, Scab!"

Mark glanced up and, much to his dismay, saw the insult had been directed his way. Its author was a large, rough-looking, bearded man who looked more like a lumberjack than a waterfront worker.

"Yeah, I'm talkin' to ya!" The man strode briskly toward Mark, closing the gap between them quickly.

"You're the reb who stole my job, ain't ya?"

This nut was the man Mark had displaced when he'd gotten a job at the factory a few days ago. *Why couldn't it have been somebody without a temper?*

Mark nodded politely, sincerely wishing to mollify him. "I'm sure you'll find a better job, sir." A fight would draw unneeded attention.

"Maybe in the next life!"

The man was clearly enraged. It was going to be tough to defuse him.

There was no time for diplomacy. The man took a swing. Mark deftly stepped aside. His military training ensured this fight would not be a fair one. The brute came at him again. Mark swiveled and artfully redirected the man's momentum, causing him to fall flat on his face. Chuckles murmured through the crowd that had gathered to watch.

Suddenly, stars swam in Mark's vision as he felt a jarring blow to the back of his neck. He fell to one knee. A skinnier man stood behind him, wielding a two by four and grinning like the Cheshire Cat. Probably one of the brute's friends.

Instinct took over now. The situation had just become dangerous. Mark's leg shot out, pounding the skinny attacker in the kneecap, hard. The man yelled painfully and dropped to one knee himself. Next, Mark threw a double punch, one to the stomach, which knocked the wind out of the man, and a second to the throat. He made sure not to hit him hard enough to collapse his larynx, but the man would be out of commission for a while.

The burlier man who'd started the fight had recovered and charged at full speed. Mark tried to dodge again, but the goon's long arm reeled him back in, and then they were dancing.

The man put a lot of power behind his blows, but Mark knew how to angle his body to deflect most of the force naturally. Meanwhile, Mark's strikes were much more measured and strategic. He had to hand it the guy though. He was certainly determined. It took 15 to 20 cycles of this violent dance before the man was disabled enough that he couldn't continue the fight.

He collapsed onto the street in a fetal position, moaning.

"Aggieeeee! Oh Aggie, I'm soooorry!" He rolled back and forth, from side to side, weeping, his agony on display for all to see.

"His name's Angus Todd," came a voice from behind. The speaker was another worker from the factory. "Aggie's his wife. This job was the first time he'd been able to put real food on his family's table in months."

Lord, did everything have to be painful?

***

Fog rolled in from the bay, forming a mystical atmosphere along the wharf like a scene from an old mystery movie set in London. Herbie and one of his friends walked a ways ahead of Mark, idly chatting and cracking jokes along the way, oblivious to their surroundings. Mark knew that somewhere just ahead, death awaited one of them.

A single arc lamp made a poor attempt to light the wharf with its weak white light. A dark alley opened into the lit street about twenty feet in front of the boys. Its mouth was pitch black. If someone were going to lie in wait, that would be the ideal spot.

Mark's experiences in past efforts to change historical events had taught him a thing or two about potential problems that could arise, so he'd planned accordingly. There would be no mistakes this time. Unless that unseen force froze him in place again.

That alleyway had to be the source of the attack. As the boys were about to pass in front of it, two men, no more than common thugs, rushed them from the darkness. The leader drew ahead of his partner. A ready jackknife in his hand glimmered wickedly under the light like a silvery snake darting back and forth, searching for its next victim. The other thug held a heavy baseball bat menacingly.

Mark did not recognize either of them from the factory. They were probably just common thieves. No inside job, no on-site jealousy, just a plain old mugging, and Walker was at the wrong place at the wrong time.

Mark could see how it was going to go down. The knife-bearing thug would arrive first, and stab Herbie, probably fatally.

Herbie's young friend had seen the thieves out of the corner of his eye and was already instinctively turning to run away, which is probably what saved him.

Mark broke into a hard sprint. He needed to get into the right position, which depended on the exact positions of the other players.

The first thug didn't give a warning. He just thrust his knife into Herbie's abdomen. The boy let out a surprised cry, a startled and weak call for help.

Don't worry, Herbie. Help is on the way.

Mark noted the exact moment of the stabbing on his shifter, but he didn't slow down. He needed to get as close to the scene as possible. He was running silently and the thugs hadn't noticed him yet; they were too focused on the other boy who was getting away.

Mark halted immediately to the left of Herbie's fallen form. Startled by his sudden presence, the lead thug jerked around and slung his knife Mark's way.

The blade arched toward Mark's abdomen, but he pushed the red button and shifted out of the scene a second before being seriously wounded.

Same street, but now it was empty. He was 8 hours in the future, and there was a blood stain on the pavement where Herbie had fallen.

Mark had carefully taken note of the exact positions of both Walker and his attacker, and he knew the exact time the knife had struck. Mark moved forward a couple of steps and shifted back to several seconds before Herbie would be stabbed.

Instantly, he was in the middle of the murder again. Herbie's face was fixated on his approaching attacker. Mark reached out, wrapped his hand tightly around the thug's wrist, and yanked hard, deflecting the blow. The hoodlum's mouth dropped open in shock.

Mark snapped the wrist upward sharply, and the crack of bone confirmed he'd broken it. The thief hollered in pain and his knife clattered harmlessly to the ground. Mark scooped it up and shifted out of the scene again.

He calmly walked around the now once again empty pavement to a spot immediately behind where the attacker would be standing hours earlier. The blood stain marking the concrete where Herbie fell was gone now. That made him smile. Mark shifted back into the fight exactly one second after he had left.

The thug was now in front of Mark, grasping his wrist in pain. Mark plunged the knife into his back between his shoulder blades, felling the hoodlum for good. Then, he shifted right back out again.

Mark had become all too familiar with killing while in the Marines. He'd long ago reasoned out his code of ethics regarding it. Murder would always be murder, but all killing was not murder. A soldier must learn to kill the enemy wherever he finds them without hesitating or second-guessing.

This was clearly a case of defending the innocent. True, he could have saved Herbie by simply disabling the thug, but what about the next victim? A man who would so callously take the life of someone over a few dollars would just do so again another day if given another chance. No, the thug could no longer be trusted with life. In fact, it would be irresponsible of Mark to let him live.

He was feeling a little nauseous now, so he took a breather. He'd shifted too many times in a row. He waited until the shops along the waterfront opened up. He ate breakfast at a nice sidewalk café and then strolled around town until he found a sporting goods store, where he bought a baseball bat.

Feeling rested, Mark returned to the scene of the crime. Before leaving, he'd marked with chalk the approximate spot where the second attacker would be standing. Now, he placed himself in a spot he guessed would be behind the guy. Then, Mark shifted back in.

He'd been a little off in his guess, but not enough to matter. The second attacker stood in front of him, motionless, catatonic after having witnessed his partner decimated by a phantom who appeared and disappeared in the blink of an eye. Only two seconds had passed here.

Calmly, Mark strode up behind the man and swung his bat silently through the air.

Crack!

The thug went down in a heap. Mark would be surprised if his skull were not fractured.

He turned to the boy who looked upon Mark with a mixture of horror and disbelief, which melded into relief when he realized Mark had saved him, but then to fear again wondering if Mark might mean to harm him also. The boy had seen the phantom popping in and out of his reality too.

Mark didn't feel the need to say anything. Herbie was safe. That was all that mattered. His young friend had seen what happened and was returning to come to Herbie's aid.

Mark shifted forward to his own time. Mission accomplished.

Chapter 17

10:00 AM, June 8ᵗʰ, 2012, Atlanta, GA

Hardy Phillips was already waiting in Mark's office when he got there. Phillips was lounging in his leather-backed swivel chair with his feet propped up on Mark's desk, a lit cigar in one hand. That peculiar smell, which belonged so distinctively to burning cigar tobacco, permeated the office. Wisps of blue smoke floated in disappearing swirls. The man certainly looked pleased with himself.

Another newspaper article lay on the desktop, awaiting Mark's perusal. It was dated fifteen years ago.

"Congratulations," Hardy said enthusiastically.

Walker Donates Building

Last Thursday evening, at a banquet commemorating the event, Herbert Walker Jr., donated a large industrial facility in downtown Chicago to the local Boys & Girls Club for use as a new gymnasium and athletic center for inner city children.

Walker also plans to donate materials and the use of his construction company's services in order to remodel the building. Total expected cost to the Boys & Girls Club will be just one dollar. The property has an estimated value of $15 million, and remodeling costs are expected to run close to five million.

Construction is expected to begin later this month.

"Philanthropist Herbert Walker has once again surpassed all expectations of generosity," commented Mayor Richard M. Daley in a speech at the banquet.

Previous contributions by Walker to the Chicago community are innumerable, among them being a large fund established to combat illiteracy which has helped over 10,000 young adults to date, and a revolutionary job training program, Job Corps, which has provided countless opportunities for the training of poorer individuals who find themselves unemployed. Walker has also been known to sponsor small business loans for high-risk individuals trying to pull themselves out of poverty.

Hopes are the gymnasium will be ready to open by next March at the latest.

"This is the same Herbert Walker I saved back in 1934?"

Hardy nodded.

Mark dwelt on that for a moment.

"It looks like he did a lot of good with his life."

"Yep."

"How did you know he would turn out this way?"

Hardy grinned, shrugging uncommittedly.

"You knew he was going to do all these good deeds, *right*? I mean, that's why you picked him. But....until I saved him, all you could know is that he died in 1934, so, how could you possibly know what he would or wouldn't do in a hypothetical future?"

Again, a silent shrug accompanied by a smirk.

"Has anyone ever told you how irritating your shrugs are?"

They were beyond irritating actually.

"As a matter of fact, they have." His grin now extended from ear to ear.

"What's that supposed to mean?"

He shrugged.

Mark couldn't help but laugh. It felt good to have helped that boy, and even better to know that he had turned out so well and had gone on to help so many. Plus, Mark was getting used to Phillips stonewalling him on answers. It could be frustrating, but he was learning that there was no way on earth he could pull information out of Hardy Phillips unless Hardy Phillips was ready to give it.

"So, what's next?"

"What do you mean, 'What's next'?"

"I mean....what's the next assignment? You do have something else for me to do, don't you?"

"A little anxious, aren't we?"

Mark's eyes narrowed, "If you've got something to say, spit it out, but don't play games."

"Sorry, sorry. Yes, I've got another mission if you're up for it, and it seems like you are. I must warn you, though, this one may be a little more mundane."

"That's okay."

"No, I mean it. This will be different. This mission is to go to Boston, shift back to 1926, and locate the residence of Mr. Randolph Vinson. On the evening of September 19th, sometime between 5:00 PM and 7:00 PM, you are to steal his cravat from his bedroom."

"That's all? Sounds odd."

"Take it or leave it."

"I'll take it, don't worry." Mark leaned forward in his chair. "By the way, *who* exactly am I working for? I think I should know."

"Do you really want me to shrug again?"

Chapter 18

"The only reason for time is so that
everything doesn't happen at once."

~ Albert Einstein

September 19ᵗʰ, 1926, Boston, MA

The Vinson estate was more like a castle from the Middle Ages than a home. Upon seeing the stony mansion four nights ago when Mark had first shifted into 1926, he'd had to double-check the setting on his watch, thinking he'd mistakenly shifted back seven hundred years instead of ninety.

Unlike a castle of old, however, this fortress was lit up by electric lights both from within and without. It was ready for a party.

Model T's had been arriving intermittently for the past twenty minutes. The guests all appeared to be high society, dressed in the finest attire of the day. Styled women hung onto the arms of their men as they strolled inside. Their short hair and straight lined dresses were right out of a movie set in the roaring twenties. Many of the women sported cigarettes, held in those old-fashioned, long, slim cigarette holders.

Mark dropped a bag of refuse outside the service entrance, careful not to dirty the white sleeves of his waiter's uniform, and turned to go back inside. It was almost time.

Four days ago, Mark had applied for a job as an assistant to the caterer who would be servicing the party and had gotten it.

Locating the residence had been a fairly simple matter. Randolph Vinson had been a wealthy man and socially very active, so he'd left lots of records. Land deeds had showed this address as belonging to him. Although the home had been destroyed along with the street in the 1960's for a new housing development, older city plans had pointed Mark to the right place.

He'd found an old newspaper article reporting on the social event at Vinson's castle the night of the 19th, and the article had mentioned the name of the caterer. If the caterer hadn't taken Mark on as a hire, he would have found another way in, but as it was, they had, so no need.

He didn't understand the reason for stealing the man's cravat, but he was operating on faith that there was a darn good reason for it. If this turned out to be Phillips' idea of a practical joke though, he might find the cravat stuffed somewhere unpleasant after Mark was through with him.

Mark's plan was to snatch the cravat right before the official beginning of festivities. Vinson was not dressed yet. A formal dinner was planned at 7:00 to kick off the evening. Vinson would greet his guests then.

Even with the shifter, this was going to be tricky to pull off. It would all be in the timing. If Phillips had just said, *'steal the cravat'*, and left it at that, the task would have been as easy as pie. *But no*, it had to be done *this* evening, between five and seven, no sooner and no later.

Mark guessed the cravat would be in the man's bedroom suite where he would dress. The problem was, Randolph Vinson hadn't left his suite since Mark had arrived on the premises at 3:00 PM.

Mark had risked as many trips upstairs as he could without raising too much suspicion. He had to catch Vinson outside of his room. Just one moment would be enough.

Twice already he'd had to offer flimsy excuses when he was caught upstairs outside of his permissible territory. One of those was to the head caterer. If caught again, they'd probably throw him out on his ear. Still, he had to keep risking it.

He climbed the stairs once more. *Oh, sorry, I was looking for the linen closet.* That's what he would say this time.

Halfway up, he heard a door open and shut in the hallway above. Mark stealthily raced up the last of the stairs to see who it was.

It was Vinson himself, headed for the bathroom. Finally. The man had left his room. A maid, however, was dusting in the hall. Mark wouldn't be able to stroll into the bedroom of the master of the house without her taking notice.

He noted the time, ducked out of sight, and then shifted forward nine hours to 4:00 AM, when he hoped everyone would be asleep.

Unfortunately, they were not.

The hall was pitch black, but someone was walking down it toward Mark. No time to find out who. Before he was discovered, he hastily shifted back to 6:31 PM....right into the arms of another caterer who'd come up the stairs behind Mark. The man startled and let out a yell.

Cheeks flushing red, Mark fumbled with his shifter, changing his target time from 4:00 AM to 8:00 PM. The caterer stood there flabbergasted while Mark manipulated his buttons, pretending the man wasn't there. Mark shifted out, leaving the caterer on the stairs staring open-mouthed.

At 8:00 PM, the hall was lit — and empty. At last. No maid. No caterer. Vinson would be at the party.

Mark entered the suite. It was extravagant, a testimony to the times. A large four-poster Mahogany bed was the centerpiece of the room, expensive looking linens covering its high mattress. A bearskin rug, head and all, adorned the floor at its foot. Two red divans filled a sitting area by a large bay window. A silk vest hung from a Mahogany dresser, and various porcelain knickknacks sat atop the numerous furnishings.

Taking a deep breath, Mark shifted back to 6:31 PM, the time when Vinson had gone to the bathroom before he'd gotten dressed. At that time, there was nothing different about the room, except the sun outside was a little brighter.

Queasiness reared its ugly head once more. Why did it always seem like circumstances forced to him to shift one more time than he wanted? He detested this nausea.

The cravat was strewn on the bed, along with a few other articles of clothing.

Mark took it.

Easy enough. Time to skedaddle.

He knew he was approaching the limit on the number of shifts he could do, and worse, he knew the next one was going to be unpleasant.

Hopefully, the party would still be going by 11:00 PM and Vinson would still be entertaining his guests. Mark shifted forward to that hour, ready for a full onslaught of nausea, and he was not disappointed.

Before he could even make sure he was alone in the suite, Mark fell to his knees, retching and vomiting onto the bearskin rug.

Luckily, he was alone. Once he recovered, which took several minutes, he staggered to his feet and exited into the hall.

Still alone. Blessing after blessing.

He made his way downstairs, through the kitchen, and out through the rear service entrance, unopposed and unnoticed. Mission accomplished.

He walked all the way to the street, cravat in hand, and shifted forward to 2012 where he'd left his vehicle.

Oooooh. What in the world had he been thinking?

An hour passed before he was able to stand after the attack of dry heaves which overcame him. He should have walked around for a couple of hours back in 1926 before shifting again. Of course, the shift sickness would be terrible after so many times.

His shifter's face glowed red. In other words, inoperative for 24 hours.

Oh well. At least the task was done.

***

9:33 AM, June 10th, 2012, Boston, Massachusetts

This time, Mark and Hardy's pre-planned rendezvous point was a park bench in downtown Boston.

Mark had studied the life of Randolph Vinson before he'd begun his latest mission. He'd wanted to know everything he could about his target. He'd been surprised to learn that, unlike Herbert Walker, Randolph Vinson had not been a kind philanthropist, just your run-of-the-mill greedy aristocrat clawing his way to the top of Boston's high society in the 1920's. His holdings had taken a dip in the crash of '29, but nothing crippling. He'd gone on to even better investments, but nothing remarkable. He'd died an alcoholic at the mild age of 58.

Before meeting with Hardy this morning, Mark had taken the time to re-research Vinson's life now *sans cravat*, but Mark couldn't see anything significantly different about it. A few of the names of the companies with which Vinson was associated changed, but nothing more. He still drank himself to an early death and left a good bit of money to his heirs.

However, it was interesting to see that a single piece of clothing could somehow affect someone's life enough to impact which businesses they invested in. How that worked itself out, Mark had no idea. The complexities involved in calculating such factors were beyond him.

So far, the day was cool and breezy, unusually so for June, even in Massachusetts. The sky overhead glowed a rich, vibrant blue and was filled with large puffy clouds that stretched from horizon to horizon. His dad would have called it a travelin' sky. A travelin' sky was the kind of sky you could only find in summer, one whose colors and depth made you want to keep going over the next hill just to see what was there. You always felt restless under a sky like that, like you couldn't feel at home till you knew what lay beyond.

"So....you wanna know what the whole cravat thing was about?" Hardy asked.

"Figured if I asked, I'd probably just get another one of those shrugs."

Hardy chuckled.

"Forget about it," Mark said.

"I'll try to pick another gesture to demonstrate non-committal." He grinned and Mark couldn't help but chuckle too.

"Nah, I like you Phillips. Well, I guess I do anyway. You seem like a decent guy. I just can't stand being left in the dark. Not knowing tends to get under my skin."

"All right. Let's enlighten you a bit. Randolph Vinson was a very vain man, I don't know if you caught that from watching him or not...."

"Yeah, I definitely got that impression from his room."

"....and he was fanatical about climbing Boston's social ladder. The night you were there, he had invited many prominent businessmen to dinner along with their wives, of course with the intent of impressing them. Many a momentous business deal has been made during social events such as that. Probably more than in actual boardrooms.

"Anyway, Randolph made it a habit to never let himself be seen by his guests until dinner was served. Once all his guests were seated in the dining hall with food on their plates, he would make his dramatic entrance, right on time, and take his seat at the head of the table. Some might call that immaturity, others a flair for the dramatic.

"That particular evening, Vinson had specifically invited Sir William Hirsch of England as an honored guest. His intent was to sufficiently impress Mr. Hirsch and perhaps enter into one or more business ventures with the wealthy British knight. In unaltered history, he did just that, and the pair became strong business partners.

"However, your cravat-stealing changed everything. Because of your intervention, Mr. Vinson could not find that crucial piece of attire, and he was not about to go greet his guests inappropriately dressed. He went ballistic tearing apart his suite and turning his closet upside down looking for it. Since he knew he'd left it on his bed, he was all the more determined to keep looking.

"In the meantime, his guests waited obediently, yet uncomfortably, around his dining room table while their food grew cold. After 30 minutes, he finally gave up and descended to greet everyone without his blessed French cravat. By then, he'd waited too long to pick a new outfit.

"The long-short of it is this: Sir Hirsch was not overly impressed, in fact, he developed a negative idea about Vinson, and the two never became business partners. That in itself did not affect either man much, but it did others associated with them.

"Raymond Jones was one of Vinson's good friends, a good-hearted man without the same naked ambition Vinson displayed. He owned an architectural firm in Boston which helped develop many different civil engineering projects.

"In the unaltered history, through Vinson, Raymond Jones met Sir Hirsch, and later on down the road, Hirsch asked Jones to hire his nephew as a project supervisor, which he did. Unbeknownst to good-hearted Jones, Hirsch's nephew was corrupt, and on at least one major project, he skimmed a large amount of funds off the top by scrimping on materials.

"That nephew of Hirsch's supervised the construction of a certain apartment building and shorted materials from the project to line his own pockets a little more. Two years later, its roof collapsed in the middle of the night, killing 7 tenants. All the blame landed on Raymond Jones and his firm, though it was Hirsch's nephew who did it. Jones was ruined socially and financially. He eventually committed suicide. His son grew up to be an alcoholic, regularly beating his wife and kids. Jones' other children grew up to similar fates and lived in different states of poverty throughout New Jersey.

"However, since you changed things and Vinson never partnered with Hirsch, that means Raymond Jones *also* never met Hirsch, and so was never asked to hire Hirsch's nephew at the firm. Jones went on to become a successful and well-respected builder in the community. There is no suicide, no alcoholism, no abuse, and no hopelessness. Amazing what one little tie can do, huh?"

Mark sat dumbfounded. "Yeah" was all he could manage to say.

"As long as it's the *right* tie, that is."

Mark considered the story, amazed at the effect of one small object on the lives of so many. It was mind-boggling. It made time feel like a giant minefield, and if you took the wrong step, it might blow up a few hundred lives here, or another thousand over there.

"Did anything else change?"

"Yes, actually. Vinson was convinced his maid had done something with the cravat, and there were reports of a mysterious caterer who appeared and disappeared like a ghost, so Vinson fired everybody."

"The maid became destitute, and because Vinson ruined her reputation with every notable family in the area, she was eventually forced to prostitute herself out to survive. She overcame it though, not like Jones."

"The catering company also had trouble getting jobs after Vinson started badmouthing them around town. After a year, the owner had to close up shop. That result was unexpected, but it was directly due to your posing as a caterer."

"You mean, something happened which you guys *didn't* predict?"

"Maybe."

"Hallelujah! I didn't think that was possible!"

In spite of his exuberance at catching Hardy off guard, he felt terrible. The original mess, with the collapsed building and the suicidal architect, had at least been the result of natural history. This other was directly due to Mark's intervention.

Natural History. Now there was a reinvented term if he had ever heard one.

As soon as he got a chance, he would have to make sure the maid and the owner of the catering company were taken care of financially so they wouldn't face ruin.

Chapter 19

12:08 PM, June 10th, 2012, Boston, MA

The coolness of the morning evaporated as the day wore on. The sun grew hot and beat down on them as they strolled through downtown Boston. Every now and then, a slight breeze broke through and wafted up through the streets, barely cooling their skin in a tantalizing and unsatisfying way.

Businessmen and women in stifling suits traversed the streets in all directions as they hurried to squeeze in what they could before their hour break was up. Mothers herded their children through crosswalks, and persistent street vendors pushed their wares on every single person who passed by. It was lunch time.

The restaurant they chose was really nothing more than a small sidewalk café. There was something quaint about relaxing at an outside table while the city passed you by. The waitress took their orders and promised to have their food out shortly.

"Tell me, Phillips, how is it that in the Vinson case I altered history like a finger dragging through water, producing ripples whether I wanted to or not, yet every single effort I dreamed up to save my kids was to no avail?"

A homeless man came to a stop right in front of their table, struggling with his shopping cart full of useless junk. A wheel had caught in a hole in the sidewalk. He finally freed it and as he passed by, Phillips handed him a twenty dollar bill.

"I don't know the answer to that, Mark, I'm sorry."

"No shrug?"

"This isn't something I know the answer to, but don't want to reveal. It's really something I don't know, plain and simple."

"Then, how do you know where to send me for these missions? How do you know I'm going to be able to make a change for the positive?"

"Should I shrug now?"

"Ha, ha."

Mark waited, but Phillips wasn't budging.

"Where do these watches come from, Phillips?"

"Call me Hardy."

"All right."

"We don't know the answer to that."

"What do you mean you don't know....and what do you mean by *we*? You keep saying we. Who else knows about these things and how many of them are there? Are you with the government or not?"

"Take it easy. No, I'm not with the government, for the millionth time. I'm going to take a pass on answering all your other questions for now. Don't worry, I promise you'll find out in due time. What I will tell you is that *we* is not a very big number."

"But surely you know how these devices work? I mean....I thought time travel was impossible. Well, I should say, I was *sure* it was impossible — until I lived it. I took Physics in college. Aren't you supposed to have to travel the speed of light to achieve time travel? And isn't it actually impossible to reach the speed of light without an infinite amount of energy?"

"We have our theories, but so far, we don't really know for sure how the watches work, nor where they came from."

"Amazing."

"Yep."

"I mean it's amazing you've got no idea what you're dealing with, but you keep using them."

"Yep. Same as you."

"Touché. Haven't you had engineers take a look at them?"

"It's a bit difficult to reverse engineer something you can't remove from a person's wrist. Plus, there is no apparent way to open the device without damaging it. We'd have to force or cut it open, and that could be disastrous."

"Surely you could set up instruments around a person before they shift and take measurements of the magnetic fields or something."

"We've done that."

"And?"

"Later."

If a grown man could pout, Mark was doing it right now. While Hardy was a naturally likable person, Mark still grew more and more frustrated with each evasive answer. Yet, he had no choice but to let his need to know go. He was too green at this to put up a decent fight. Understanding would have to wait.

They ate and paid their bill. Then, Hardy asked Mark to follow him back to his office, which surprised him. Mark hadn't known Phillips had an office here in Boston.

The office was located in an older building that had once been a town home. It looked to have been built sometime in the late 1800's. They walked up several flights of stairs until they reached the third floor.

It was a large open space, bright and airy; large enough for three desks with plenty of room between them. One desk was empty, clear of any sign of an occupant. Another supported volumes of piles of papers and books, though all were neatly arranged, as if they'd just been straightened by someone with severe neurotic tendencies.

At the third desk sat a muscular man with skin a shade somewhere between a cinnamon stick and ebony. He wore shorts, a T-shirt — which only accentuated his strong physique — and sandals. His hair was trimmed close to the scalp. He didn't look like the kind of guy who ever let it get much longer than that.

His desk was the opposite of the other, papers and other clutter strewn chaotically across its surface. If asked, Mark bet the guy would know exactly where every last scrap was. Mark liked him right away.

"Mark, this is Ty." Hardy motioned to the man. "Ty's an ex-marine, just like you."

Mark moved forward and extended his hand.

Ty took it, his grip was strong. "Ty Jennings. Nice to meet you."

Mark gripped the man's wrist with his free hand and turned it up. Another shifter gleamed in the florescent light

"Just how many of these things are there?" Mark asked.

"Have a seat." Hardy pointed to an empty chair behind Mark.

Arrgh. Typical Hardy — never answered a dad-blamed thing if he didn't have to — and he never seemed to have to. Mark was getting sick of it.

"We've got another mission, but this time, Ty is going with you."

Mark reclined in the chair, listening while Hardy explained. Ty appeared relaxed, absently twirling a pen in and out of his fingers and staring at the blank wall behind Hardy. Despite his appearance to the contrary, however, Ty was very much paying close attention.

Hardy continued, "You're going back to 1863, Mark. To Madison, GA."

"I've never gone back that far."

"We know that. It's not a problem."

"Just surprised me is all."

"That's one of the reasons Ty is going with you. He is much more experienced than you in operations during many of these eras."

"I appreciate that."

"To be truthful, though, the main reason *you* are going is to accompany Ty. Middle Georgia in 1863 is not exactly the time or place where a person of Ty's color is able to move about freely. He needs you as cover."

"What's our mission?"

"Ty will explain later. For now, there's a few other items we need to go over. By now, I'm sure you've noticed that there's a limit to how many times you can shift within a short period of time?"

"That particular feature has been quite annoying. The watch shuts down for 24 hours."

"Yes, your device will shut down if you shift six successive times within one hour, or eight successive times within twelve hours. It's a self-protection mechanism. Your "watch" begins to overheat after too many shifts, so it shuts down to give itself time to cool off."

"I'd kind of figured that out already."

"Well, don't push it. We believe over-shifting may affect the life span of the device somehow. Try to always keep your number of shifts to a minimum.

"Which reminds me," he continued, "No more of this Shift & Strike hot doggin', okay?"

"What are you talking about?"

Hardy slid another newspaper article from his pocket and spread it out on the desk.

Boys Saved by "Phantom"

Two boys, Herbert Walker Jr., 12, and Charles Johnson, 11, of Chicago were saved from attackers last night by what they claim was a phantom. Early yesterday evening, they were attacked while walking along the waterfront by two thugs in an apparent attempted robbery.

Police found both the thugs dead at the scene. Walker and

Johnson were in a very agitated state claiming that the "Shadow" had killed them, appearing and disappearing at random throughout the attack, only to disappear again afterward. "The Shadow" is a radio program about a mysterious crime fighter that can appear in any situation without being noticed.

In spite of the fanciful nature of the boys' story, police noted that the deceased men were locally known hoodlums and criminals. They identified one as Malcolm "the Mick" O'Leary. Police also pointed out that the boys would be incapable of inflicting the type of wounds sustained by the men.

Police are asking any witnesses to please come forward.

"I see."

"Once in a blue moon is okay, but more than that draws too much attention to us."

"Sure makes things easier, especially in a fight."

"Maybe. But you don't want...*we* don't want that kind of attention. Too much attention inevitably will come back to bite us when we least expect it. Do your best to find ways to accomplish every mission without having to shift in front of others."

"Got it. Don't shift too often and don't shift in front of others. Anything else?"

"Never use your shifter for personal gain in a way that brings harm to others."

Mark nodded silently. That went unsaid — at least for him. The possibility of using his watch in that way hadn't even crossed his mind, but he could see how a certain kind of person might. For him, the thought of it made his gut twist in distaste. He would never do that.

"Those are the three rules. Can you abide by them?"

"I can."

"Good. Come with me."

Hardy led him to a metal cabinet on the wall. He swung open one of the doors and retrieved a thick briefcase. Inside was what appeared to be a folded costume. Definitely dated, slightly worn and dirty, but not aged.

Hardy pulled it out. "This is the typical attire the average southerner would have worn in 1863. You should blend right in."

Inside the briefcase was also an antique, yet well-oiled pistol, along with a Bowie knife and several other key accessories.

"Ty's outfit is a bit different, but also fitting for the period. You can leave any time."

Mark turned to his new, over-sized partner who just sat there grinning at him.

Chapter 20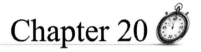

Would you go with me
If we rolled down streets of fire

"Would You Go With Me"

~ Josh Turner

June 11ᵗʰ, 2012, Madison, GA

Since airplanes fly a lot faster than horses trot, they flew to Atlanta before shifting back to the 1800's. Since Mark had left his car in the Atlanta Hartsfield Airport parking lot before traveling to Boston, they just picked it up and made the hour drive to Madison, Georgia.

Madison was one of the few towns to escape General Sherman's wrath on his famous march to the sea in 1864. Legend had it the town was so beautiful Sherman had refused to burn it. The truth was Madison had been the hometown of a pro-union senator named Joshua Hill, and Sherman spared it for political reasons. Regardless, the result was a perfectly preserved city reflecting Georgian architecture prior to the Civil War. Large antebellum homes lined both sides of the main street and were in such good shape, visitors could feel like they'd gone back in time to the Old South. That is, if they could ignore the telephone poles and asphalt.

Ty Jennings was a big man. Thick neck, thicker chest, and burly forearms. Enough muscle to intimidate most people. High intelligence shone behind his dark amber eyes. He looked like a Marine. For the most part, he seemed to be a man of few words, the kind of man people are naturally inspired to place their trust and confidence in.

It felt as if Ty didn't know quite what to do with Mark. He seemed fundamentally uncomfortable with their partnership. Yet every now and then, it was like he would slip up and break into friendly banter, only to revert back to stiff formality a short time later. Mark didn't know what to make of it.

"Tell me about yourself, Ty," He said to break an uncomfortably long silence.

"What do you want to know?"

"Normal stuff, where you're from, places you've seen....."

Ty grimaced. "Not much to tell. I was born outside Chicago, 1944."

"1944! You can't be that old...."

In answer, Ty lifted the wrist bearing his shifter into the air. Mark nodded in understanding. *How easily we forget.*

"Yeah, Mama was alone and never had much to offer us kids. Never knew my dad. Scraped by growing up, barely stayed out of trouble. Joined the Marines when I got out of high school so I wouldn't get drafted into the general army. Best decision I ever made.

"They shipped me off to 'Nam and attached me to a special recon unit. Gave me lots special training for the jobs they wanted us to do. Tough missions, hard decisions. The worst scrape I was probably ever in was during the Tet offensive. But that's a long story. I'll tell you about it some other time."

"How did you end up becoming a time-shifter?"

"Later."

Ty was apparently going to be as evasive as Hardy.

"You haven't asked me what our objective is," Ty noted.

"I figured you would tell me when you were ready."

"Yeah, Hardy said you were a Marine too."

It was Mark's turn to grin. "So, what *is* our objective? Why are we going back to 1863?"

"We're going to save my great-great-great grandfather's life."

***

10:03 AM, April 15th, 1863, Madison, GA

Mark had never gone this far back before. Dashing between decades within the 20th century didn't seem like such a big deal, but somehow standing in the middle of Georgia during the Civil War left him awestruck.

The dusty road wound ahead lazily, disappearing around a bend in the trees in the distance. They had waited to shift until they were far enough out of town nobody would notice. Out here, the only difference from the modern era he had noted so far was there were no paved roads. Granted, trees and barbed wire fences were the only other sights they'd seen till now, and those would look the same in any century. It was still odd though. You would think you would be able to tell what century you were in by the way the trees looked. Of course, that wasn't true.

Come to think of it, there *was* something different about the trees. There were much fewer of them. Apparently, a lot of what was forest in modern times had been cleared farmland back in 1863. More fields, more farms, less forests. Weren't environmentalists always complaining about how we were stripping the world of its trees? Plant a tree, save the world. Well, based on what he was seeing here, modern times had plenty of trees. Much more than the world used to have anyway. Wouldn't be the first time environmentalists had treated *pseudo-science* like it was gospel.

Behind and to the right of Mark, Ty shuffled along demurely, dressed in the torn, soiled rags of a slave. Mark had strenuously objected to this, but Ty had insisted. He was a veteran of the mid-1800's. Having visited several times before, Ty knew not acting the part of a slave would have drawn them undue attention. A slave and a white man walking side by side like friends wouldn't just catch people's eye either. The south was in the middle of a war for its survival and such behavior would be attributed to a union sympathizer, an association that could get them killed. It was wiser to play the parts.

"Ty, what's it like being a black in America these days? Uh, I mean...back in our day."

Ty hesitated, then he smirked. "Honest question deserves an honest answer. I grew up in the 1940's and 50's, so it was tough. We moved around a good bit, so I experienced the best and the worst of the south, the north, out west, you name it.

"I felt like a second class citizen, all the time. Told where to sit, stand, drink, and even ride the bus. Made me feel worthless....and helpless. Once, when I was young, a white man tried to force himself on my ma right in front of my eyes. I was about twelve. It was only by the grace of God she was spared from it.

"That's hell, man," Ty continued, "Watching your mama being attacked like that and not knowing which is better, to protect her or do nothing, so they don't come back on both of you later. In those days, there really were people who seethed with hatred just because of your color, and the KKK was still alive and kicking."

"How about in my time? In 2012."

"It's better. A lot better. Some black leaders keep hyping up how oppressed we are, but it's nothing like it was. Many don't know any better because the younger generation never lived it, and some of the older ones have forgotten. But I know. I've lived both.

"Don't get me wrong. There's still real prejudice out there. It's not all imagined. Been called the "N" word a few times. Been followed around stores. Had some punks wave the old confederate battle flag at me from their car once. Back in the 50's, the south was worse than the north, but to be honest, I think that's flipped now. Most of the flak I get these days is from northerners."

"Guess I can't really know what it's like."

"Maybe not. Then again, there had to be some time in your life when you didn't fit in to some group, some time when you were despised because of something you had no control over."

"Yeah, I guess."

They walked without speaking, their eyes glued to the dust passing beneath their feet.

"How many times have you shifted back to the 1860's?" Mark asked.

"Four or five."

"How does it compare? I mean....the racism here must be worse, but how does it feel to be walking in an era when your ancestors were slaves?"

"Hard to describe. Wasn't exactly what I expected. Sure, there's a lot more blatant racism in 1863, but I knew it'd be that way, so I haven't really paid too much attention to it.

"It's frustrating to feel like I'm not free, like I can't go where I want without an escort — unless I wanna risk getting shot, that is. Makes my blood boil seeing my people forced to work themselves to death in the fields. Other times, I'm just resigned to the fact that it's just the way things are here.

"There's a lot that might surprise you, though," he continued. "Nothing is quite as cut and dry as history teachers make it out to be in the 21st century. First of all, there aren't as many slave owners in the South as you might think. Only about 10% of the southern population actually owns a slave. 90% of whites don't, usually because they can't afford any, but often because they're morally against it.

"The poorer whites are the hardest to figure out. Some are envious of the jobs slaves take from them. Many of those would love to set 'em all free and send 'em up north. Some hate all blacks and will turn you in as a runaway faster than you can blink, while others are downright cozy with us, sharing liquor, good times, whatever.

"Same thing with the owners. Not all of them treat their slaves badly. Though too many do. I've seen some real bad stuff since I started coming here. On the other hand, there's some owners that believe the best way to get the most work out of their slaves is to treat 'em well. Even though we're viewed as property, we are *valuable* property. Mistreating us can be bad for business. Unfortunately, for every good owner, there's probably two with just the opposite philosophy, though usually it's the foreman who decides how things are gonna go.

"There's a rare few among the plantation owners who wish to God they didn't have to have slaves but don't think they can make it without them. Then, among those, there's some who actually give in to their moral convictions, free all their slaves, and shut their plantation down, because the bottom line is, they're right. It's not possible to keep a plantation running in 1863 without slaves. The local economy won't support it.

"I admire those men. They're willing to give up all financial well-being, even put their family's welfare at risk, just because they are so convinced of the evil of slavery.

Ty shot him a sly look.

"Wanna know a dirty, little secret? I don't worry about my people. There's no denying they suffer, and terribly. There's also not much I can do about it, but many of them have made their peace with God.

"No, I tremble for the owners. Absolute power corrupts absolutely, and slavery corrupts the slave owner down to his very core. It's not uncommon for owners at death's door to summon their slaves to their bedside in their last moments, begging for forgiveness. That actually happens *a lot,* and it's rare to hear of an owner who doesn't pass into eternity screaming in utter terror of figures and shadows they see lurking in the darkened corners of their rooms, waiting to drag them down.

"Whips draw blood, but physical wounds heal. And even when they don't, there's a healing salve waiting in heaven above. I'd choose the whip over eternal burning any day."

Mark scowled. "I didn't realize you were so religious."

"It's not religion. Facts are facts."

Mark took it all in. It was eye-opening to hear these things from a black man who'd experienced the best and worst of all eras.

"You should have studied sociology, Ty."

"Ha!" He snickered, "I am. That's what I do in my spare time."

They both laughed.

Chapter 21

For years, Ty had longingly pondered his roots, wondering who his ancestors were, what they'd been like, what they'd endured. Growing up, the only living grandparent he'd known had been his grandmother, and her history-telling had always been a bit sketchy. He'd pieced together as much as he could with the crumbs of fragmented memories that she could recall, but it wasn't much to go on.

Many blacks he knew didn't care much for genealogy. He could understand that. It was a much easier hobby for whites to take up. Better paper trails. Illiterate blacks weren't always issued the proper birth and death certificates, etc.

Whites were also more likely to find something in their family history in which to take pride. Blacks tended to think they already knew where the trail would end up....slavery. Not only was slavery not something to be proud of, it hurt to think about. No one really wanted to dwell on the inglorious and painful suffering of their forefathers, especially when subconsciously you had to recognize that their suffering made possible your future, comfortable life in the good old U.S. of A.

A third reason Ty suspected some didn't care for long family trees was the futility of it. Slavery capped every family tree as sure as rain. It was almost impossible to trace one's line through that historical obstacle all the way back to Africa. Still, family history had always fascinated Ty, as had history in general, and he had wanted to try.

When he first received his shifter, he saw no reason why he couldn't use his free time to go back and investigate his family line in person rather than on the dusty pages of some ledger.

It turned out to be an easy exercise when you had the right tool. First, he'd traveled back to the town where he'd been told his grandparents had grown up. He'd shifted to a year when he thought they'd be kids (Though he was very careful to limit his contact so he wouldn't inadvertently create some kind of time paradox that would prevent his own birth).

He met their parents (His great-grandparents) who looked shockingly, though appropriately, young, and then simply asked them where they'd grown up. He repeated this process for his 2nd great grandparents. It turned out that his 2nd great grandfather, Jefferson Jr., had been born during the Civil War. In as long an interview as Ty dared risk, Jefferson Jr. revealed that his father, Jefferson Sr., Ty's 3rd great grandpa, had been killed around that same time. Jefferson Jr. hadn't known any of the circumstances of his father's death, only that it had happened in Madison, GA.

After investigating further in Madison, Ty learned that in 1863 Jefferson Sr. had been lynched for the crime of stealing a chicken.

This discovery steeled Ty, and he became determined to save him.

Mark absorbed the account intently as Ty explained the history.

"So....*did* he steal the chicken?" Mark asked.

"Does it matter?" Ty spat on the ground. "Stealing a chicken isn't a hangable offense."

"Relax. I wasn't saying it should be. Just curious."

"No. Near as I can tell, he was innocent. It was a trumped up charge so some plantation owner could get revenge for something else."

"What's the real story then?"

"A lot of men were involved in the lynching, but the whole thing was instigated and led by two men in particular who owned large plantations nearby, Stephen Plageanet and Vincent Regnier. I've been told they hated my grandpa because he walked in on Plageanet while he was trying to rape some poor white woman named Ruby. Plageanet is a known womanizer, by the way.

"Most slaves would have meekly snuck back out of the building, knowing what it would mean for them to interfere. But not my gramps. Jefferson Sr. went right up to Mr. Plageanet and stood there, staring him down. Never lifted a hand in violence, just stared hard from no more than a foot away until Plageanet stopped.

"His aggressiveness cooled Plageanet in the way that mattered right then, but it also made his blood boil in another. If Jefferson had done anything else, Plageanet would have had an excuse to skin his hide right then and there, but there was no clear offense he could point to without incriminating himself in front of other whites. Plus, Jefferson belonged to the Martin plantation, and a man had to have a good reason to harm another man's slave. We *are* considered valuable."

Mark noted how Ty kept referring to local slaves as "we" instead of "they", a subconscious act of solidarity.

"Jefferson went home proud, but nervous. He knew Plageanet wouldn't forget the humiliation, not for a long time, if ever. Plageanet couldn't stand the idea of being bettered by a slave. So, he bode his time. A few months later, he hooked up with another plantation owner, Vincent Regnier, a man who hated all blacks and treated his own slaves horribly just for the sake of being mean, together with some other like-minded folk. They stole a few chickens from the Martin plantation, cooked themselves a nice lunch, and then claimed they'd caught Jefferson with them red-handed. The lynch mob hung him that same afternoon."

Mark couldn't imagine the horror of having to live like that, always on guard lest you step out of line and put your life at risk. "What about Jefferson's owner, Martin? Why didn't he stop it?"

Ty sighed. "John Martin is indifferent, as you'll see. He's got a lot of slaves, so losing one didn't bother him too much, as long as he felt there was cause. Plus, Plageanet's stealing the chickens from Martin's own farm stripped Martin of the ability to protest very loudly."

"So where did your family get the name Jennings then? I haven't heard of anybody named that yet. Didn't a lot of slaves take the last names of their former masters when they were freed?"

"Well, there's a fourth gentlemen I haven't told you about yet by the name of Jacob Jennings. He also has a large plantation in Madison. From all I've heard, he's a good man and treats his slaves very well. Some ridicule him for it, but when my grandpa was hung, Jennings went to Martin and offered to buy Jefferson's wife and son, Jefferson Jr. He overpaid by a substantial amount just to make sure they had a safe place, and Martin, of course, took it, being the businessman that he was. My family took Jennings name from then on out, and ever since I learned this story, I've been proud to wear it."

"But we're going to try to save Jefferson Sr.? Aren't you afraid we'll screw things up in a way that might forever change your family's history or even cause you to cease to exist?"

"It's a risk. But, it's one we're gonna take."

"Okay. Count me in."

After that, as hard as Ty tried to maintain proper decorum for 1863, he kept finding himself drifting forward and walking more alongside Mark than behind him.

"Just don't forget who's boss, got it?"

"Got it." Mark grinned.

1:57 PM, April 15th, 1863, Madison, GA

They lay silently in the brush lining the beginning of a ridge line. Both had been through sniper school in the Marines, so they felt right at home. Their bodies were well disciplined in lying for hours at a time without movement.

Ty's previous research had led him to this grove. There was an oak tree down in the vale about fifty yards in front of them. That was the tree where they would hang Jefferson Sr later in the day — at 2:12 PM to be specific. They even knew which branch the mob would swing the rope over.

This time, however, events would not proceed as they always had in unaltered history. Ty and Mark had neatly sawed most of the way through that branch and hidden the traces of their work. When Jefferson's weight was suddenly thrown upon it, the branch would snap off cleanly, dropping Jefferson to the ground without any pressure on his neck.

Ty had prepared well. On some previous visit, he'd stashed two sniper rifles in a camouflaged dugout. This was their only concession to modern times. It was a risk to their identities, but as long as no innocent bystanders walked into this brush, no one would be the wiser.

Each rifle was well-oiled, wrapped in waterproof plastic, and was outfitted with a decent silencer. They each took one and set it up, messing with the tripod and the scope until they were satisfied they would be able to perform.

Then, they waited.

A few minutes after two, a group of men on horses entered the clearing. An obviously exhausted black man dressed in rags stumbled along behind them, his wrists tied to the last horse. He was barely keeping up.

The men wore neither hoods nor costumes. They'd made no effort at all to hide their identity. Masked lynch mobs would come later in history. There were ten men in all, four of them seeming to be the leaders of the group. Mark guessed that one well-dressed figure who, even from this distance, gave off an air of arrogance, had to be Plageanet. Another shorter, burly man stayed close by his side and had a cruel look to him. That was probably Vincent Regnier. Mark had no idea who the others were.

They reached the lone tree and swung their rope over the fated branch. After some heckling and jeering, they got down to business and sat Jefferson on a horse. Plageanet wrapped the noose around his neck, an expression of sublime satisfaction inscribed on his face.

Both Ty and Mark readied themselves. Mark sighted Plageanet through his scope. The man's eyes were not cruel like Regnier's, just cold. Cold, arrogant, and merciless.

"May I?"

Ty nodded. "Be my guest."

Plageanet slapped the rear of Jefferson's horse. The horse bolted and Jefferson slipped off, dropping fast. *Crack!* The branch snapped as planned, and Jefferson fell all the way to the ground. Plageanet's eyes opened wide in surprise, which would be the last expression the man would ever wear.

Mark calmly depressed the trigger, and then Plageanet was no more, his face disappearing in a cloud of red. His body slid lifelessly from his horse.

The silencer kept the rifle's report from being heard by the other men. Initially, no one saw the blood, except a man standing to Plageanet's right. Mark took him out as well. Ty dispatched Regnier almost simultaneously.

Three down in a matter of seconds. The men were beginning to realize they were under attack, but not hearing the customary, loud crack of gunshots, nor seeing the expected puffs of gray smoke, they had no idea where to search for their ambushers. Controlled panic ensued as they raced their mounts in circles, desperately seeking the source of the shots. All had drawn their pistols, but they held them impotently pointed to the sky.

Ty swiveled and fired again. Another man toppled from his saddle. Several of the lynchers were now spurring their mounts to the safety of the tree line like there was no tomorrow. One bold individual, however, rode over to Jefferson and brought his pistol to bear on the kneeling man's head to finish the execution. Mark almost saw what was happening too late. He whipped his rifle around and dropped the executioner before he could pull the trigger. A second shot killed another of the scoundrels at that man's right.

With six dead, including their leaders, and two others in flight, the last two gave up as well and rode off like bats out of hell in full retreat.

Jefferson Sr. just knelt in the dust, palms up to the sky, a look of shock painting his visage.

Mark and Ty leaned back and raised their muzzles.

"You thinking what I'm thinking?" Ty asked.

"This ain't gonna to work, is it?"

"Don't think so. My plan sounded great until we actually did it. There's gonna be relatives and friends who'll want revenge. They've no idea who we are, but they'll sure know who Jefferson is."

"Yeah, he's a dead man. Not much way we can protect him now. There's always going to be someone after him."

"So what now?"

"We could whisk him and his family away."

"With this many white people dead, they'd probably pursue him to Siberia."

"Why don't we hang around the Martin plantation for a while, see if we can learn anything from the aftermath of our handiwork? Maybe we'll stumble across a better way there."

"Sounds good to me. Nice thing about these shifters," Ty tapped his watch, "History's never final."

Chapter 22

"Massah Martin shal' be dow'n fort-wit."

Mark had trouble believing he was standing in an actual functioning plantation home. Expensive hand-made furnishings dotted the interior of the home, all finished in a dark walnut stain. Plush, burgundy rugs blanketed the floors. The wallpaper coverings were ornate and full of dark, but vibrant colors. He waited in the parlor for the master of the home to attend to him. Ty stood outside, waiting patiently.

"Sir? I do not believe I have had the pleasure."

The man's smooth southern accent rolled off his tongue in a refined drawl. His face was ordinary except for a slightly hawkish sharpness to his features, which was mostly due to a hook in the tip of his nose. His dark hair was plastered flat with some kind of oil. He had a lanky figure, which belied his imposing personality.

Mark stood.

"Phillip Trudeau, at your service, sir," Mark responded, "Sorry to bother you, but we were traveling along the road near here when my slave fell and injured his leg. He's sprained it quite badly, I fear. We were on our way to Covington, but it appears he will not capable of continuing without some rest. Might we trouble you for room and board for a few days. I'd gladly reimburse your kindness, of course."

"Mr. Trudeau, it would be our pleasure to host you," the man flashed a slick smile, "Hospitality is a pillar of our society, is it not? No payment will be necessary, of course. You shall be our guest."

The man's head twitched to the side, an unusual look entering his eyes. "Are you sure the injury is sincere?"

"Sorry, what?...No. Uh, yes, I mean, I do know my slave quite well and feel I could tell if that were the case. No, his injury is quite real and incapacitating, I'm sorry to say."

"Some men would force him to continue regardless."

"I believe in taking good care of my property."

Martin smiled. He understood that line of reasoning.

"Well, you are welcome to stay here while he heals. My servants will take your things to your room. Your man shall find a bed down at the slave quarters."

"You are too kind."

"On your way to Covington, eh?"

"Yes, we have relatives down there."

"Ah, I see. Well, I must excuse myself. I have business to attend to, but perhaps we can chat more at dinner."

Cool night air washed the plantation in tranquility. Crickets chattered their comforting song to rich and afflicted alike. Oak and magnolia branches waved in the blue moonlight under the influence of light breezes that came and went like ripples on a calm sea. From somewhere down the row, the faint rhythm of slaves singing evening hymns drifted his way. Smoke from a campfire mingled with the aromas of roasting meat and baked beans.

It was an altogether pleasant atmosphere, which Mark never would have imagined could belong to this oppressive time and place in history.

Intellectually, his mind knew in which time he stood. Freedom was denied here to so many, yet right now, his heart couldn't feel it. For the moment, all was at peace.

Mark ducked through the low doorway into the warm interior of the shack. It was warm now only because Jefferson Sr. had stoked the fire well for the cooking of the evening meal. By morning, all the holes and cracks in the walls would allow the invading cold to dominate once more.

Mark and Ty had shared with Jefferson that they were the ones who had saved him, but only because it seemed easier than remaining incognito. They had warned him to keep a tight lid on it, but the warning was unnecessary. He knew the risks better than they. He was curious to how they'd happened to be at just the right place at the right time, and what kind of magic guns could shoot without noise, but he was also used to keeping his mouth shut, so it wasn't hard to avoid his pointed and difficult questions.

Having a meal with a regular family was a nice respite from lonely bachelorhood for Mark. Jefferson's wife, who they called Gabi, served some sort of vegetable stew and fresh cornbread. She was kind and hospitable, though the idea of a white man eating with them in her shack obviously made her nervous.

Their baby, Jefferson Jr., was only three months old. He cooed and giggled, oblivious to the problematic world around him. He'd rolled over for the first time that very morning.

After dinner, Mark stepped outside for some fresh air. He knew he was making Jefferson and his family uncomfortable with his presence, but he wanted to keep a close eye on them. He felt responsible for their welfare now. Plus, he couldn't stand the idea of lounging around up in that mansion while they were down here with Ty. That just wasn't his style.

It certainly confounded the Martins as to why he'd want to fraternize with slaves and deny himself comfort, but he didn't care. He wouldn't be here long anyway. Just long enough to get a feel for things, have a chance to hear local gossip, and come up with some other way to save Jefferson.

Whump!

Something heavy struck Mark hard in the back of the head. Before he could turn to see his attacker, his legs gave out. The last thing he saw was the ground rushing toward his face.

***

7:47 AM, April 16th, 1863, Madison, GA

"Wake up, boy."

Cold water splashed his face, shocking him back into full consciousness. Gasping, Mark sat up and sputtered, struggling to get a grip on his surroundings.

He was in some kind of shack with a dirt floor. It smelled of damp soil and smoked meat. His back was to the wall.

His arms ached from being pinned behind him for some length of time. When he tried to bring them around, he realized a cord had been wrapped tightly around his wrists. His hands were tied behind his back.

His hands were tied behind his back!

He had no way to reach his watch. No way to shift out of whatever mess he was in. Desperately, he strained against the bonds to see if he could break them or slip out, but they held firm.

"No use strugglin'. We gotcha tied up good."

His ankles were also wrapped with a thick rope, which was knotted around a rafter in the ceiling. The rope had a little play in it so he could move around a bit, but if he tried to go too far, the rope configuration would yank his feet out from under him.

Ty sat against the opposite wall, similarly bound like Mark. He was awake too. His face looked beaten and a trail of dried blood ran down one of his cheeks. His head hung low, eyes to the ground, as if defeated. Mark hoped that was an act for the sake of their captors. The Ty he had gotten to know over the past few days wouldn't give up so easy.

"Listen here, boy, Ah wanna know if you the man kilt my pa."

"Who are you?"

"Hugh Plageanet. You two kilt my pa, I'd bet my life on it."

"Never heard of you, nor your pa. I don't have any idea what you talking about. We were traveling to Covington to visit some family. We stopped at the Martin house to rest while my slave's leg healed. Now, I demand you untie us!"

"Likely story I say. If'n that so, whatcha you doing in Jefferson's shack, the same slave pa was gonna hang for theft when he was kilt by some skirmisher?"

"I was looking for a bunk where my slave could sleep, and Jefferson offered his shack. I don't think Mr. Martin would look to kindly on you kidnapping his guests in the middle of the night."

"Oh, John Martin, he's all for it! Once I told him six men were dead, including my pa, and that somehow his slave Jefferson was involved, why he was more than happy to help see justice brought. When we found you two down at the shack, we knew you had to be involved somehow, bein' strangers and all. It only makes sense. Mr. Martin, he agreed."

"Martin may not think like us Plageanets as to the treatment of these no account negroes, but he sure ain't gonna stick his neck out for one. Much less for some stranger who don't even sound like he's from the South."

They were on dangerous ground now. Anybody not from the South was by definition a traitor.

"I'm from Richmond."

Richmond, VA was close enough to Washington DC, that the lack of a strong southern accent could be explained.

"Could just as easily be from the other side of the border."

Mark shrugged. He glanced at Ty who still sat motionless. This could get ugly for both of them fast.

"I obviously can't convince you of the truth, so what are you going to do?"

"We gonna hang Jefferson and your'n slave too, jes' for the heck of it. We gotta talk some about you. I reckon you'rn a northern spy, but there's a chance you ain't. I'd hate to kill another southern boy when we's so short on 'em already."

Turning, he walked out the door and closed it behind him. Ty lifted his face. He sat more erect and his defeated spirit melted away. No, he had not given up.

"You got some plan going, Mark?"

"I'm thinking. We've got to get our hands free somehow."

"You ain't kidding. This situation right here is noooo good. No good at all."

"We'll think of something. Regardless of what they decide about me, I won't leave you."

Ty smiled a smile that came from the heart. "Didn't think you would, buddy. Still, I appreciate you saying it."

"In a way, it'd be better if they let me go. Then, I could go back and get our rifles and shoot you out of this."

"Sure am glad you finally woke up. They must have hit you harder than they hit me. Plageanet's spawn was having a good old time roughing me up before he decided to wake you. By the way, Jefferson's tied up outside."

They heard footsteps and Ty changed back to intimidated slave mode. Hugh Plageanet stormed back in, furious determination blazing in his eyes. Three other men trailed behind him.

"You're gonna hang, boy. Same as your slave. My men who saw what happened didn't tell me about how pa died for fear I'd think they were crazy, but now they done spoke up. Said pa an' the others were kilt by guns that made no noise.

"Don't know what kind of trickery that is, they thought it were witchery. I think it's some kind of new-fangled fabrication from up north. Same as that band on your wrist. First time I saw that, I knew something were wrong. Puttin' two an' two together though, says yer some kind of northern spy fer sure. Not sure what you're doin' round these parts, but by gosh, I don't care. You're gonna hang."

He grabbed Mark's elbow and yanked him to his feet. The other men did the same with Ty. He was about twice the size of any one of them. The men cut the ropes around their ankles that tied them to the rafters.

Now, Mark and Ty could make a break for it if they wanted to, but where would they go? They still couldn't shift with their hands tied behind their backs. Still, if both of them could somehow escape at the same time, Mark could push Ty's shifter for him....

There was no time for that unfortunately. Before they could even protest, they were both hoisted up and seated astride a horse. The men secured their ankles together again with ropes that ran under the horses' bellies. If for some reason, they were to fall off the horse's back on the trail, they'd most likely be drug to a gruesome death.

After a twenty minute ride, they arrived at the top of a cliff, with a view overlooking a small valley. The drop was at least 100 feet straight down.

Hugh Plageanet stopped Mark's horse short next to his own.

"You ever read about Judas, spy? Bible says after he betrayed the Lord he went and hung himself on a tree overlooking a field. His body hung there in that tree until it finally fell into the field and all his guts spilt out. Fittin' end for a traitor, don't you think?

"Well, that's what we're gonna do with you. See them three trees there by the edge? We're gonna hang all three of you, one on each tree, just a overlookin' that valley there. An' then, we're gonna leave your bodies to hang and rot. Just like Judas. Whatcha think about that, spy?"

"I think if you really believed in the Lord, you wouldn't be doing this."

"War is war." Plageanet spit on the ground as he said it.

"Jefferson's got nothing to do with this war. You just want revenge."

Plageanet grew red in the face, "He ain't a person, you fool!"

"Could've fooled me."

With venom, the predator spun to his men.

"Get on with it! Hang 'em all. An' put the spy between his two beloved slaves!"

Their ankle bonds were loosed once more so they could dismount. Once on the ground, Mark played his last card.

"One last request?"

"Wuz that?" Plageanet sneered.

"Let me take a whiz before I go. I heard that hung men will pee themselves. Spare me some dignity at least."

"Forget it, spy."

One of Plageanet's men piped up, "That don't seem so unreasonable to me, boss." Another man echoed the sentiment.

"I'll decide what's reasonable and not! All right, fine. Untie him so he can empty his bladder, but keep your guns on him!"

To heck with Hardy Phillips and his Shift & Strike rules. It was either that or die. As soon as his hands were loose, it would only require one quick motion to push the button on his shifter and be safe. Then, he'd have all the time in the world to figure out how to go back and save Ty.

They cut his bond and he breathed an audible sigh of relief. He brought his arms around, reached for his shifter, saw the alarm dawning on the faces of his captors, saw the guns coming up....and then he shifted out.

What happened next came as a complete surprise. Instead of standing safely in the future, Mark found himself airborne, about 100 feet off the ground. Instantly, that sickening feeling you get at the top of a roller coaster hit his stomach like a baseball bat, and he was falling to his death.

He could only think the shifter must have somehow malfunctioned and moved him horizontally off the cliff's edge as well as through time. Reflexes took over and before a second had passed, his hand was moving back to the shifter, pressing the button to return him to 1863.

This time, his body underwent a wrenching sensation unlike any other he had ever experienced. His bones felt as if they were literally being stretched and the pain was agonizing. Nausea came upon him, tremendous and overwhelming. He felt like he was being pulled apart piece by piece, and he very nearly was. In that brief second, he'd fallen at least 15 to 20 feet.

The shifter would always work to push him out of the way of unexpected objects occupying his projected position in the target time. This time, because he had fallen, he would have shifted to a place 20 feet underground. The device had never had to transpose him that far before. He realized now that the transposition could actually hurt.

Luckily, when he returned to his lynch mob buddies, a glitch in the transposition feature had caused him to reappear just outside the line of fire of his attackers, slightly to their left.

He had just one second to try and assess what he needed to do. There was no time to change a setting on the watch. Apparently, in the future, the cliff edge was in a different place than it was 1863.

In that brief moment of falling in 2012, Mark hadn't had time to judge distances very accurately, but he guessed he'd been about 50 feet away from the future edge of the cliff. Somehow, he had to move himself and Ty at least 50 feet away from the current edge in order to shift to safety.

Mark dove headfirst into the man closest to him. The blow knocked the gun out of his hand and the wind out of his stomach.

Ty stared at Mark. He'd seen Mark shift out, only to instantly reappear, but not in an ideal position as expected. He could tell something was wrong from the look on Mark's face.

"Ty, move back! Move! Move!"

Marine instincts kicked in and Ty drove his body into that of a second man. Mark was back up now and he kicked a third man's gun away. If these men hadn't been so distracted by Mark's disappearing act, he doubted he and Ty could have achieved this much.

Plageanet hadn't had his gun drawn, but he was drawing it now. Mark grabbed Ty and yanked him up off his knees. They ran in a short zigzag pattern, which made Plageanet's first two shots miss. The other men were regrouping quickly.

Had they gone fifty feet yet? No way to know for sure, but Mark was out of time. It was either now or never. If they hadn't gone far enough, Ty would certainly fall and die with his hands tied behind his back, but if they didn't shift now, they'd be shot for sure.

Mark knocked Ty to the ground. "Pray, buddy." He pushed Ty's shift activator, and then his friend was gone. Mark pushed his own next.

Chapter 23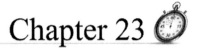

And if all you ever really do is the best you can
Well, you did it man

"Something to Be Proud of"

~ Montgomery Gentry

8:42 PM, June 11th, 2012, Madison, GA

They lay side by side, chests heaving, hearts racing, two feet from the cliff's edge. Now, Mark could see clearly what had happened. The shifters had not malfunctioned. By 2012, this hill had been strip mined. The entire area where their fight had taken place in 1863 no longer existed, and the cliff's edge had moved east by about fifty feet.

Lesson learned. Never shift into an unknown set of circumstances.

"That was a close one," Mark breathed.

"You aren't kidding."

The sun was beginning to set over the hills to their west bathing the clouds in beautiful shades of pink and purple. It had been morning in 1863 when they'd shifted out. The few times in Mark's life that he had come close to dying, it seemed a super heightened appreciation for living always followed. Too bad he couldn't feel this way all the time. Life tasted so wonderful when you came close to losing it.

"We need to go back for Jefferson," Ty said.

"I don't think that's such a good idea."

Ty's face clouded. "We need to go back for Jefferson," he repeated firmly.

"I agree we need to save him, but do you really think our going back to that scene is going to help him? Even if we save him from those guys, then what? He's never going to be safe since we killed those men."

"We just need to get him away from this lynch mob and then we can smuggle him and his family north."

"I've got a better idea, but we'd have to start over."

"All right, let's hear it."

"How about we just go to Jacob Jennings before the original lynching, ask him to buy Jefferson Sr. and his family from Martin, and give him the funds to do it."

"Then, we have Jennings free them and send them up north?"

"Basically."

Ty's brow knotted in agitation. "The only thing I don't like about that plan is that we'd be going back and changing things before we shot Plageanet, Regnier, and those other KKK wannabes."

"Yeah, but it's safer for Jefferson long term. We'd still wait till after he saved that woman from being raped."

Ty eyed Mark suspiciously. "Why? 'Cause she's white?"

"You know that isn't it! It's just the right thing to do."

Ty was silent.

"Fine. If you want we'll save Jefferson before he stumbles on the attempted rape, and then we'll save the woman ourselves."

"Man, I just can't stand the thought of those men living on peacefully, knowing what they are and that they're gonna hurt more of my people. We're gonna leave 'em dead."

"Fine with me, but it puts Jefferson in more danger in the long run, even after he's up north."

"I know it. We'll cross that bridge when we get to it."

"You're the boss."

"We're gonna go back and kill the son, Hugh Plageanet, too. Wipe the Plageanet line off the map."

"I don't know if I can go along with that, Ty."

"Why the heck not?"

"I mean....the others, sure. Plageanet Sr. tried to rape a woman and then he and the others tried to murder Jefferson just because he stared Plageanet down. They're murderers, and I have no problem killing murderers. But Hugh Plageanet was avenging his father. We don't even know how he'll run his plantation yet. He might be all right once he cools off."

"In my book, the apple doesn't fall too far from the tree."

"Could be. Still, we don't *know* that. It's a heck of a thing to kill a man without evidence."

"I say we're gonna do it."

"I say I'll go along with you on the others, but till I have evidence, count me out on Hugh."

"All right. Just don't sit around waiting for that evidence to fall in your lap, Carpen."

"All right."

Ty was irritated with him, but Mark just didn't feel right about taking out a man without justification.

***

4:22 PM, April 15th, 1863, Madison, GA

The Jennings' plantation was humbler than Martin's and more orderly than Plageanet's. The main set of buildings consisted of a smallish main house, which was a simple square building painted white, a separate cooking shed, various barns, and some white-washed cabins behind the main house. The cabins were probably slaves' quarters, but if they were, they were certainly much nicer than Martin's slave shacks.

Jennings was heavyset and had a jovial manner about him. His smile was quick, and his handshake warm.

"What can I do for you, Mr....?"

"Smith. John Smith."

"I see."

"Could I have a word with you in private, sir?"

"Why, of course! Come into my parlor."

They moved into the parlor and sat in a pair of opposing plush chairs. The room was decorated with burgundy wallpaper and dark, cherry wood trim.

"I have an unusual request, Mr. Jennings. There is a slave on the Martin plantation who I feel is in grave danger. I have reason to believe that Hugh Plageanet may try to lynch this slave, unjustly, I might add, sometime this evening, and I was hoping you could help me save him."

"Why is this slave in trouble?"

"Hugh Plageanet's father, Stephen, was killed earlier today while he was trying to lynch this slave, and Hugh thinks the slave is to blame."

"Plageanet's dead?" Jennings leaned forward in disbelief. "When did this happen?"

"A few hours ago."

Jennings leaned back in his chair and let out a shocked gasp.

"What is this slave's name?"

"Jefferson Sr."

"I know Jefferson, he's a good ma...a good slave, I mean. He wouldn't have hurt Plageanet unjustly."

"Glad to see you're a good judge of character. He didn't hurt him *justly* either. He didn't hurt him at all. It was someone else. We want to give you enough gold to buy Jefferson and his family and pay for their train fare up north."

Jennings snorted derisively. "For that matter, I'd gladly buy him with my own money if he's really in danger."

"He is, and we're happy to. I've got the money, and we want you to make Martin an offer he can't refuse. Offer double the going rate."

"All right."

Silence cooled the air.

"Where'd you come from anyway, son? I don't recall seeing you around these parts before."

"Just passin' through."

"I see."

"So, will you do it?"

Jennings sat quietly, staring at the floor.

"I don't really cotton to slavery, you know?"

"Then, why do you have them?"

"Several years ago, a fellow up Covington way freed all of his slaves in a fit of conscience. Within a couple of weeks, half of them came back begging him for work just so they could eat. The majority of the rest were trapped and claimed by other plantations as if they'd never been freed. Those few who actually made it up north weren't much better off, having to scramble and fight for factory jobs.

"I'd free 'em if I thought they'd be better off. Heck they really are free anyway, I just haven't told 'em officially. If one of 'em ran off, I wouldn't chase him. I don't bust up families, and I certainly would never sell a man to somebody else. I've paid extra a couple of times just to keep a family together.

"I try my best to make sure they've got plenty to eat, nice places to stay. They get sick, I take care of them. I limit their work hours to the normal work week. There's absolutely no beating or anything of the sort on my land. I'd buy all my neighbors slaves if I could just to give them a better life, but the God's honest truth is I can't afford it. When you run a plantation the way I do, your profit isn't quite as high.

"I set a man by the name of Thomas free a couple of years ago. He knew how to read and write, so I gave him a loan and set him up with a business in town. He does pretty well too. The others just don't have the skills to make it on their own, and I don't have the resources to teach them."

"Sounds more like a commune to me."

"What's that?"

"Nevermind. So, what do you say?"

"Well, Mr. Smith. You've brought me some shocking news, but you seem to be an honest man, with the exception of your name, of course. I need to verify what you've told me first. Meet me at the train depot around 8:00 this evening. If I don't show, the answer's 'No'."

"Just remember, we're pressed for time."

"Understood."

"And when you pay Martin, give him a little extra to keep his mouth shut about who bought Jefferson."

Chapter 24

7:51 PM, April 15ᵗʰ, 1863, Madison, GA

The sun was low enough in the sky the whole town was dressed in a late afternoon, golden hue. Mark and Ty waited on a bench at the depot. The train had pulled in a few minutes ago and was scheduled to leave again a little after 8:00. Their conversation had dropped off into a lull a few minutes before. Until it became clear what Jennings was going to do, the tension would remain thick.

"Why don't you pop into next year and see how ol' Hugh actually turns out," Ty suggested. "Then, we can settle this issue."

"Sounds good to me. Anyone watching?"

"Nope."

Mark set his shifter to a couple of years in the future. Give the man more time to define himself.

The café/restaurant was rustic, small, and quaint. A couple of men seated at a table drinking some coffee were the only patrons. The waitress/cook was an older woman in her fifties, her streaky, brown hair put up in a bonnet.

"Can I hep' you?"

"Just coffee, ma'am, if that's all right?"

"Fine."

He sat and sipped from his cup. The other two men were heatedly discussing Northern reconstruction efforts and carpetbaggers. Mark was in 1867 and the civil war had ended two years ago.

"Excuse me, gentlemen, don't mean to bother you, but I'm looking for a Hugh Plageanet. Know anything about him?"

"Yeah, we know plenty, son. Who's askin'?"

"Name's Smith. It's just a business matter."

"You ain't got no northern accent. Whatcha you doin' round here?"

"I'm no Yank, just looking for Plageanet."

"Well, if'n you were one of them carpetbaggers, we'd have sent you right on to him. But seein' as how you ain't a Yank, I'd recommend you steer as clear of him as you can. He don' live 'round here no more anyhow."

"Why? What's wrong with him?"

"The man's just plumb *mean* is all. When the war ended, he kilt as many of his slaves as he could rather than let 'em go free. Mean ol' turd. A few escaped, but he finished off most. Since, he's taken to robbin' banks and hangs with some thieving outfit out west. Last I heard, he'd kilt some folk south of Indian Territory."

"Thanks. Maybe I will steer clear after all. Thanks for the advice."

"No bother."

Mark finished his coffee and then left the café to shift back to Ty.

***

"Okay, I'm in."

Ty smiled for the first time in hours. "Simple as that?"

"Simple as that. Didn't have to do much research either. First couple of guys I asked knew all about him. When the war ends, he kills all his slaves rather than set them free."

Ty cursed under his breath.

"So, how to you want to do it?" Mark asked.

"Wait here," Ty ordered.

Ty stood and walked over to the town's general store. He was good at playing his role. He hung his head demurely and shuffled a bit, just like a fearful slave might do.

Ty entered, hat in hand.

"Can I hep' ya, boy?" The man behind the counter was of average age, balding, and had a slight paunch. He removed his reading glasses to see Ty better.

"Ma Massah, he wan' sum dahnomite."

"Who's ya master, boy? Ain't never seen you before."

"Massah Plajnay, suh."

"All right. Now what was it you wanted again?"

"Dah-no-mite."

"What's that?"

"Dynamite."

"Never heard of it. If this is some kind of joke, boy, I'll..."

"Ne'ermin'"

Ty left quickly and crossed the square again.

"Hey, Mark."

"That was quick."

"Yeah. When was dynamite invented? This guy hadn't heard of it."

"Uh...not sure. You always see it in Western movies, so I'd guess 1880 would be a safe bet."

"All right. I'll be right back."

Ty shifted out.

***

Same clerk, now seventeen years older.

"How many sticks does he want?"

"Ten, if'n dat okay."

"Whoo-ee. What's he want with all that dynamite, anyway?"

"He's gon' blows up sum stumpy trunks he got o'er der."

"Stump blasting, huh. Well, all I've got at the moment is seven sticks. That'll have to do for now. Tell him our next order don't arrive till next week."

"Ah tell 'im."

"Here, gonna need some blasting caps and fuse wire too."

Ty handed the man some gold and walked back out into the sun.

***

Jacob Jennings showed up at the train depot right at 8:00 PM in a cart pulled by one horse. In the cart rode Jefferson and his family. They stepped up to the loading platform.

"Your story checked out, Mr. Smith," Jennings said, "Granted, I've got the feeling there's quite a stink brewing back there. Best get Jefferson on this train before Hugh's got a chance to catch up with him."

Jefferson Sr. and his wife looked very scared.

"Will they be safe?"

"Should be. I've freed them and given them notarized papers saying as much. This train will take them straight to the Mississippi. From there, they can take a steamboat north. I've given 'em more than enough to cover the fares and to tide them over till they set some roots wherever they stop. I'm going to talk with the conductor, make sure he looks out for 'em."

Jennings walked off toward the front of the train. The whistle wailed loudly. The train would be leaving soon.

Ty looked longingly at his ancestors. They were completely unaware of his relationship to them. Holding his hat in hand, Jefferson never removed his gaze from the ground.

"I'm gonna go for a short walk," Mark said. "Ty, keep Jefferson company please."

Ty would want some time alone to speak with his great, great, great grandpa.

***

There was no moon, so they had to work by starlight, which was not easy. They dared not even light a match, lest it give them away. Successfully wiring a detonation device is complicated enough, but it can be downright scary in pitch blackness.

Mark and Ty lay in the long grass behind the Plageanet house. Thankfully, there were no hounds or other animals to give away their presence. About halfway between them and the main house was a rickety, unpainted outhouse.

In the refuse pit beneath the outhouse, they'd stashed seven sticks of dynamite directly beneath the hole where a person would sit to use the facility. A wire ran inconspicuously (even more so in the dark) from those sticks of dynamite, up the hole, out through a crack in the back wall, and through the tall grass until it ended a hundred feet away at a detonation device in Ty's hands. The wire would not be noticed by anybody in the outhouse, even when sitting down.

"Here he comes."

"Shh....wait. I'm going to make sure it's him."

Mark snuck off into the grass silently. He got as close as he dared to make the identification. After a minute he returned. The man had just entered the outhouse and was going about his business.

"Well?"

"It's him all right," Mark assured him. "Go ahead."

Ty hesitated for a long moment, weighing what he was about to do. Just when Mark thought he wasn't going to, Ty plunged the contact down. Before two years had passed, Plageanet would kill over fifty men, women, and children. There was no forgetting that.

A violent explosion rocked the night, shattering the peace that had reigned just a moment before and filling the yard with a burning, orange glow. Pieces of wood and other matter rained down with dull thuds all around.

"Ready?"

"Yeah. Let's get back." Ty hit his shifter and Mark followed.

***

Back in 2012, Ty thanked Mark and asked him to meet him and Hardy at the office the next day.

"So, what'd you and Jefferson talk about while you were alone?" Mark pried.

Ty let out a slow smile.

"I asked him what his father's name was."

"I suppose he told you."

"Not only that, he told me his grandpa's name too."

"What'd that be? Your fifth great grandpa?"

"Yeah. He also told me what tribe in Africa his ancestors had come from."

"That's great, man." Mark was sincerely happy for him. Ty was thrilled to uncover more of his family's roots.

"Yeah, my fifth great-grandpa. Can you believe it? I was stuck. Didn't know who Jefferson Sr.'s father was."

"I've never been that much into genealogy myself, but you really like it, huh?"

"Yeah."

"All right. Well....see you tomorrow?"

"Yeah, see you tomorrow."

***

The office was abandoned.

The three desks were still in their places, but that was all. The rest of the office furniture was missing, the potted plants, the pictures from the walls, even the window blinds. A few scraps of paper lay strewn about the floor. The air felt stale, still, as if the room knew its inhabitants were not coming back.

Mark moved to the first of the desks, the one that had been Ty's. He checked every drawer, but they too were empty. Each of the other two desks were the same.

Where had they gone? What was going on?

Mark was too astonished to react. A million thoughts raced through his mind. Had this all been some kind of elaborate con game? If so, what was the con? He hadn't given them any money.

Worse, had they used him as a patsy, setting him up for some kind of fall? No, that didn't really make any sense.

Maybe something had happened to them. Maybe some government agency had caught on to what they were doing. Could they have been arrested? Was Mark next? Or were they themselves part of some covert government agency after all?

They couldn't have been arrested. They would just shift out of custody to another time.

Had he done something to offend them?

Mark remembered the lonely shack in the woods. It had appeared empty at first, but in the end, he'd found a very intriguing watch which had changed his life forever. Maybe there was something like that here he'd missed.

He searched the office frantically and left nothing unturned. He pulled each and every drawer fully out of its desk and flipped them over, looking underneath and on their backs for some hidden item. He ran his hand over the interior surfaces inside the desks where the drawers had been in case something had been taped up in there. He checked every nook and cranny of the bathroom and the closets. Under the sink, behind the toilet, he even disassembled the light fixtures.

There was nothing to be found. Not even dust. The scraps of paper strewn about were of no importance. Most were blank, the rest were just a few old utility bills.

Mark sat and waited. He waited until dark. He waited through most of the night. Why he was waiting, he wasn't sure. Hardy always seemed to know when and where to find him if he so desired. By waiting, perhaps he subconsciously hoped to stave off the inevitable sense of loneliness assaulting the walls of his heart.

They weren't coming, he finally admitted to no one in particular. He felt like the office in which he sat.

Abandoned.

Chapter 25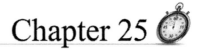

June 13th, 2012, Boston, MA

He had no clue where to find them....nor *when* to find them for that matter. The only places Mark knew for sure they'd be were times where they'd met with him already, and he didn't have the guts to meet his own alter ego yet. Who knew about possible time paradox problems and things like that.

He didn't think foul play was behind their disappearance. He considered shifting back a day or two to see if he could catch them before they abandoned their office, but, in the end, he decided to just drop it. *If they want to disappear so bad, let 'em.*

Besides, if their goal was to hide, it wouldn't be hard. Time really was the fourth dimension.

Imagine trying to find a certain person somewhere in the world without knowing their exact location. It would be an impossible task, of course, like finding a needle in a Mt. Everest-sized haystack. Yet, if you knew that same person's exact location within the three physical dimensions, you'd find them with no problem.

Unless, you didn't know *when* to find them there. Time added a fourth dimension. You could know a person's exact physical location, but if you had no idea when in history they were going to be there, you would be back to square one with the needle in a haystack problem.

Add to that the ability to shift around instantaneously within time, and it became even more impossible to pin down a person's location within the *four* dimensions.

Mark was faced with a daunting question. One that he would have to answer now, it appeared, by himself:

What should he do with the rest of his life?

He was filthy rich. So rich, in fact, that it would be pointless to try and increase his wealth any further. It just wouldn't make any difference to him.

Women? Kelly's abandonment had left a sour taste in his mouth that hadn't quite gone away yet.

Travel the world? Skydiving? Climb the Himalayas, sail the Caribbean?

None of those things felt worthwhile. He had this shifter for a reason. What that reason was, though, he had no idea. So far, Heaven had not opened up in a glorious display of angelic music and light to reveal its will to him. There had been no booming voice telling him what to do. He would have to figure it out on his own.

So many people talked about changing the world, but now he was in a position to truly do it. Maybe more so than anyone else in history. He had unlimited financial resources and a powerful tool in the shifter. He wanted to help people, to make the world a better place, but where should he start? What to do?

His life was an open slate, like a chalkboard that had been erased, the residue of previous smudges still marring its surface, but clean enough to be written on anew. It was time to pick the chalk back up.

***

The Stanford Costume Company was a simple affair. The walls of the small front area were painted in warm shades of beige and accentuated by a few pieces of cherry wood furniture, namely a few chairs and bookcases. It had a sparse, but lively, homey feel.

The moderate sized workroom was in the back, but all customers were attended in the front by whoever was sitting at the elegant cherry desk.

"I'm sorry, *who* did you say you represent again?"

The young lady squinted her eyes so quizzically, Mark thought the creases in her brow would undo her tightly wound bun. The bun and her thin-rimmed spectacles made her look like a mousy librarian, though she presumably was not one. Her eyes were a cool-water blue, and deep. Glossy pink lips were accentuated nicely by the light, creamy hues of her unblemished skin. Her honey-colored hair being pulled back and up revealed a slight and graceful neck. Her manner was soft and professional.

"Historical Enterprises."

"....And what is it 'Historical Enterprises' does again?"

"We have a number of interests, but at the moment we're looking to create a variety of historically accurate costumes"

"About how many costumes are you wanting? And from which era?"

"Let's say somewhere between one to two thousand, from all different eras."

She almost choked on the water she was sipping. The crease in her brow deepened in confusion. "I'm sorry....but did you just say one *thousand* to two *thousand*?"

"Yes." Mark couldn't help but smile.

"Eh....Okay....well, this is really my mother's business. I'm just watching it for her today. She does all the sewing, I just do the research. We're both kind of part-time."

"Okay."

"She only does this to keep busy since she retired, you know. I help out as I can, when I'm not in class or working. We typically make just a few costumes every now and then for local theater companies....or sometimes costume shops."

"Yes, I realize a lot would be involved. You'd definitely have to hire several seamstresses for an extended period of time."

"Uh....I'm not sure mom would want...uh....to go to that much effort. It'd be a lot for her."

"You'd probably have to help out full-time for a while too. A big, big part of the work would be research. I've come here because I believe your mother is the only one with the expertise in town to do this well. What's your normal rate?

"Anywhere from $250 to $750 per costume, depending on the detail involved."

"Well, these will be very detailed. I'll give you a $400,000 deposit to get started, and I'll pay you double your rate for each costume finished. I'll also pay as you deliver to prevent any cash flow problems. I'm going to need numerous historically accurate costumes for every 25 year period in history since the year 1500. For each 25 year period, I'll need distinct costumes representing a myriad of countries and cultures, from Mexico to Europe, for all different economic levels of society, both male and female.

"Historical accuracy is very important," Mark continued. "I can't stress that enough. A person shouldn't be able to tell these costumes from the real thing. I won't need anything from Africa or Asia for the time being. Here's my card. Any questions?"

She gulped and slowly shook her head to say no.

"And your name is?"

"Savannah....Savannah Stanford."

"Nice to meet you, Savannah. I'm Mark. Mark Carpen."

***

The first coin specialist Mark sought out was more suspicious than Savannah Stanford of the Stanford Costume Company had been. Mark wanted to place an order with an antique coin dealer for accurately made historical coin molds, reflecting the coinage of various countries throughout the past 500 years. The first seller he initially approached was concerned that Mark was planning to counterfeit a bunch of antique coins and try to pass them off in the rare coin market as the real deal, so the man refused to do the work. Unable to allay the specialist's fears, Mark was forced to seek help elsewhere.

If needed, once the costumes were ready, Mark could bypass the need for a coin dealer by taking gold bars back to the different historical eras and exchange them for real coins, but such a plan would be extremely labor intensive, not to mention time-consuming.

Instead, Mark tried a second rare coin specialist, one who was less scrupulous, and though the man was surprised by the sheer size of the request, he gladly took the project on. Especially, when Mark explained what he was willing to pay.

From this dealer, Mark commissioned authentic coin molds which he could use to stamp new copies of every major coin from over 20 different countries that had been in circulation since 1500 AD. All in all, he commissioned around 1,000 molds, which was a painstaking process for even a trained specialist. That type of work wasn't something you could train run-of-the-mill employees to do.

It took the coiner over two years to complete the project, but for Mark, patience no longer had to be a virtue. He simply placed the order, shifted to a couple of years in the future, and then picked the molds up.

He could have asked the coiner to actually make the coins, but he didn't want the man knowing just how much in gold coin he planned to produce. For discretion's sake, it was better to keep the right and left hands from even knowing the other existed.

Once he had the molds, Mark recruited a metallist to stamp several tons of gold and silver into large quantities of authentic coins from each period of history. If he ever ran out of a certain kind of coin, the molds would allow him to just make more.

Next, he hired a team of artisans and carpenters to create an armory of authentic weapons, tools, and other accessories from each historic period.

Finally, he funded the founding of the *Institute for Historical Studies* on the campus of Harvard University. Through the institute, Mark had a team of professors and graduate students working to prepare detailed "Manuals for Living" for various historical periods. Savannah Stanford had also been a big part of this project, being a PhD student in World History at Harvard. These manuals explained in simple terms the customs, verbal expressions, philosophies, current events, and the extent of scientific knowledge of any given generation in western history.

Perhaps it was due to the historical ambiance of the city, or just the fact that he was using Harvard so much in his research. Maybe it was because Boston was the last place he'd seen Hardy and Ty, or maybe Atlanta just held too many bad memories for him, but whatever it was, Mark decided to move his base of operations from Atlanta to the Boston area permanently.

To house his giant historical arsenal, Mark built two large hangars at a local private airport. One hangar actually housed an airplane, a Gulfstream jet Mark could use to get to any part of the world quickly. At least much more quickly than having to drive to the airport, park, and pass through security, only to travel at painstakingly slow commercial airline speeds.

Inside the second hangar, which was adjacent to the first, were hundreds of small areas sectioned off from each other by painted yellow lines on the concrete floor. These rows and rows of rectangular sections and the aisles between them filled the entire hangar. Each area was clearly marked with the year-span and country it covered and had a tall wardrobe containing the appropriate attire for those years, as well as a chest with drawers full of leather pouches holding coins, tools and weapons from that era. In the top drawer of each chest, next to the pouches, always lay the "Manual for Living" for that time period.

So, if Mark planned to visit any country in the western hemisphere during the past 500 years, he could, in about 15 minutes, clothe himself, arm himself, study up on the era, and be assured to have no money problems as he traveled.

To a stranger, the hangar would seem nothing more than a giant furniture warehouse at first glance. If they opened the drawers, they might decide it was an enormous antique bazaar, but no one would ever suspect it for what it really was. A time-travel armory.

Nevertheless, Mark made sure no strangers *would* stumble upon it. Each of the hangar's doors was welded shut from the inside, and he had an elaborate alarm system installed which would monitor any activity around those entrances. The only way in was through a tunnel in the floor, which led to a hidden door in the mechanic's ditch of the first hangar where the Gulfstream Jet was. Even if someone were to surveil Mark day in and day out, they would only see him entering the first hangar and never associate him with the second.

Mark scheduled the completion of every part of this project so that he would only lose a few days from the natural progression of his home time. Regardless, even with his new ability to shift through time instantaneously, it still took Mark a little over six months of his "real time" to get everything set up right without arousing too much suspicion. Confidentiality was a must.

When it was finally finished, Mark looked over the armory, satisfied with his effort.

He was ready.

Chapter 26

The question was: Now what?

There were literally trillions of injustices that needed undoing in the world, yet there was no way on earth Mark could make even a small dent in their total, not even with all the time in the world.

He needed some method of choosing, some way to focus his efforts on those problems that would make the most difference.

He could always try to stop some of the largest tragedies in history, like the Holocaust — or he could randomly select individual crime victims to rescue. He could transport inventions into the past in a hope to accelerate technological advancement and better the quality of life for billions ahead of their time. That last one seemed a little far-fetched, but why not?

Yet the question remained: *Who* should he save? In what year? And why them? Mark didn't have any good answers for those questions.

He drummed his fingers on the glass-topped breakfast table, pushing around his now cool eggs absent-mindedly with a fork in the other hand. He picked up the newspaper and began to browse the previous day's police reports.

Ironic. He'd just spent months making it easier to travel hundreds of years into the past and now he was going to stick with the present?

Oh well. He had to start somewhere.

Several incidents gripped his attention right away. The prior afternoon, a man had fallen from his roof while trying to repair it and had died at the scene. He'd left behind a wife and two young children.

Later that evening, a young woman had been assaulted in the Boston Commons (Newspapers never said so explicitly, but Mark guessed she'd probably been raped).

A two-year old had also been killed in a fatal car accident. That one in particular broke his heart. Accidents involving children probably always would.

Picking up the phone, Mark dialed the Boston Herald. After a few rings, an automated answering system picked up. He pushed "0" to get an operator.

"Police Briefs, please"

"Certainly, sir."

A few more rings.

"Becky Thompson."

"Hello, Ms. Thompson. My name is Mark Carpen. I've got a business proposal for you...."

Police reports in a newspaper never provided enough of the detail Mark would need if he wished to stop a crime, like an exact time and location, etc. For a couple thousand dollars a month, Becky Thompson agreed to fax him on a daily basis the more detailed crime reports, the unedited versions containing addresses and other in depth detail that wouldn't fit into the small space allocated for them in the paper. He was overpaying for the service, but this way he wouldn't have to worry about how well the job was being done or whether she'd forget.

***

It was Saturday and today, John Wilson, father of two, would try to squeeze in a load of household chores. It was his day off, and like most working men, his "honey-do" list was likely a mile long. His roof had sprung a small leak in one of the kid's rooms and he would attempt a small repair about 3:00 PM. He would fall backwards off that same roof at around 3:15 PM. He would impact at an angle and snap his neck decisively when his head struck the ground before the rest of his body. Death would be instantaneous.

Mark had gone over the scenario a thousand different ways on the drive over to the Wilson home, but he couldn't come up with any sure-fire, easy way of preventing the accident. He could think of all kinds of ways to get the guy down off the roof, or to delay his starting on the repair, but none of them would insure Wilson wouldn't just get back up there later that same day — or another day for that matter — and fall off then.

A seemingly simple accident was proving to be more insidious than it first appeared. In the end, Mark decided on an equally simple solution.

He parked his car in front of the Wilson home and got out. Then, Mark shifted back to 8:00 AM, before the family had fully started their day. Hastily, he scribbled a note on a stray piece of paper from his car:

To: John Wilson
You are planning to fix your roof today.
If you do, you will slip off and be killed.
Please do not fix your roof today or be very careful.

Mark wrapped the note around a rock he found in front yard and secured it with a rubber band. Winding up with a flourish, he chucked the rock through the large window in the Wilson's family room.

The crash of shattering glass resounded and Mark was already shifting out of the scene before the last shards had finished tinkling to the ground.

Back in his car, he re-checked the newspaper lying in the passenger seat. He breathed a sigh of relief and smiled. The report of a new widow and two orphaned kids was no longer anywhere to be found. Wilson had apparently gotten the message and would still be around at the end of the day to tell his kids a story before bed. The man would probably tell the story of the strange note thrown through his window for years to come.

1 down, 2 to go.

***

According to the police briefs, Jennifer Scott would be attacked right after taking an evening jog in the Boston Commons.

When she returned to her car, she would discover a flat tire. A stranger would appear playing the good Samaritan, ready to lend a hand. Nervous about being stuck in an abandoned parking lot so late at night, she was happy for the help.

Her brief gratitude would turn to horror as his true intention quickly manifested itself. After the assault, he would beat her senseless. She wouldn't regain consciousness for several hours, and during those crucial hours, the trail grew cold, making it more difficult for the police to follow.

Mark opted for simplicity once more. He first determined the make, mark, color, and license plate of her vehicle. Then, he drove to the park, waited until the right space freed up and parked his car right next to hers.

He purposefully left his lights on and the motor running. He also turned on the interior light in his car, so passer-bys would not miss his presence. He picked up a book and pretended to read as his eyes scoured the area for any sign of the attacker.

A couple of policemen on bicycles stopped once and inquired what he was doing. He made up a story about waiting for his daughter to get off work. Frankly, their timing stunk. Twenty minutes later and they would have been in time to save the girl.

Obviously, it would be the attacker himself who would flatten the woman's tire in order to put her in a vulnerable position. Mark hoped that by making himself so blatantly visible, the attacker would not dare get close enough to knife the tire.

And it worked. She emerged from the park a little after 8:30 and jogged up to her car, finished with her run. She mopped her face and neck with a white sports towel, got in the sedan, and drove off without a hitch. She would never know the danger that had faced her, or that the stranger she'd glanced at sitting in his car and reading a book had been so integral to her salvation.

It felt *good* to help people this way. Mark was beginning to feel a true sense of purpose. Finally.

With this case, however, there was a tinge of regret. This guy, *this sicko*, who'd attacked her in the alternate past, was still out there in the darkness somewhere. Based on the nature of the crime, he had to be a serial rapist, and now he was free to go after someone else. Because of the strategy Mark had chosen, he now had no way to bring the guy out of the shadows.

He would do it differently next time. It wasn't enough to save someone from a crime if the potential criminal would simply select another target.

Mark shifted forward to his true present and checked the newspaper. He was stunned to see the story of Jennifer Scott's assault was still there, only the details, including the location, were different. The guy must have followed her in his car. When she'd turned onto a more secluded road, the attacker had bumped her from behind.

Naturally, she'd stopped because of the accident. When she got out of her sedan, he overpowered her and the rest of the story read the same from there.

It wasn't random. This attacker must have been stalking her in particular. Either the guy knew her or he was a serial rapist and had been following her for some time.

Strangely, Mark was happy that he would be given a chance to rectify his earlier mistake.

He drove to the roadside where the revised police report now said the attack would take place. The area was roped off with yellow crime scene tape. He found the tracks of the two vehicles and took a guess at where he needed to stand.

He shifted back to fifteen minutes before the approximate time of the assault. The vehicles hadn't arrived yet, so Mark walked up a small incline beside the road and hid himself in some bushes. The only light came from a lone street lamp near the road and it was so dark where Mark was he didn't have to try very hard at concealing himself.

Within ten minutes, the two cars came into sight. The rear vehicle was following too close and when the girl slowed, their bumpers met with a light crunch of metal. They both pulled over to the shoulder

Mark waited until both occupants had emerged from their cars. Jennifer looked visibly distressed. It was late, she was tired, and now she'd been in an accident. She was probably worried about insurance premiums and having to wait for the police and all the other headaches that accompanied a fender bender. She had no idea what greater tragedy would shortly befall her.

The man wore a slithering smirk, a malicious little grin that twisted his mouth unnaturally. Evil lurked behind those oppressive eyes. Mark didn't care what the man's name was. It didn't matter.

With an acquired agility, Mark swiftly and silently descended from the incline. He was dressed in black, so neither the attacker nor the woman noticed him. This was the kind of operation for which he'd been trained.

In a single smooth motion, he raised his right arm and fired three shots from his .45 into the side of the attacker's head, the third shot striking home before the man's body could collapse from the first. Without a doubt the man was dead.

The girl was screaming bloody murder, but she was safe.

"He was going to attack you," Mark stated simply, trying to calm the terror in her eyes, but she was so panicked he wasn't sure the words got through.

He returned to the bushes and shifted out.

***

The car accident case made Mark nervous. He had purposely put it off until last.   It just hit too close to home. What if he couldn't save the boy? What if it turned out to be like his own kids?   What if there was some cosmic force mandating that children could never be saved?   Could he take that? Failing to save the boy would crush him all over again, and there was only so much grief he could withstand. It would rip the wound in his heart open so wide.... to say it might even kill him wasn't necessarily an exaggeration.   He'd heard of people dying from a broken heart. And if he didn't, he might wish to have.

Yet, if he could save the boy, maybe it could help him heal.

Mark stopped at a corner store and bought a pack of cigarettes.   Smoking was not his style, but he needed something.   Fingers shaking, he fumbled with the lighter, finally getting one of the sticks to burn. He took a few puffs while staring vacantly at the sidewalk.

He knew he was just delaying.

You can't outrun your fears, Son. You either face them, or they rule you.

His father had said that the summer Mark had first tried out for football. He hadn't ever played on a real team before, and most of the other boys had. He'd come away from that first practice with pains and bruises all over his body, but the worst damage was to his state of mind. After getting slammed to the ground repeatedly, each hit jarring him senseless, he'd been thoroughly intimidated.

He hadn't wanted to go back, but his father had taken him aside and told him different. Holding both shoulders firmly and looking him straight in the eye, he had said, "You can't outrun your fears, Son. You either face them, or they rule you. You conquer them, or they will conquer you."

That fateful day in 2009 had been the biggest hit of his life. Now, just seeing a photo of his kids wrenched his heart from his chest and slammed it to the ground. Worse than any hit he'd ever felt so many summers ago as a young football player, worse than any battle wound he'd ever sustained as a Marine.

Mark pulled the cigarette from his lips and stared at the butt. He dropped it and crushed it on the black asphalt with his boot.

This car accident, a different accident, would occur about noon at a four-way stop in a suburban neighborhood outside Boston. The mother would be leaving her home to run errands with her two-year old, but before she got more than a few blocks, another mother would run a stop sign at full speed, totaling both vehicles and killing the little boy. No alcohol was involved, the driver at fault had simply and carelessly missed the sign.

There were a number of ways he could try to stop the accident from happening, but basically, Mark had to stop or delay one of the cars before it made the intersection.

He *really* didn't want to watch (or hear) the accident take place over and over again, which is what he would have to do if he wanted to stop the vehicle at fault before it ran the stop sign. In the end, it felt easier to mess with the victim's car. From the police report, he knew their address. He drove to their home and shifted back to a few hours before the accident.

The shift startled Mark because he hadn't expected to immediately see the little boy playing outside on the sidewalk. Thankfully, the child didn't notice him phase into solidity. He was a cute little kid, probably about two and a half. Brown hair, blue eyes. He was playing with some toy cars, rolling them up and down the walkway leading to his front door.

The mother soon emerged from the house, her arms overloaded with miscellaneous bags to load in the car. Mark had thought it was odd she'd leave the kid unattended there. He was a little young to be outside by himself, but she was apparently ferrying stuff back and forth from the house to the car and watching him from inside while she did.

"Tyler!" he heard her call, "Come inside honey, it's time for lunch."

The boy pretended not to hear, he was so engrossed in his game.

"Tyler! Come on! If you don't come right away, there'll be no Goldfish after."

That seemed to get his attention. Reluctantly, he abandoned his cars on the sidewalk and waddled inside.

Mark stayed where he was for a few minutes to make sure the coast was clear and then went into action. He checked the driver's door. It was unlocked. He popped the hood, and the rest was quick work. He loosened a battery cable and then disconnected three of the lines running from the plugs to the distributor cap.

That would delay her for hours, if not a couple of days. She would be frustrated by the ruined plans, and then angry when she discovered someone had deliberately sabotaged her, but if she only knew what being on time today would cost her, she would embrace this frustration like a long-desired birthday present.

Even if she turned out to be a roadside mechanic in disguise and figured out what was wrong, while she could fix his tricks pretty quickly, it would still be too late. Mark would be gone and she'd be held up for at least a few minutes, which meant little Tyler would live to be a three year-old.

Chapter 27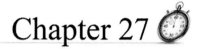

For weeks, Mark continued acting on information gleaned from the daily police reports to save people from the worst tragedies of the day around Boston. He was getting pretty good at it too. He'd learned to be more efficient in how he solved things.

Since he could only shift six times within 24 hours, if he returned to his home-time after each event, he could only stop three horrors per day, and that was without any glitches. However, if he timed things right, he could shift back to early in the morning of the previous day and just drive from scene to scene changing what he wanted as he went. When he did it that way, he was only limited by how fast he could drive and the path he chose, though he often had to shift out of a scene quickly due to the manner in which he stopped a crime, like when he'd killed the rapist that first day.

There were re-dos, panicked escapes, and cases when several events occurred in too quick a succession, forcing him to use his shifter in order to have enough time to get to both. In short, his goal was to stop 7 or 8 bad events each day while only using 3 shifts to do it. That way his watch never shut down and he could work each and every day. On the days when he did hit six shifts, he was forced to take the entire next day off while the watch recovered, and that was annoying.

He was hitting his goal more often than not lately, which elated him. Still, he longed for company. This job was a lonely one. He had two more unused watches sitting in that old backpack. Perhaps it was time to do something with them.

***

September 8th, 2012, Boston, MA

The late afternoon sun gleamed streaks of gold upon her hair as she walked in, like the glimmering halo of an angel. The effect was momentary, but striking. Savannah Stanford moved further into the office and out of the light, returning to the realm of mortal women. She bore an armful of antique-looking costumes.

"I've got another fifty ready for you, Mr. Carpen. They're out in the van."

"Please. Call me Mark."

"Okay, Mark."

"I'll help you carry them in."

He wheeled a large cart outside and helped her unload the van onto it. Her mother had purchased the van with Mark's initial contract. Their goal back then was to get him fifty costumes per week. Once they'd reached a thousand, he'd gone ahead and set up his armory in the hangar. They still had another thousand to go after that, so Mark met Savannah here once a week to collect their work. The weekly rendezvous was a nice respite from his crime-stopping routine.

"Savannah, would you consider coming to work for me full-time?"

"Uh....well....I've got my classes."

"Sure. We could work around those. I'd pay you well."

She blushed. "What kind of work would I be doing?"

"Some of it would be receptionist type work. I have need of that. But a lot of it would be historical research. Right up your alley."

"I'd have to talk to Mom about it."

"Is that a yes?"

She smiled.

***

June 2ⁿᵈ, 1987, Fort Bragg, NC

The morning was cool and breezy. Pleasant. Gray skies hung low over Fort Bragg, the remnants of a pre-dawn fog that had lifted recently. About a hundred yards away, a platoon of soldiers jogged along an asphalt path, the abrupt calls of their sergeant easily carrying through the morning air.

A large flag flew atop a nearby pole, its bold stars and stripes waving proudly in the breeze. Seeing flags fly always stirred memories of his previous service. For him, this base felt like home.

Mark was dressed in the uniform of an army captain, with all the proper insignia. This rank would be sufficient enough to impress authority, but not high enough to garner unwanted attention.

The platoon was closer now, which meant his target was approaching. The sound of their unified cadence blended with the measured beats of their deep-voiced chant.

As the soldiers passed, Mark whistled sharply and barked, "Phillips!"

Hardy Phillips slowed and then broke from the rest of the platoon once he recognized the rank on Mark's uniform. He jogged over. Their eyes met, but Mark saw no sign of recognition in them.

"Sir!" Hardy snapped to attention and saluted. Mark returned the salute.

"Follow me, soldier."

Mark led Phillips into a currently empty office next to the mess hall. He enjoyed giving Hardy instructions for a change instead of the other way around, even if Hardy didn't know him from Adam.

"Sit." Mark motioned to a chair. "You are Hardin Phillips, rank Sergeant First Class, Delta Force. Is that correct?"

"That is my rank, sir."

"But you are not in Delta Force?"

Hardy remained silent, unsure how to answer. Delta Force was a secretive unit and he was not free to divulge his membership to just anybody. Even though they were here at Delta Force's home, Fort Bragg, Hardy did not know who Mark was.

"You don't know me, do you, sergeant?" Mark studied him for a reaction.

"I'm sorry, sir. I do not."

"No matter. I know you. That's what's important. And I know you're Delta."

Phillips was puzzled.

Mark continued, "If you did know me, you'd see how ironic this whole meeting is."

"I....I'm sorry, sir, you've lost me."

Mark gestured dismissively. "Don't worry about it. I'm not exactly who I appear to be, but you'll find that out soon enough. Here. Take a look at this."

He flipped a newspaper onto the desk in front of Phillips.

"What's that look like to you, sergeant?"

"A newspaper?" Phillips tilted his head curiously.

"Of course, it's a newspaper. What do you notice about it?"

"I dunno." Hardy studied the front of it. "It's dated June 4th, today's just the 2nd."

"Yep."

"So what? It's a misprint."

"You hang on to that paper. Keep it tucked away, under wraps, if you know what I mean. Till the 4th. Meet me here at 0700 on June 5th. Come alone and tell no one of this meeting. Dismissed."

Hardy was clearly confused, but had just received an order from a superior officer. Reluctantly, he rose and left the building.

Mark waited until Phillips was out of sight. Then, he set his watch to 0700 on June 5th and hit the button. Mark loved not having to wait for things. He could have set the time to slightly earlier than 0700 to be sure and arrive first, but this way would be more fun.

Phillips nearly fell out of his chair in shock as Mark materialized in front of him with an electric hiss. The Delta warrior leapt to his feet, completely unnerved.

"Who....what....who are you? What just happened?" He was paler than a Canadian at the beach.

"Son, how would you like a chance to be involved in a project that has the potential to impact the entire world for good, as well as serve your country?"

"Did....uh....did you just *teleport*? How did you *do* that?"

"In a way."

"This has to be classified, sir!"

"I repeat, son, how would you like the chance to be involved in a project that has the potential to impact the entire world, as well as serve your country?"

"That's what I'm in Delta for, sir." He was recovering some from his initial shock.

"Yes, I know. This, however, would be....different."

"That paper you gave me!"

"Yes?"

Understanding dawned on Hardy's face.

"That paper you gave me. It was full of things that hadn't happened yet! Sports, crimes, weather, even a bombing! It was yesterday's paper. I know — I saw copies."

"Yes, that's true."

"But how?"

"Take a look at my watch. Have you ever seen anything like it?" Mark extended his wrist.

Hardy examined it thoroughly.

"No."

"To be blunt, it's a time machine."

Hardy drew a sharp intake of breath.

"It's true," Mark affirmed.

"I....I guess, I know that. I mean, how else can I explain what I've just seen? You just appeared out of nowhere....and this paper. It's....crazy."

"I actually just left our meeting three days ago. For you, it's been three days. For me, just a matter of seconds."

"Huh? Oh....yeah." He was processing. "Who are you, sir? I mean, why me? This has gotta be way over my security clearance."

"My name is Mark Carpen. I'm actually no longer on active duty, and this has nothing to do with any military project."

Hardy's eyes narrowed sharply. "What? Why shouldn't I turn you in then? This is a tightly secured military base."

"You could try. I'd just hit this little red button and quietly shift back to the time from which I came, leaving you to look like a total schmuck."

Hardy frowned. "I don't get it. Why are you here? Why are you showing *me* this?"

"Because I've researched your record. I think you would make a great addition to my company."

"What company? What kind of company?"

"My time-travel company."

"Look, I'm no mercenary. I took an oath to the United States of America, and I intend to keep it."

"I'm not hiring you for an army, son. I'm calling you to something higher. I intend to use this powerful tool to help people in a thousand different ways, and we'd probably help our country too. I am an ex-Marine for goodness sakes. There's no way on earth I'd want to see this thing misused for anything like you're thinking."

"What do you want me to do?"

Mark set his bag on the table and unzipped it. He reached in and pulled out one of the two extra shifter/watches he'd had since that first day in the woods. He now had a home for one of them. He extended it to Hardy.

"Take this and put it on. A warning though, once you put it on, you will not be able to get it back off." He also handed Hardy a slip of paper. "Go to your superior officer and tender your resignation, effective whenever you want. Time makes no difference to me, as you can see. It's just a matter of how much of your life you want to lose before we get started.

"Once you're ready, that paper has an address and some numbers on it. Go to that address and set your watch to match the numbers. Then, push the red button, and I'll meet you there."

Chapter 28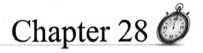

Ty proved to be much harder to locate than Hardy. Mark had to do a good bit of research to figure out where and when to look for his friend.

He finally found him in the middle of a bloody battle in Vietnam. At a time when many young men were dodging the draft, Ty had actually gone and volunteered to be a Marine. Of course, before the ink was dry on his sign-up papers, they'd whisked him off to the war.

Mark didn't have a lot of options when it came to contacting Ty. He couldn't approach him before Ty entered the military or had a chance to fight in the war. Mark needed him to have received all his training and gain some real fighting experience if he was going to be of use to Mark.

What really made it difficult, though, was that military records showed Ty as killed in action at Khe Sanh in 1968. That meant Mark had to travel to Vietnam to intercept Ty in the middle of the battle of Khe Sanh before he was killed.

Some red dirt, splotches of grass, and a feeble concrete monument that resembled a broken tablet were all that remained of the battlefield of Khe Sanh in modern times. Large clearings surrounded the former marine base and broken hill peaks covered by jungle brush stood visible in the near distance.

In 1968, Khe Sanh had been a US military base located 12 miles south of the border with North Vietnam and had been manned by two regiments of Marines. Ty's company had been stationed there.

This trip proved to be a bit more complex than most for Mark. He'd had to fly into communist Vietnam, which had opened back up for tourism in the 1990's, and then travel to the former site of Khe Sanh before he could shift.

Once he reached the site, Mark set his shifter to 2:00 AM on January 19th, 1968. That was two days before the North Vietnamese would begin their offensive against the marines.

Appearing in the middle of the night, Mark was challenged by no one. He bode his time until morning when the base began to stir and then went to look for Ty.

Mark hadn't thought it possible, but Ty looked even more muscular and toned than during their mission to save Jefferson Sr. Now that he thought about it, was that trip to save Ty's grandfather in their past....*or their future?* It was definitely in Mark's past. Was it in Ty's future or would it never happen now? Mark was creating a heck of a paradox here and it was making his head hurt.

He approached Ty when he was alone so they could talk in private. Since time was short, this initial conversation would have to be more direct than the one with Hardy.

"What's up, Captain?"

Ty did not stand to attention or snap a sharp salute. Instead, he slouched on top of a crate with his back to a tent, acknowledging Mark only with his eyes. His manner was relaxed, unimpressed by rank and decorum. The formalities of soldiering often evaporated on the extended battlefield, especially in Vietnam.

"Jennings, you don't know me, but I know you. This conversation will sound very odd, but there's no help for it, so let's get started. Take a good look at my watch. Have you ever seen anything like it?"

"Uh...no." His forehead creased in puzzlement. "Is that new Marine issue?"

"No, sergeant. It's a time-travel device."

Ty broke into a large grin, and guffawed. "Shoot, sir, you had me going there for a minute."

"This isn't a joke, *Sergeant*. I'm here on false pretenses. I'm not a Marine....at least not any more. I'm a civilian now. I'm here because you are going to die in 3 days and 11 hours. I'm going to get you out of here before that happens."

Ty's face revealed uncertainty but masked a much stronger incredulity. "Hey, ya know. It's been fun an' all, but this joke, man, it really ain't that funny. Pretty mean sayin' sometin' like that."

He turned to walk away, but Mark grabbed his arm. Ty swung back around, the beginnings of anger simmering in his eyes. The Ty he knew did not have much of a temper and Mark was not used to seeing such flares in Ty's normally jovial face. When Mark was sure he had Ty's attention again, he released his arm.

"Watch this." Mark touched his shifter and disappeared.

Ty's mouth still hung open when Mark popped back into existence a few seconds later. He was speechless.

"Listen closely," Mark continued, "At noon today, the first song to come on the radio will be "A Whiter Shade of Pale". Peggy Fleming is going to win the US Female Figure skating championship tomorrow, and Houston is going to beat UCLA 71-69. When those things happen, come find me. I've got important information for you."

Mark clapped Ty on the shoulder and began to walk away.

"Hey, Mac!" Ty called out behind him, "UCLA is on a 47 game winning streak if you hadn't heard! Houston ain't never gonna beat that."

Mark didn't look back.

January 21st, 1968 12:00 PM, Khe Sanh, Vietnam

At 0530 that morning, the North Vietnamese Army had begun bombarding the marine combat base at Khe Sanh with heavy mortar fire and 122mm rockets. This first day of the siege of Khe Sanh, most of the base's fuel and ammunition supplies would be destroyed.

Resupply helicopters would work frantically over the next few days to keep the marines supplied with everything they would need to fight back. Marine units would be sent out into the hills on patrol to root out the NVA positions and relieve the base of some of the pressure.

Ty would be sent on patrol with his platoon tomorrow evening. Right about sunset, he would be killed along with almost all of his unit and a significant portion of his platoon.

The base had initially descended into chaos at the onset of the initial surprise bombardment at dawn, but marines are well-trained, and they quickly took control of the situation and began to counter-attack.

If you could ignore the current barrage of mortars and rockets, you might say things had calmed down significantly since sunrise. At least, there was no longer a sense of franticness in the movements around the base.

Mark found Ty, whose eyes widened in awe upon seeing him.

"*Who* are you, mister?"

"Do you believe me now?"

"Yesterday at noon....that first song was just like you said "A Whiter Shade of Pale.""

"And the undefeatable UCLA?"

Ty hung his head. "They lost. 71-69. News came in on the radio about midnight last night."

"Well?"

"I ain't heard nothing about no figure skating yet, but unless you're one heck of a lucky guesser, *I'm* guessing that you are who you say you are." He paused, thinking. "So, how does that thing work anyway?"

"I don't know."

"What do you mean, you don't know?!"

"Look, I just inherited this thing, okay? I use it just fine, but I don't claim to know how it works."

"And you're not with the government?"

"No."

"Why are you here, then? I mean....this is pretty weird showing up in the middle of all this....in 'Nam. Why me? Why now?"

Mark kicked the gravel with his shoe.

"Why you? You'll understand that soon enough. Too complicated to explain here. Why now? To be frank, I had to reach you after you'd gained training and experience in the Marines, but before your....er....your death."

"You said that before. So....what? According to you, I'm supposed to die in a couple of days?"

"Tomorrow."

Ty grimaced. "Why should I believe you?"

"Remember UCLA?"

No answer.

"Look, I know it's a lot to take in. I know it sounds fantastic, but why would I lie? Why else would I be here right now, risking my own neck. Any one of these incoming mortars could land a direct hit on yours truly at any moment. You've seen what I can do. Why would I risk coming here if talking with you weren't important?"

"I guess. It's just crazy, man. I mean, cert'fiably insane. What is it you want from me then? You want me to be some kind of mercenary or something?"

"No. I want you to join my time-travel company."

"Why? To make money?"

"No, to save lives."

"I'm saving lives here, man. I've got the backs of all my buds."

"Not after tomorrow you won't."

Silence.

Ty was chewing on it hard. The offer would be difficult for him to accept.

"How could I go? They'll declare me AWOL."

"I've got a shifter for you — another watch just like mine. When you go out on patrol tomorrow, we'll both just shift out once the firefight begins. You'll be classified MIA."

"What happens to my platoon?"

"Most of them don't make it."

More silence.

"All right. Look. I'll go with you, but not now. I ain't gonna abandon my unit. Gotta get them through this alive. If that thing is what you say it is, then use it to save me somehow, but I ain't leavin' my unit!"

"Look, it doesn't quite work that way...."

"Just do it, or it don't matter, got it?"

Mark was frustrated. The firefight in the jungle tomorrow would be intense. With the shifter's limitations, Mark would only be able to take out three shooters at the most, not to mention the constant risk random flying metal would make to his own health. One stray bullet and his time-traveling days would be over.

He reached down and unzipped his duffel bag.

"Fine. I was afraid you'd say that. Put this on at least." Mark pulled a Kevlar vest from the bag and handed it to Ty.

"What is this?"

"It's a bullet-proof vest. It won't stop everything, especially larger ammo, but it'll help. I've got one too."

"All right."

"Here. Take this also." Mark extended the last unused shifter to Ty.

It seemed like he had been destined to find three watches, and now he'd found the home for the last one. One for himself, one for Hardy, and one for Ty.

Ty shook his head vehemently. "Don't want no part of that till we're done here. Get me?"

"Sure."

Ty stormed off, oblivious to the explosions in the distance.

***

January was a cooler month in Vietnam, so at least the temperatures weren't stifling. There weren't even any mosquitos to deal with yet. Not at all what one would expect for tropical South Asia..

Mark had gotten himself assigned to Ty's unit fairly easily. He'd brought along falsified papers for just such an instance which identified him as a intelligence officer who should be afforded every courtesy. If such an officer wished to have himself assigned to a perilous patrol in the middle of a intensely heated gun battle, well, it was only courteous of Ty's superior officers to allow it.

Their platoon broke up into four units of ten men each. Each unit was independently attempting to covertly scale Hill 881 in order to shake up the mortar positions on top. Ty's unit was making its way through a flat wooded area where two streams came together.

The fight began suddenly with the crack of a single rifle shot, followed by a torrent of ensuing gunfire. That very first shot, though, was the critical one. It had killed Ty. His body fell limply to the ground by Mark's feet, blood pouring from the side of his head.

Fortunately, Mark had seen the shooter's location. Ducking behind some brush for cover, he shifted forward 30 years into the future. Then, calmly, he walked to the spot where he knew Ty's shooter would be.

This one's for you, Hardy. Shift 'n' strike.

Mark popped back into 1968 two feet away from the VC sniper who was aiming for Ty's head, three seconds before the sniper would pull the trigger. Mark pulled his instead and the sniper slumped over, dead. Mark had used a silencer, but gunfire still erupted on all sides. He scrambled back to Ty's position.

Ty was all right now, sitting with his back to a tree trunk, using it as cover.

"I got the sniper that was supposed to take you out," Mark called over the deafening staccato bursts.

"Great!"

Ty turned and sprayed some bushes with automatic fire.

"This is getting out of control. Let's get out of here!" Mark yelled.

Just then, a well-liked, young private nicknamed Sandy, who was hunkering down nearby, fell over. He'd been strafed by a stream of bullets pouring out of some brush about 20 yards away.

Ty's face twisted in anger. He stood, grabbed Mark by the shirt collar and thrust him up against a tree.

"*Marine*! My unit is dying around me! Get fighting! Or is there no Marine left in you?"

Mark felt it then. The call. The rush, the over-whelming fury that filled your veins in the heart of a battle for survival. It was a fierce anger that sharpened into an even fiercer determination. He knew one's duty to a fellow Marine.

Mark nodded firmly.

"Good!" Ty released his frenetic grip. "Start by saving *him*!" He pointed to Sandy's bloody figure.

A wild war whoop burst from Mark's lungs, and he ran toward the brush hiding Sandy's assassin. He shifted, disappearing from Ty's view in mid-stride. He shifted back to exactly the right moment and killed the VC before the communist could send the strafing fire Sandy's way.

Only a couple more shifts before the watch shut down. A third sniper was hidden up in some branches about ten yards away. Mark shifted out and in again, taking that sniper out before he could fire.

Mark's shifter was now blinking that all too-familiar red. Any further heroics on his part would be unassisted by time-travel.

Mark tossed a grenade at a nearby pocket of resistance and sent a parade of bullets toward some other brush as he ran back to rejoin Ty.

"I can't shift anymore!"

"What?!"

"You can only shift six times in an hour. Then, it shuts down." They both dove for a ditch and covered their heads as an NVA grenade went off nearby.

They fought well together. Mark laid down covering fire for Ty as he advanced, and vice-versa.

Then, Hog went down. Hog was a corporal, another one of Ty's pals. Ty turned to Mark with pleading eyes. Mark was at a loss. Then, he remembered.

He searched his pack and found the third shifter. He held it out to Ty.

"If you put this on, it's on for good! You will not be able to get it off again!" He shouted over the gunfire.

Ty nodded that he understood. Mark pulled him close and hurriedly explained how to use the watch. Then Ty was off into the brush.

The first thing Mark noticed was that Hog was no longer down. It was an odd thing to see history unmade in front of your eyes.

Next, several grenades among the VC went off almost simultaneously. A few moments later, Ty staggered back. Vomit covered the front of his uniform.

"Does this thing make you sick?" he croaked.

"Yeah, but you'll get used to it."

The enemy fire was dying off now. The VC were in retreat.

Chapter 29

September 12th, 2012, Boston, MA

Ty and Hardy sat before Mark in leather-backed chairs, a thick, cherry wood desk between them and him. More than ever, Mark was struck by the sheer irony of the situation. Originally, Hardy and Ty had recruited and trained him. Then, after they'd disappeared, Mark had hired Ty and Hardy and was now beginning *their* training.

The question was: *Who* really started the company? *Who had hired whom?*

The paradoxes involved were mind-boggling. Mark could philosophize with the best of them, but when things needed getting done, he didn't ponder such questions long. If the answer wasn't obvious, he moved on. There would be time to dwell on it later.

"Good to see you both, gentlemen." Mark smiled sincerely. It *was* good to see them. They were his only real friends left in the world, even if they didn't know it yet.

Hardy piped up with a hesitant "You too....Sir."

Ty remained silent.

"No need for formality. Call me Mark. Hardy, this is Ty Jennings. Ty, meet Hardy Phillips." They shook hands awkwardly.

"We're all ex-military here. Ty and I are both Marines, Hardy is Delta." That made the men a little more comfortable.

"I think you both understand that the devices I gave you are time-travel machines, correct?"

They both nodded.

"One thing that *is* different for the three of us is our home times. I am from 2012, Hardy's from 1987, and Ty's from 1968."

Ty broke in, "Why me...well, I mean, why us? Out of all the people you could have picked."

"Gentlemen, due to the nature of these watches, I was obviously privy to information about both of you that neither of you could possibly know about yourselves yet. I will not elaborate more than that at this time, other than to say that you *will* understand some day."

Hardy's blank expression belied his deep contemplation of what Mark was saying.

"I'm not sure I can accept that," he said. "I just don't get it."

"Believe it or not, neither do I," Mark replied smugly.

Mark was thoroughly enjoying turning the tables on Hardy with cryptic answers, confusing the Delta man even more. A little payback wouldn't hurt. He might even shrug a time or two just for the heck of it.

"Tell us about the watches."

"I call them "shifters". You'll notice your shifter has an upper and a lower digital display. The two displays will always represent two different moments in time. One will be the time you are currently in, the other is the time you will go to upon pressing the red button underneath the displays."

"The settings do not switch places as you switch times. In other words, if you are in 2012, and the upper display reads 2012, then the upper display represents your current time. Let's say, in such a case, the bottom display read 1987. That would be the time to which you would shift.

"If then, you did shift to 1987, the numbers would not shift positions. So, 2012 would remain in the upper display, but now it would represent the target time you would shift to, not the current time, and 1987 would still be in the bottom display, now representing the current time.

"That feature can save your neck. If you ever shift and there turns out to be some urgent reason why you need to shift back immediately, you only have to hit the red button again. No need to reset any dials.

"Each display has a series of 6 numbers followed by a letter and a dash, and then 8 more numbers. The first six numbers represent the time in terms of hour, minute, and second. The letter will always be a "P" or an "A", reflecting PM or AM. The last 8 letters represent the date. Month, day, and year, in that order."

Both men were staring at the watches on their wrists, fingers playing with the miniature buttons on the sides, changing the displays to random dates.

"Don't do any shifting yet, not until I've explained more. You can easily get yourself into trouble."

"Who made these?"

"I don't know."

"What do you mean you don't know?"

"I mean, I don't know. Really. I don't know much more about them than you do, other than what I've learned through experience."

"Who gave them to you?"

"Nobody. I just found them."

"Where?"

"In the woods."

Hardy grunted.

Ty slapped his knee. "You've got to be kidding me. So, this really isn't a government project?"

"Nope."

Ty wore a bizarre kind of smirk on his face. Hardy stared at the floor.

"I'll tell you what. Why don't you both finish listening to my little orientation seminar? Think you can keep your yaps shut till then?"

They grinned, happy to hear the assertive tone in his voice. Being military, strong leadership made them comfortable, weak leadership, uneasy.

"When you shift, you'll notice your body being yanked around some. Most times, it's quite subtle, but every now and then, you'll feel like you're on a roller coaster.

"That's because whenever you shift to another time, there will be slight variations in the elevation of the terrain, location of plant growth, etc. Buildings and floors settle over the years as well. Things change. Most of the time, this is no problem.

"However, every now and then, your position in your target time will be occupied by another object you weren't expecting. Your shifter is somehow able to detect this and moves your physical position along with your temporal to compensate and prevent you from appearing in the middle of a tree, or a wall, or something else unexpected. When this happens, you'll experience a severe wrenching sensation as your body is moved to an unoccupied position. It is *not* pleasant when that happens, but it normally doesn't hurt either. Usually, just leaves you feeling very disoriented.

"This not only works horizontally, but vertically as well. Once, I shifted to a time when the ground was about twenty feet higher than the time from when I'd shifted. It felt like I was being ripped to pieces as it yanked me upward. It did hurt that time. Try to avoid doing that. I'm not sure what the shifter's limitations are. There may be a limit to what it can handle and you could wind up shifting into the middle of a fifty foot pile of dirt. Not fun.

"Another time, I shifted to a future year where the hill beneath me had been strip mined. If I hadn't been able to shift back at the punch of a button, I would have fallen to my death. So, be careful.

"You can only shift six times successively within one hour, or eight successive times within twelve hours. After about the third time, you'll notice yourself becoming increasingly nauseous with each successive shift. After six times in a row, I guarantee you'll be heaving your lunch. And your watch will shut down. The displays will flash red and you won't be able to shift again for about twenty-four hours.

"Any questions?" Mark leaned back in his chair, fingers interlaced behind his head.

"What about your clothes?" Hardy asked.

Ty snickered.

"What do you mean?"

"I mean....why don't you show up naked when you shift?"

"Not sure. The best we can figure is the shifter is somehow able to detect the dimensions of the person it's attached to along with any small objects touching that person. Of course, you never lose your clothes when you shift, or the fillings in your teeth for that matter. The change in your pocket stays with you. Small to medium-size objects you hold in hand will go with you. I've transported all kinds of things with me, weapons, money, papers, electronic devices."

"Can you take another person with you...one who doesn't have a shifter?"

"Uh....not sure. Never tried that."

"Might be worth a shot."

Mark nodded.

Now Ty spoke up, "So, why are we here? What do you want from us?"

"Guys, I'll be frank. The devices I've given you are *yours*. Even if I wanted them back, there's no way to get them off your wrist short of cutting your hand off. Obviously, you can do all kinds of amazing things with them.

"If you want to get rich, it's easy as pie with these shifters. I can show you how to do it the simple and quick way. Heck, if you prefer, I'll give you however many millions you want. I've already made billions and it just keeps increasing.

"What I'll tell you though, is that after I accumulated all my wealth, something was still missing. I felt empty. I wanted....I needed something more. I knew I had to use this thing to help people.

"Millions of tragedies happen every day on this mess of a globe, and I decided I was going to undo some of them. It's a heck of a thing to see a widow's tears dry up, a lost child brought back to life, to see life spring up where there had been only death and suffering a moment before. I'm trying to make this world a better place.

"That may sound corny, but I know what it's like to lose somebody. I lost my own kids several years ago. Drunk driver."

Hardy let out a low whistle. "Man! That must have been awesome, being able to go back and save 'em. That's cool!"

Mark's jaw quivered. His eyes swiftly welled with tears as he struggled to maintain composure. The two men sensed the grief he was holding in. Against his will, a lone tear broke rank and trickled down his cheek. He quickly wiped it away with his sleeve, trying to pretend it hadn't happened. He made a couple of failed attempts to speak again, but could only manage a muffled choke. Hardy's exclamation had taken him completely off guard.

"You mean....you didn't save them?" Hardy asked.

Mark shook his head.

"Why not? You've got the only tool in the universe capable of such a thing."

Mark fought to relax the constricted throat muscles preventing him from talking. After a minute, he regained control. "Not everything...." he croaked, "Can be changed."

Ty leaned forward.

"What do you mean 'not everything can be changed'?"

"I mean I tried everything under the sun to save my kids and nothing worked. I just can't bring them back, all right?"

"Okay, okay. Sorry. We didn't know. We're new at this."

"I....I know."

"Do you mean like....your kids....that they were somehow fated to die?"

"Something like that."

"I don't get it. How can we change things in the past if they were fated to happen?"

"I don't understand it myself. All I can tell you is that there are a lot of things I've been able to change, but there are a few things....I couldn't."

"And you want us to help you change history?"

"Pretty much. There's a lot to do, and I can't do it all by myself. I had two extra shifters, and I knew you two were the right guys for the job."

"What if we just walk away?"

"You won't. I know you better than you think."

Ty and Hardy looked to each other and then back at Mark, big grins plastered on their mugs.

Chapter 30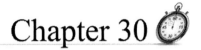

August 9th, 2012, Washington, D.C.

Alex Rialto drummed the pencil eraser on his desk as he perused the file one more time. His intercom buzzed.

"Alex, Mr. Pennington wants to see you in his office."

"All right. Tell him I'll be right over."

Rialto was a senior investigator for the IRS. He knew very well that specific three letter sequence was probably the most dreaded in the English language, at least for citizens of the United States. Just a letter or phone call from any agent within the agency made most people quake in their boots, and he was now near the top of the service's pecking order.

He'd begun as an ordinary clerk at the bottom rung of the agency's ladder. Through naked ambition and a healthy bit of talent, he'd scrambled up the food chain pretty quickly. In his early thirties, he was still young, yet he'd already earned enough authority to choose his own cases, follow his own hunches.

He was good at his job. To date, he'd been responsible for the imprisonment of more drug lords and other mafia types than several entire FBI field offices. And just because he knew how to see patterns in the financial data others couldn't. Finances always left a paper trail. There was no avoiding it.

He had the growing reputation of an agent who always got their man, a reputation that was now reaching important ears in other governmental agencies, ears that belonged to people who might be instrumental in getting him out of the IRS and into something even better.

"Alex! Have a seat."

Sanford Pennington was in his sixties, portly, balding, and oddly commanding in the way only senior government officials can be.

"What can I do for you, sir?"

"What projects are you working on right now?"

"A guy named Mark Carpen."

"Never heard of him."

"You wouldn't. He keeps a very low profile, though he's a billionaire several times over."

"How'd he get his money?"

"You name it, he's done it. Stocks, real estate, etc. All your normal investment stuff."

Pennington slapped his knee. "By gosh, we could use a piece of that, that's for sure! How'd you flag him?"

"His name crossed my desk because he's got so many accounts spread across the world, like he's trying to hide something. He may just be covering the fact he's a billionaire. Could be a privacy thing. On the surface, he does seem to be on the up and up. His returns have all been filed appropriately, but something in his file keeps nagging at me."

"What?"

"Not sure yet, but something's not right."

"Well, put that one on the back burner, okay. While it would be quite a coup to catch a couple billion in back taxes, it's an election year, and the main issue is crime. The President is breathing down my neck to break the Santos ring in L.A. FBI thinks we're the key."

"Okay."

"Here's what we're gonna do...."

***

Rialto obeyed the letter of Pennington's law, even if he couldn't obey the spirit of it. He worked on the Santos case for the rest of the day, but he couldn't get Mark Carpen out of his mind, so he took the file home with him that night. Not just that night either. Due to the sheer volume of records involved, the study of Carpen's returns quickly became a nightly hobby for the next few weeks.

He just couldn't quite put his finger on it, but something was off about the man's financial history. Rialto had scrutinized the records over and over and over again, yet he still couldn't see what was gnawing at him.

Carpen's tax returns had all been filed on time, and he seemed to have paid every penny in taxes he owed. He'd used all the normal loopholes rich guys use, and even then, there were several he'd failed to take advantage of.

It seemed like your typical silver spoon case. A lot of rich kids blew their inheritance once their parents had passed on, but this guy had turned his father's millions into billions. How had he done it? Stock purchases, real estate deals, business acquisitions. Carpen had been very lucky.

When you got right down to it, that's what was really bothering him. Carpen was *too* lucky. He seemed to have gotten in on the ground floor of every wealth-making stock five years before they were ever valuable. Either the guy had a great nose for picking them, or something was fishy.

At first, Alex figured the stock picks had to be bogus, a front for some nefariously gleaned financial gain, but when he put in requests for official records from the SEC, he found that Carpen had indeed made the stock purchases at the times he said he did. All of Carpen's other deals checked out similarly.

Maybe he should kick it back to the SEC. Could it be some kind of long-term insider trading deal? That wouldn't explain the overly fortunate real estate deals though, or the gambling wins.

Alex Rialto had a nose like a bloodhound. He could smell a crook a mile away. Something was up here, but *what*?

According to the file, Mark Carpen was actually Mark Carpen III. He'd inherited his wealth from his father, Mark Carpen Jr., who'd inherited the family fortune from Mark Carpen Sr. Alex had to pull their files from Archives since their returns were so much older. He'd studied those files as well, and they were just like Carpen III's. They were also filled with fortunate business deals. Yet, he couldn't see anything in them that shouted "Criminal!" either.

Something that did stand out was the timing of the filings. The year Mark Carpen Sr. died was the same year Mark Carpen Jr. first began filing tax returns and having transactions in his name. The same held true for the transition between Jr. and Carpen the Third.

What did *that* mean? Probably that the sons were completely maintained financially by their fathers until the death of the fathers. Still, it seemed odd for a wealthy father to turn a great financial empire over to his son without having him get his feet wet first. *To each his own*, he mused.

However, now that he thought about it, there was something else unusual about those transitions. Carpen III had only been 17 when Carpen Jr. had died in 1984. He'd filed his first tax return when he was only 17 years old. Surely, he'd had accountants who'd managed his funds for him as trustees until he was of legal age. Could it have been some anonymous accountant making the fantastic stock picks?

As Alex browsed through the returns, new and ancient, for the umpteenth time, one item finally riveted his attention. The signature. The signature was much too flowery, too developed for a 17 year old to make.

A forgery? If so, who forged it? Why was it forged? Was it one of the nameless accountants?

He checked the other returns. All of them, up to last year, had the same flowery signature. Had the signatures been forged every year, or was the original signature real after all?

Alex looked back over the files of Carpen Jr. and Sr. He noticed something else, something very odd. Neither man had ever indicated a spouse. Ever. Yet, they'd had sons.

He checked the signatures.

Pay dirt! The signature on every return going back almost 70 years was made by the same person with the same flowery scrawl. Mark Carpen III had been born in 1967, so he couldn't be the author of all those signatures.

The same signature for 70 years! What in the world? Did the Carpen family use the same accountant for all those years and have him forge their signature every time? That would mean they'd started using the accountant when he was around twenty and that he was now over ninety years old and still processing the books for the Carpen empire. Didn't seem likely.

Maybe Mark Carpen wasn't really a person. Maybe it was a fictitious name being used as a cover for a long-term mob organization.

The truth was, Alex couldn't come up with any scenarios that would explain it and still sound plausible to a rational person. It definitely required further investigation. *Personal investigation.*

To heck with the Santos gang. There was something big going on with Mark Carpen, and Alex Rialto intended to figure out what that was.

Chapter 31

September 14th, 2012, Boston, MA

"Gentlemen, we need to develop an operational plan."

They sat around an antique mahogany table, long and rectangular in shape and full of character. The simple table would work just as well for research work as it did meetings. Mark wasn't into luxuries.

He had created a rustic rec room for the main gathering area of their new headquarters, complete with leather couches, a couple of La-Z-Boys, a billiard table, dartboard, foosball, and a chess board. Their round table stood in the middle of the rec room next to the billiard table. He'd set a large screen TV in one of the corners, but they hardly used it. They already knew the outcomes of most of the sporting events, and for movies, he'd built a theater upstairs when they wanted to relax, so it looked like they wouldn't really need it. He'd probably just give the TV to Savannah.

Hardy was still dressed in gray sweats from his morning run. Ty sported a pair of long beach shorts and a T-shirt.

After their first meeting, Mark had asked both of them to set up a dummy corporation, in which Mark had then "invested" $100 million dollars each. They'd both stared at him dumbfounded when he'd told them what he'd done.

The reality of his wealth and his willingness to share it with them hadn't really sunk in until that moment. To be yanked out of your home time, your entire life as you knew it, given the ability to travel though time, and then be made a super multi-millionaire overnight had to be quite a shock. They seemed to be coping wonderfully though.

He didn't care about the money. It required no effort to earn back those amounts, any amount really. In fact, a couple hundred million was only two months interest in a bad mutual fund for him. What he gained was two dedicated employees who wouldn't need to waste time on frivolities and would instead focus on the assignment at hand. Friends really, not employees. Well....they *would be* friends, as they once had been, but for now they were still getting to know him.

Ty interrupted, "What are we going to call our company?"

"I've been calling it Historical Enterprises for any business dealings with the public, but how about ChronoShift?"

"I like it."

"Me too."

"Okay, done." Mark smiled inwardly. They had just created the very company that Hardy claimed to represent when he'd first hired Mark.

"Now how are we going to change the world?" He said.

That was the hard question. The three of them pondered the plethora of potential answers.

Hardy piped up first. "In my opinion, there are two main categories: present day crimes and major historical events."

"What about historical crimes?" Ty added.

"What do you mean?"

"Like...crimes that didn't happen yesterday, but years or centuries ago."

"Okay, so forget 'present day'. Just 'crimes' and 'major historical events'."

Ty spoke up again, "What about improving the quality of life of peoples in the past. What if we take certain technologies back to previous generations? It could hyper-accelerate the quality of life for people all over the world in our present time."

"I did that once, on a very limited basis," Mark said, "but I don't think it's a good idea to do something like that in a big enough way it might change an entire society's future."

"Why not?" Ty frowned.

"Well....because history is *history*. The smallest change in the past can hugely impact the present. If we were to introduce a new technology to an old culture, the level of change that act could wreak on the present would be astronomical."

"So, what? They could be great changes."

"Except we can't predict what those changes would actually be. Knowing human nature, the changes very likely wouldn't be great. For example, let's say we took machine gun technology back to the American colonists during the Revolutionary War to help them beat Britain faster. Sounds good on the surface, but the colonists didn't have much industrial capacity at that point. It isn't hard to conceive that somehow the British would also get hold of the technology. They had plenty of industrial infrastructure and might prove capable of fabricating the automatic weapons on a massive scale. They'd massacre us in either the Revolutionary War or the War of 1812, and the United States we know and love would never be.

"Or, even if the colonists could use the technology to their advantage, how do we know the South wouldn't be able to use it later to give them the slight edge they needed over the North to win the Civil War?

"Or what if we were to help someone like Benjamin Franklin create the light bulb 100 years before its time? What if that accelerated the advancement of science so much that nuclear technology became available to Hitler before the US was ready to take him on? What if science had advanced so much by then that he would have access to shifters like ours? He would conquer the world and commit genocide on levels that would make the Holocaust seem minor by comparison.

"It's too risky," Mark concluded, "I think we should stay away from that kind of thing."

The reality of how easy it might be for them to screw up history, the whole world even, began to sink in.

Ty capitulated, "I see what you mean."

Hardy nodded in assent.

Mark was scribbling notes on a pad. "Okay, so are there any other possibilities? Or is it just 'Crimes' and 'Major Historical Events'?"

"We could help the government with espionage and special ops," Hardy added.

Each of them looked to the others, considering whether or not they wanted to use this new power that way. The idea died a silent death in the air between them. Each had been in the military and knew how the government operated. In a heartbeat, all three men would jump to help the U.S. government if it were needed to protect the American people, but if they weren't careful, the *wrong* people in government would get a hold of the technology. Then, they'd be sucked in. Slaves to the system. And when that happened, it was always for the wrong causes.

"Okay 'Crimes' and 'Major Historical Events' it is." Mark slapped the desk for emphasis. "I think we ought to break the 'Crimes' category into present day crimes and historical crimes. The current ones will be pretty easy to research, but the historical cases will be a little tougher to figure out. Granted, I've already got the Harvard Institute for Historical Studies doing reams of research for me. I can redirect Savannah and them to give us reports listing the most tragic crimes and tragedies across the country for each year."

"So, how are we going to distribute the work? Are we going to rotate assignments, or are we each going to specialize?" Hardy asked.

"Good question," Ty added.

"I think we ought to specialize. The military trains that way because it's the most effective method," Hardy commented.

"What do you think, Mark?"

"Hardy's right. We each need to pick a category and take it by the horns. Who wants 'Current Crimes'?"

Hardy raised his hand.

"All right. Ty, what do you want?"

"If it's okay with you, I want 'Historical Crimes'. Not only does it sound good, but I just don't feel comfortable with all this new-fangled technology you've got here in 2012. I feel more at home....back in the past."

"Guess that leaves you with Major Historical Events, Mark. You happy with that?"

"Yeah, I think we all got what we wanted. But I don't think we should work in isolation either. We should all try our hands at each type of case from time to time to keep ourselves fresh and versatile. Plus, there will be a lot of cases that require the involvement of the whole team, so we need to build team unity and be familiar with every environment."

"So, where would the MLK assassination fall in these categories? Would that be a historical crime, or a major historical event?"

"What's MLK?" Ty asked.

"Martin Luther King."

"What?" Ty jumped out of his seat, clearly upset.

"Ty didn't know about that yet, Hardy. He shifted out of 1968 three months before it happened."

"Oh, sorry, man. I would've figured....well, I figured you would have heard about it by now."

"Well, I didn't! I can't believe it! Who killed him?"

Mark motioned to the chair. "Have a seat, Ty. There's a lot I need to tell you *both*."

***

September 28th, 2012, Boston, MA

Rialto had followed Carpen for several weeks now. Discreetly, of course. Unfortunately, he couldn't find anything amiss.

If Carpen was a front for some mob organization, it was cleverly disguised. In addition to shadowing him, Rialto had used laser directional listening devices and even wiretapped his phone, but had turned up nothing.

In fact, it seemed that Carpen managed most of his financial transactions himself. He had an accounting firm, but it was a reputable firm that had been around for decades and served many of Boston's larger and most respected companies. He doubted they would be willing to jeopardize their entire reputation by corrupting themselves for one guy. Unless it was a rogue agent inside the firm forging the signatures, but they wouldn't trust an account of Carpen's size to anybody other than a senior CPA, and no single accountant would have been at the firm for seventy years. No, the answer did not lie with Carpen's accountants. The man himself was the source of the mystery.

Rialto was able to identify a couple of men who met with Carpen on a regular basis, Ty Jennings and Hardin Phillips, both of whom were ex-military. Whenever they met, though, they remained deep inside Carpen's office building away from any windows, so the directional listening devices were useless. Somehow, he needed to get inside that building and plant some bugs.

***

June 24th, 2010, Juarez, Mexico

"You guys ready?"

They gave him the thumbs up. Hardy and Ty crouched on the broken sidewalk of a small alley, their backs to a pockmarked, concrete wall. Mark squatted facing them and was in a better position to observe their target. It was his turn to train them, and this was their first mission.

"All right. Run through the rules one more time for me." Mark said.

"Minimize your number of shifts," Hardy offered, "Don't shift in front of others."

"Don't contaminate a historical scene with modern weapons. Never use the shifter for personal gain in a way that will harm others," Ty finished.

"Good."

"You've only gone over it about fourteen times," Hardy said dryly.

Mark laughed. What they didn't know was, with the exception of the last rule, he wasn't very good at following them himself. So what? Hardy had made *him* learn them. It was their turn, and they were pretty good guidelines anyway.

Mark's eyes narrowed as he turned his gaze back to the object of their mission. It was a squat four bedroom house, built of concrete in the style of most middle class Mexican homes. It'd been a while, however, since this home had been occupied by someone of the middle class, not that there was much of that particular gentry left anywhere in Mexico these days. The exterior paint had once been white, or cream, but was now mostly peeled off, revealing large areas of bare, butchered wall. Thick, black iron bars covered the windows and blocked every opening in the partition wall separating the front yard from the street. Sharp, broken shards of glass had been imbedded in the concrete along the top of that wall, which was also crowned by various layers of curling razor wire.

In the States, this house would have stood out as especially ugly, the dwelling of a paranoid security freak. In Mexico, it was the norm. The fact that it was so run-down wasn't even out of the ordinary. What did make this house stand out was the level of luxury apparent in the types of vehicles parked in front and the frequency with which they changed out with others, also just as luxurious.

Juarez was dominated by drug cartels that smuggled narcotics and other illegal items into the United States. The Mexican police and military had proven completely incapable of reining them in or even dampening their influence. Every now and then, under pressure from the United States, the Mexican government would launch a new initiative to root them out of the border towns by sending in the army, but the cartels always won in the end. If soldiers wouldn't take bribes to look the other way, they weren't asked again. The cartels simply put them in an early grave. The police were even less of a challenge to dominate.

This house was a base of operations for one of the cartels. This particular cartel had just committed an act that would be extraordinarily heinous in the eyes of most decent people, yet unfortunately was just another day in the life of Juarez.

They had kidnapped a pair of teenage American girls who lived across the border in El Paso. The girls had come to Juarez to attend a concert that evening and had approached a local police officer to get directions. Instead of helping, the corrupt official immediately radioed his boss in the Alvarez cartel, which was none other than Antonio Alvarez himself, to advise him of the presence of the two attractive young teens. Within ten minutes, the girls were swept off the streets and brought to this safe house where bad things were about to happen to them.

Mark guessed the vehicles coming in and out were bidders. The girls were being auctioned off.

"I'm going to hang back here," Mark informed them.

"Chicken."

"It's good policy for one man to stay back in case the other two get in trouble. Plus, I've had plenty of experience fighting with a shifter. You guys are the newbies."

"Yeah, yeah."

"Now that you've got the rules down so well, we're going to break the first two like crazy."

"Thank goodness."

"Those jokers have got top of the line assault weapons, as well as a healthy stash of grenades and even RPGs, I'm sure. They're armed to the teeth. Any ideas on how to breach?"

"Just shift in," Ty said.

"Good, but how?"

"We'll shift in at opposite sides of the house," Hardy added. "We'll each take out one or two bad guys, shift out, then shift back in somewhere else in the house, and repeat."

"Good. Never, and I mean *never,* shift into a fight on your sixth shift. Having your watch shut down in the middle of a battle would be....problematic." They chuckled. "Instead, take a twenty-four hour break in another time before going back in."

From his equipment bag, Mark pulled out several pair of what looked like overly thick binoculars.

"These might help."

"Night vision goggles?"

"Infrared."

"What do they do?" Ty asked.

Infrared technology had not yet been in wide use during his time in the Marines. Hardy had used infrared vision before while in Delta, but never equipment this sophisticated.

"Put them on."

They did.

"They detect heat signatures, even through walls."

"Awesome!" Hardy was elated, counting in the air with a finger the colorful figures he now saw inside the safe house.

"See anybody that looks like they could be one of the girls?"

"Yeah. There's two smaller figures lying down in a back room," Ty confirmed.

"I'd shift into that room to start. That way no one can slip in and execute them while you're fighting elsewhere. Once you've cleared that room, the girls will be safe as you clear the rest of the house. Got any questions?"

They didn't. He didn't have to train them on how to perform an assault or insure a successful rescue; they already had plenty of training and experience in those areas. The only new factor was the shifter, which was a powerful new weapon in their arsenal. They just needed to get used to using it in a battle scenario.

The men grabbed their weapons and disappeared from Mark's view as they shifted out. They would use the year 1900 as a rendezvous year for this mission. In 1900, this neighborhood was nothing but empty, arid terrain, so the task should be an easy one for them. They only had to walk about fifty yards into the desert and then pop into the middle of that back bedroom. Piece of cake.

Plus, he knew from his own past that Hardy and Ty would survive to recruit him later. Still, he found himself a bit anxious, like a mother hen releasing her chicks into the wild for the first time.

A few moments later, the hollow staccato of rapid gunfire erupted within the house. Which was *not* good. Ty and Hardy had silenced weapons.

Then, an explosion roared behind the house. Two more blasts tore out the front rooms. Shards of window glass showered the street like jagged strips of hail. The roof lifted off its moorings and collapsed back in on itself, caving in the walls as it went. Then, one by one, each of the luxury SUVs parked in front burst apart in a torrent of unexpected explosions. The force and heat of these explosions set Mark back on his heels. It was like the apocalypse had descended onto that house and that house alone. No one inside could have lived through that.

"Hey, Mark."

He whirled. Ty and Hardy stood behind him, smiling proudly. Each held one of the girls, both of whom were very much alive. Hardy cradled one in his arms; Ty was hugging the other, comforting her. The girls' faces were pale and fearful, but they were safe. Seeing their clothing intact, Mark was thankful. They had mostly likely gotten them out before the cartel had time to touch them. Needless to say, he doubted these girls would be coming back to Juarez any time soon for another concert.

"What happened?" Mark asked. "You were just supposed to get the girls out."

"We did. First thing. That only took a minute. Snuck 'em out a window in the side wall of that back room after just a couple of shots. But....we decided we couldn't let that garbage go unpunished, so, we went back."

"What was with all the automatic gunfire?"

"They were firing at ghosts. Couldn't figure out where we were."

"And the explosion in the back?"

"They were having a cookout in the back yard, so we crashed their party. Threw a grenade underneath their propane tank."

"It was a big tank," Hardy added.

"I reckon."

"Then, we put a couple of strips of C-4 in the front rooms, as well as under the vehicles. I think we got them all."

"I'd say so. How in the world did you do all that with just six shifts?"

"Spent a night camping in the desert. That gave us twelve shifts each."

Mark shook his head. "Amazing," he muttered. They'd left him just one minute before, but had lived a full day and a half outside of his presence in that minute. It felt different when you observed the effect as a bystander.

"Relax, man. We know what we're doing."

Mark smiled. "Yeah. You sure do."

Chapter 32

4:07 AM, September 30th, 2012, Boston, MA

The woman would be here soon.

In less than two minutes, a man would attack her somewhere along this block, but so far, Mark hadn't been able to determine where he was hidden.

He would have to wait until the perp made his move. In this current version of history Mark hoped to correct, the attacker would grab her from behind, clamp his hand over her mouth and force her into a vehicle. He'd drive her to a nearby park, force himself upon her, and then dump her in the gravel, unconscious and half dead. She would never see his face nor the exterior of his car, which would make it impossible for the police to catch the animal.

Hardy was handling most of the current crimes like this, but Mark couldn't get started on historical tragedies until Savannah completed some research he needed. In the meantime, he'd been splitting the crimes with Hardy, and there were plenty to go around.

The woman's name was Laura Kingsley, and Mark intended to make sure this tragedy never befell her.

He saw her. Her stride was purposeful. Even in the dim light emanating from the windows of businesses closed for the night, he could detect a slight sashay to her walk. The faint glow illuminated her left side while her right half remained eclipsed in the darkness of the street.

Her beauty was exotic and striking. Glossy, dark auburn hair flowed down in long, loose, wavy tresses, a perfect frame for her well-chiseled face. Her skin was the color or silky caramel. Her figure....was perfect. She strode confidently, oblivious to the danger lurking nearby.

She passed in front of a small alleyway, and the attacker showed his hand. He suddenly leapt from the black opening like a trapdoor spider on its prey, ripping her head back and strapping a hand over her mouth before she could scream. She fought with the strength of a tigress to escape the man's grasp, but he proved too strong.

She managed to stomp the insole of one of his feet, causing him obvious pain. That move almost allowed her to get away, but he recovered too quickly and merely tightened his grip.

The very moment Mark had seen a flicker of movement in that alley, he'd launched into motion. This vigilante business had refreshed his military training well, honing the skills he'd acquired years before. He no longer had to think about what to do in moments like these. His body just went into action, like a natural dance.

Mark crossed a distance of about fifty feet in under five seconds. Before the attacker knew what was happening, Mark had struck two successive blows to his head and kidney. The man lost his grip and dropped to the pavement. As he released her, Laura fell as well, landing flat on her back.

WHAM!

Something heavy struck Mark in the back of the head. He tried to step forward, but was too stunned from the blow. His vision swam and his right knee gave out unexpectedly.

He was falling. He landed on top of the woman. There was no time to think. If he passed out, the guy would kill him. Dazed, he reached for his shifter, hit the red button, and shifted out.

***

He experienced all the sensations that normally accompany a shift, but curiously, Laura Kingsley didn't disappear out from under him. Which was strange. It was hard to think. His mind felt muddled.

"Your eyes are purple," he mumbled vacuously, transfixed.

They were indeed a bright, sparkling violet, and the unexpected brilliance of their hues stole his breath. His mouth was very close to hers. Light scents of lavender nestled in her hair drifted up to meet his senses, like a tantalizing invitation to something fresh and invigorating.

Somehow, she had shifted with him. They still lay on the sidewalk, but the time was now dawn, two days later.

There must have been two assailants.

The attacker he'd seen must not have been working alone. That was scary. A team working together to assault women. Another guy must have been waiting in the wings to make sure there were no problems with the grab. When Mark took down the first attacker, the second had emerged and smashed him with something in the back of the head.

Wide-eyed, Laura was screaming bloody murder now, scratching and scrambling, trying to get out from under Mark. Her initial state of shock had worn off. Weakly, he rolled over onto the pavement beside her, doing his best to fend off her blows. He was recovering, but still somewhat incapacitated.

"Calm down, lady. I saved you," he groaned.

She scooted herself away as fast as she could and jumped to her feet. Furtively, she looked up and down the street, trying to get her bearings. Not seeing any other attackers, she slowly calmed and then stared at him, chest heaving from fear and adrenaline.

It suddenly occurred to her that it was now daylight, which caused her mouth to fall open in astonishment. Her lips worked silently as if to ask a million unvoiced questions all at once. Finally, she shut her jaws and let out an odd gasp.

Mark had always made it a practice when shifting to use a base time when no one would be around. For this mission, he'd chosen a few minutes after sunrise two days after the attack. He knew seven minutes would pass before the next car came down the street. For the time being, they were alone.

"Sit," he croaked, motioning to a bench.

She obeyed, dumbfounded. "What just happened?"

"A man attacked you. I saw it and tried to help, but there must have been a second guy, 'cause somebody walloped me from behind. Hard, too." He sat up, massaging the back of his skull.

She rubbed her eyes and blinked repeatedly, probably trying to wipe away what she thought must have been a bad dream.

Goodness, she was gorgeous. *Exotic.* That was the word that kept coming to mind. Intriguing, magnetic, it had been a long time since he'd seen such hypnotizing beauty.

"No, I mean, what happened after that?" she said, "I know I was attacked. You....I mean....I don't know....but what happened? It was....*night.* I was coming home from work. Now, it's *morning.*"

Mark knew she worked at a gentlemen's club a few blocks over. He acted groggier than he really was in an attempt to divert her questions. "I don't know. We must have both been knocked unconscious."

She swiveled her head back and forth, searching for signs of other people. "No, I fell. You fell. Then, we were here. I never closed my eyes. I know it. You didn't either. The light just changed and things got quiet." She massaged her brow and stared at her feet. "Who are you, anyway?"

He hesitated. There wasn't going to be an easy way to get out of this.

"You're Laura Kingsley," he said at last.

In mid-massage, her hand froze. Her eyes shot up and fixed on him apprehensively.

"No," he reassured her, "I'm not one of the attackers. Cross my heart." He held up three fingers like a Boy Scout as he staggered to his feet.

"So, who are *you*?"

"Look. I can explain, and you probably won't believe it, but I'm not going to tell you who I am until I'm certain you can keep your mouth shut. Sorry."

Her expression grew even more quizzical. She shook her head a couple of times as if trying to rattle some sense into it.

"You tell me right now or I'll start screaming," she declared.

"Sorry, I need to know this conversation will stay private, completely private."

He couldn't believe he was actually going to tell her. He should just shift out. She'd lose two days of her life, but she'd be safe from the attacker. It was a good trade. Still, something about her intoxicated him. If he stayed much longer, he'd probably spill everything whether he wanted to or not.

"Fine," she gave in, "Explain away, I'll keep my mouth shut. Scout's honor." She mimicked the sign Mark had made.

So, he did.

Mark sat next to her on the bench for near an hour, recounting the whole truth of his involvement. His reluctance to share his most guarded secrets with a stranger dissipated in the face of the thrill of sharing his heart with such a beautiful woman.

As expected, she was at first incredulous, but after she checked the date on the paper in the newsstand and Mark shifted in and out of her sight once, she began to believe.

"But....if this is all true, then how did I...."shift"....with you? *I* don't have a watch."

"I don't know. This is the first time that's happened to me. We've never shifted with another person before. Since we were touching, I guess the watch didn't differentiate between you and me as separate objects. I've transported objects before, but we didn't think it was possible to bring a whole other person along."

"Do it again."

"Do what again?'

"Shift. I'm having trouble believing all this."

"All right. But you're coming with me. We'll shift to the same hour, but to some date in the future. Double check the date on that paper."

"October 2nd."

"Okay, we're going to 6:40 AM, October 30th." Mark took her wrist in his hand. This was the first time he would intentionally try to bring someone along on a shift. Would just holding her wrist be enough contact for it to work?

It was.

Now, it was night again and easily 20 degrees lower than just a second before. Her eyes grew wide. In the glow of the street lamp, she read the date on the paper in front of them now.

"Not much way for me to instantly manipulate the sun or the weather, now is there?"

She was dumbfounded, shaking her head, and beginning to shiver. "No, nor the paper."

"Check out that storefront. Decorated for Halloween."

She nodded absent-mindedly. "Yeah....it's still hard to believe though."

"I know."

She stared at the newspaper dispenser in front of her, reading headlines of events that wouldn't occur for another month in her world. The bewilderment in her eyes was obvious. It was one thing to tell someone there were little green men on Mars, it was another to show them one.

"You have purple eyes."

"You said that."

"Sorry."

"They're contacts. So, what now?"

"I'm going to shift back to the morning of your attack and take care of those two guys so they don't hurt anyone else, but I have to wait 24 hours."

"Why?"

"This shifter only has enough juice for 6 shifts within 24 hours. I've already done 5. I don't like shifting into a fight with a shut-down watch. Puts me at a distinct disadvantage. If something were to go wrong, like say a third guy we didn't know about, I'd be stuck, unable to shift back out. Not good, and I'm no gambler.

"Plus, I'm already feeling nauseous. After the sixth shift, you pretty much start puking you guts out. It's an unpleasantry I'd like to avoid. So, we'll just have to hang out for a day or so."

"Okay. When you go..."

"Yes?"

"....I'm going with you."

"No way. Too dangerous."

Her brow creased firmly in determination. An endearing look for her.

"No buts. I'm going. I want to see it. I won't feel safe again otherwise."

"All right."

Something told him arguing with this woman would be futile.

Chapter 33

To say he was enamored would be an understatement. Her beauty was invasive. Her pearl-white teeth formed a smile that warmed you from the inside out. Her laugh caused his heart to accelerate excitedly.

Brief lapses back into rationality tinged his cheeks with embarrassment when he realized how much he was acting like a desperate schoolboy. Exactly how long *had* it been since he'd been out with a woman?

His wife had left him....

How long ago had his wife left him? Linearly, it was about two years or so, but he'd jumped around so much, it was probably closer to three for him emotionally.

They had nothing else to do for the entire day, so they ate breakfast together, milled around some shops, and then had lunch. Mark felt like he was on a date. They strolled through the streets, checked out more local shops, went to the park. After some espressos at a coffee shop, they took in a movie. He instinctively chose a romantic, candle-lit restaurant for dinner.

Laura was fun. She was a balm to the sting of the acute loneliness which had plagued him since Kelly left.

When Mark lost his children, the pain had been unbearable. His world had come apart at the seams. When Kelly left, instead of pain, he'd gone numb. It was a merciful, self-protective feature of the soul, deadening him to the anguish he might have otherwise suffered.

He was sure Laura didn't view their day together the same way he did. She had no reason to. What would a dancer like her want with a guy like him? At least, she seemed to be having fun too.

Mark hadn't recognized how desperate he'd been for companionship until now. Like a dying man in the desert, ignorant of the strength of his own thirst until he took the first sip of water that unleashed the full power of his need, Mark fought hard against the rising desperation he felt from the prospect of their day coming to an end.

He paid for separate rooms at a five-star hotel in downtown Boston. He'd never taken his wife to such a place, not because he hadn't wanted to, but simply because they had never been able to afford it. Now, money was no object.

"You should have the hotel give you a wake-up call," he said, "We'll leave here about 5:30 AM."

"Why so early? I mean, you've got the watch and all. Can't we just go over there any time we want?"

"Yeah, but it's best to shift when no one is around. We need to be assured we'll have the street to ourselves."

"Okay."

He hesitated, wanting so badly to kiss her, to make some kind of move, to express what he was feeling so strongly, but he feared the feeling wasn't mutual. She was his involuntary prisoner on this shift, biding her time until he took her home. He gazed into her eyes, but held himself back, not willing to force his desire upon her.

She leaned forward and bussed his cheek, a light butterfly of a kiss that melted his heart with a hope for a future he wasn't sure was there.

***

"Are you ready?"

"Ready as I'll ever be." She looked nervous, though she tried to hide it.

"Grab both my shoulders and hold on. Stay well behind me. I'm gonna try to pop in right behind the guy who attacked you. As soon as you feel the shift, let go of me and drop down as low as you can. I can't be distracted by concern for your safety."

"All right."

"Remember, I'm not the police."

"What does that mean?"

"These guys aren't gonna make it until the police arrive. Got it?"

"Oh." She grimaced, apparently not having thought through all the ramifications of Mark's planned action.

"You can always stay here. I'll come back for you."

Her jaw set firmly. "No, it's okay. I'll go."

"All right. Grab on. If you see any movement other than the two guys we know of, yell. For all we know, there may be a third one."

He positioned himself in the approximate spot he thought would work. Laura stood behind him and laid both her hands on his shoulders as if about to give him a back rub.

He was off by a few feet. The man he needed to focus on was the second attacker, the one who had conked him on the back of the head. The first attacker was still struggling to recover from the blows Mark had laid into him.

Mr. Second Attacker was obviously a body builder. He was completely bald and wore a loose-fitting T-shirt. His mug, which most of the time could undoubtedly produce the meanest of glares, now appeared quite shocked to have witnessed two people evaporate from the ground before him into thin air. His eyes were still glued to the empty spot on the sidewalk where they had been.

He would never overcome his surprise. Wasting no time, Mark raised a silenced pistol and fired two neat shots into the man's forehead. These two were systematic rapists and Mark had no tolerance for rapists.

Plus, the police couldn't arrest them. There was no crime; Mark had prevented it. If he let them go, they would just rape again, and probably kill at some point, if they hadn't already.

He turned to his right and emptied another couple of rounds into the body of the first attacker who had pushed himself up against the building, still not having yet recovered from Mark's first attack.

"Mark!" Laura screamed.

A bullet slammed into Mark's upper arm, driving him down and to the right. He continued with the natural flow of the motion and rolled, coming up into a kneeling position facing the direction from which he instinctively felt the shot had come. Two more attackers had been hiding in the alleyway and were now rushing him. One of them brandished a gun.

Mark tried to lift his arm to fire, but it wouldn't respond. He'd been shot in his gun arm. He threw himself onto his side to avoid the barrage he knew was coming. Sudden bursts of pain ran through his shoulder as the ground slammed into his wound. Several bullets whizzed over him through the space he'd just occupied.

Deftly, he transferred the gun to his good hand and took aim at the third attacker who held the gun. A couple of well-placed shots ended that threat. The fourth man turned and ran. Mark fired several rounds after him, but only managed to hit his leg before he got away.

Mark sat up, gripping his wounded arm. Blood ran down his sleeve, dripping from his wrist to the concrete below. He didn't know how badly he'd been hit yet. It was still fairly numb from the shock, but enough pain was already flaring up for him to wish it to stay in shock.

"Mark."

She wasn't hysterical or panicked, just concerned as she ran her soft hand over him, checking for other wounds. She examined his arm lightly, careful not to jostle it.

"You're bleeding pretty bad." She removed her leather belt and wrapped it around his upper arm like a tourniquet. "That should help until we get to a doctor."

"I told you it wouldn't be pretty."

"Do you make a habit of getting shot?"

"Very funny."

"You stopped them from hurting me. That's all that matters." She didn't like the way his arm looked. "We need to get you to a doctor."

"We'll shift to yesterday. The police from today will be checking the hospitals for a while looking for men with gunshots."

"Okay."

"What are you doing?"

Laura was rolling the attackers' bodies over one by one and removing their wallets.

"I want to know where these scum bags lived."

***

Sitting on the cold, steel examining table, the weak florescent lighting made Mark's face appear paler than normal. The harsh light even dulled Laura's normally caramel skin to a flat, pasty brown.

"So, what are you gonna do with those wallets?" Mark asked.

"I don't know. I figured we might need to know who they were. Thought maybe they'd done this kind of thing before."

She was holding a gauze pad to his arm as they waited for the doctor to come back and stitch up his wound. It had absorbed as much blood as it was going to, so Laura peeled it off and replaced it with another.

Mark winced in pain. "I'd bet that wasn't their first time. The newspaper report said you had been attacked by only one man."

Laura shuddered at the mention of a newspaper account of a rape she'd been spared.

"That means the group must have made it a practice to assault women together, but took turns as to who actually did the assault. The others would have been waiting in the background, like they did with us, for any unexpected trouble. Shrewd."

"Why would they do that?" She asked.

"Because the police wouldn't be as quick to link the cases that way. It would always seem like a different perp, different description, etc, whereas if the public got wind of a gang going around assaulting women, the police would be searching fast and furious for them."

Laura clenched her fists tightly. "You're right! This couldn't have been the first time. We've got to stop them. Go back and stop them from doing it to *any* woman!"

Mark nodded his head a couple of times slowly.

Laura raised her voice a pitch. "Mark, we've got to stop them!"

"Laura, don't worry. I'm going to stop them. This is what I do for a living."

"I'm going too."

"We'll see."

"I am." Arms crossed, she was resolute.

"I said, we'll see. I won't be doing much of anything for a while, not until my arm heals."

"The doctor said you'd have most of your motion back in two to three weeks."

"Yeah, thankfully it missed my artery and just nicked the bone."

Her voice softened silkily, "I want to take care of you, Mark. I'll nurse you back to health."

Warm blood rushed to his cheeks. He'd had worse wounds than this. He didn't really need the help, but he didn't want to say no.

"Okay."

***

Mark awoke drenched in sweat. His arm throbbed horribly.

Must have an infection.

Good thing the doctor had prescribed him some antibiotics. He struggled to his feet and shuffled to the kitchen, groggily squinting in the dim light.

"Mark, what are you doing up?"

"Got a headache. Infection. Need some pills."

"Here, here. I'll bring them to you, just get back in bed." Laura gently turned him back the way he came. He shuffled back to his room and collapsed on the bed, his head pounding.

Then, she was there. Feeding him his pills, a glass of water in hand. She caressed the fever-dampened hair from his forehead. He felt better already.

"Mark....?"

"Yes."

"I was thinking. Do you know how much money you could make with that thing...that watch of yours?"

"Yeah. I already made billions."

"Oh."

"You want some?"

"Boy, you *are* groggy."

"No, really. No problem. I can make more easy. I'll have a couple of million transferred to your account tomorrow."

"Oookay," she intoned sarcastically.

He'd closed his eyes and was trying to go back to sleep. '*He's actually serious*,' she realized.

"That thing really is powerful, isn't it?" She asked.

"Uh-huh." He wanted to drift off again.

"Mark, could you take care of a guy for me?"

"Who?" He was waking back up now.

"Guy named Dwayne Cole. He owns the club where I work."

"What'd he do to ya?"

"Well, nothing....to me. But most of the girls there, before he'll allow them to dance in his club, he makes them do special favors for him, if you know what I mean."

"Why would they do that?"

"It's good money."

He didn't reply.

"Then, he tries to get all the girls hooked on crack or coke or dope or something else, so they've got to give him all their money to pay for the drugs. When they run out of money, it's back to the special favors again."

"Sounds like a piece of work."

"He is, believe me."

"It also sounds like these girls got into it with their eyes open. He probably *should* be killed.....but not by me."

"Why not?" she huffed.

"'Cause I only kill killers....or rapists. There's a lot of bad people in the world. I gotta draw the line somewhere or I'll just become a common murderer."

She said nothing in response. Her arms were crossed again, forehead creased in anger. It was becoming a familiar gesture of hers.

"Look, you said it yourself. This shifter is a powerful tool. I've got to be careful to never abuse it."

"All right, fine!" She threw her arms down in exasperation. "Can't you do *something*?"

"I'm sure we'll think of something. Now can I go back to sleep?"

"Okay. Here, lay down." She patted the bed. He laid on his good side and she began caressing his hair again. Soon, he was blissfully drifting off.

"Laura?"

"Yes."

"I'm glad I found you."

Chapter 34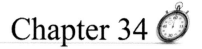

October 8th, 2012, Boston, MA

Mark, Hardy, & Ty met every Monday morning at 9:00 AM at ChronoShift headquarters. They needed to meet regularly in order to coordinate efforts. Theoretically, they could meet every day, or even every hour since time wasn't an issue, but to keep their sanity, it seemed best to maintain some kind of orderly progression of time in the present.

As it was, their bodies would still be living the equivalent of about two weeks for every week that passed in 2012.

Mark had created a relaxed atmosphere in ChronoShift's new and slowly evolving headquarters. Comfortable leather couches and chairs were plentiful, cherry wood paneling and trim gave the place a homey look. A pool table stood in the center of the large meeting room with an antique stained glass light fixture advertising some century-old beer suspended over it. The refrigerators and food pantries were all well stocked. There was even a separate apartment suite for each of them if somebody needed to crash during the day.

The TV was gone. They'd lost their appetite for mindless entertainment once they'd begun making history.

It was like a supreme bachelor pad, but well done. An ideal place to chill and hang out in between missions, yet formal enough to keep the importance of their work in the forefront of their minds.

"Pretty sweet set-up, man," Hardy admired.

"Yeah, we could just live here instead of getting our own places."

Mark laughed. He and Hardy grabbed a couple of pool cues. "You aren't going to play, Ty?"

"Nah."

Mark racked and Hardy broke, sending balls spinning to all corners of the table. He sunk two solids on the break.

"Hey, Mark, I ran into one of those cases last week."

"What 'cases'?"

"You know. Like your kids....somebody that couldn't be saved."

"Oh."

"Yeah, it was this middle-aged guy, name of Pete Bradley. Father of four."

"What happened?"

"Drunk driver hit him. Drunk guy was fine, but Bradley died from his injuries at the scene. I tried at least seven different ways to save the guy, but nothing worked. It was like....it was like there was this invisible hand over the event, keeping it from being changed."

"I haven't had one like that yet," Ty said.

Mark concentrated on making his shots, saying nothing.

"Why do you think that happens, Mark?"

"How should I know?"

"It's God, man," Ty declared.

Mark cocked an eyebrow Ty's way. This wasn't the first time Ty had indicated some kind of strong religious belief.

"Sorry, don't buy that," Hardy refuted, "It's obviously some kind of time paradox. The reason Mark couldn't save his kids was because it would have created an unsustainable paradox. Sorry, Mark, I hate to bring that back up."

Mark waved dismissively.

"Look," Hardy continued, "Mark only found these shifters because of his tragedy. If it hadn't happened, he never would have been in those woods. If he used his shifter to undo the very event that caused him to find the shifters, then how could he find the shifters and still undo the event. It's a paradox, man. Plain and simple."

Mark's complexion darkened as the conversation progressed, though neither of the other men noticed.

"Then how do you explain this guy Bradley that you couldn't save?" countered Ty.

"I don't know. That's why I'm asking. Maybe saving him would have caused some paradox we're not able to perceive ahead of time."

"Like what?"

"I don't know."

"Bradley died *after* Mark found the shifters, so there's no way his living could cause a conflict with that."

"The space-time continuum is a pretty complex thing, buddy. We'll never understand all the complexities and interactions of every event and person in history. Maybe if Bradley had lived, he, himself, or someone he knew, would have gotten a hold of a shifter in the future and gone back and stopped Mark from finding them."

"That's reaching, dude."

"Look, we, of all people, know how fictional the line between past and future actually is. The order of events doesn't mean squat."

"I'll give you that, but answer me this. Who is monitoring these potential space-time paradoxes and preventing them?"

"So, what do you think it is, hot shot? Why would God get involved?" Hardy missed sinking the fourteen ball in the corner pocket by a hair. "Your turn, Mark."

"I don't think....I *know*," Ty stated emphatically, "God has predestined all things. Nothing is accidental. And the things he doesn't want changed, we aren't able to change."

Hardy looked like he'd passed beyond skeptical and had moved on to incredulous. "If everything is predestined, then how is that we *can* change so many things."

"Simple. We were predestined to change them."

Hardy choked and spewed out some Coke he'd been drinking. "That's rich, man." He wiped his mouth with his sleeve and got some paper towels to clean up the mess he'd just made. He was trying to control his smirk to mask some of the ridicule he was feeling. After all, Ty was a friend.

"So, you're saying that God ordained Mark's kids to die."

"All life and all death is in God's hands. Nothing happens without His permission or even, to be truthful, His causing it." Ty was confident.

Mark, who'd been completely quiet on the matter until now, suddenly threw his cue down in anger.

Shaking a finger at Ty, he declared, "I don't want any part of a God who would take Daniel and Brittany from me so....so....capriciously!" He spat the last word. Then, turning to Hardy, he said, "And you! I don't care what kind of 'paradox' it creates. I'd give up these shifters and all the money in the world in a heartbeat if it would get me my kids back!"

Mark kicked over an end table, sending a lamp crashing to the floor. "And I don't want to ever talk about this again, you hear! That goes for both of you!" With that, he stormed out of the room.

Ty and Hardy looked at each other. They knew how sensitive Mark was on the subject of his kids and realized they'd been too flippant. "I'll go," Ty said.

He caught up to Mark in the hallway.

"Mark, wait up, man."

Mark stopped. "Go away, Ty. I don't want to talk about it."

Ty took his arm gently, preventing him from going further. "Look, Mark, we're sorry. I mean, we know how much it must hurt, but if we're gonna be shifting around through time, these kind of discussions are gonna be necessary. We've got to understand why things happen the way they do."

Mark sighed heavily, tension flowing from his shoulders as they slumped low. "I know," he whispered, "I'm sorry. You're right. I just can't take it. I don't want to think about it."

"Look at it this way. If we can figure out what's preventing these people from being saved every now and then, we might be able to figure out a way to get around whatever's blocking you from saving your kids."

Mark looked up, a new gleam in his eye. "But if *you're* right, Ty, then there's no way I can save them, period."

"That's true."

Mark stared at him.

***

"Sit down, Rialto."

Alex seated himself smoothly in the stiff leather chair facing his boss' desk.

"Sir."

"I got word today that you requested a wiretap on Mark Carpen."

"Yes, sir."

"I distinctly remember ordering you to drop that case, Rialto. What do you think this is? Your own private investigation agency?"

"Actually, you just said to put it on the back burner for a while, but I found some things in his file that I felt warranted a follow-up."

"Like....?" Pennington looked like he wasn't in the mood for wrong answers.

"It appears somebody's been forging Carpen's signature on all of his tax returns for the past 25 years. On top of that, this same person forged the signature on all the tax returns for his father and his grandfather. Meaning, the same person has been forging these signatures for over *70 years.*"

"Okay. Let's say I believe it. So what?"

"So what? That's forgery. There's something very suspicious going on there."

"What else you got?"

"Nothing else....yet."

"What do you have for me on the Santos gang?"

Rialto stared at his shoes. "Still working on it."

Pennington's face turned a bright shade of scarlet. His words were measured and clipped.

"Let me get this straight, Rialto. You've been traipsing around following this Carpen guy — a guy who's paid us *billions* in taxes mind you — with nothing more to go on than a hunch and a suspected forged signature, yet you have completely ignored the Santos case? Does that about sum it up?"

"Uh...."

It seemed steam might erupt from Pennington's ears at any moment.

"Let me ask you a *question*, agent." His tone dripped with sarcasm. "To the best of your knowledge, is Mark Carpen smuggling thousands of tons of cocaine into the United States each year? Has Carpen set off bombs outside government buildings in Mexico killing dozens of civilians? Is the *dreaded* Mark Carpen responsible for the murders of three United States DEA agents?"

"No, sir!"

"May I humbly suggest, *agent*, that you get your priorities straight! You're lucky I don't land your rear in a sling for this stunt. Heck, I'll be lucky if the President doesn't land mine in one. You will drop this Carpen case, and you will drop it right now. Is that clear?"

"Yes, sir!"

"You will get to work on the Santos' case and have results for me yesterday. And if I hear one more word about this Carpen nonsense, you'll be looking for work elsewhere, got it?"

Rialto nodded his understanding and slunk out of the room with his tail between his legs. He understood all right. It wouldn't be difficult to get some dirt on the Santos gang. He'd pull an all-nighter or two and get Pennington what he needed. That was no problem.

He certainly didn't think he deserved that kind of a berating, not with his exemplary record, but the President was probably breathing down Pennington's neck, as the man himself had said. No, he didn't blame Pennington for the outburst. The real culprit was Mark Carpen.

Carpen had won this round. He was up to something, of that Rialto had no doubt. For now, he was stuck, and he'd have to keep any further investigations close to the vest. Rialto wouldn't rest though. Even if it took him years, he would get Carpen for this humiliation. No one pulled the wool over Alex Rialto's eyes.

Chapter 35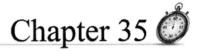

October 12th, 2012, Washington, D.C.

"Whatcha got for me, McGuire?"

Tony McGuire was a senior field agent with the FBI. He was based in Boston and he owed Alex Rialto a number of favors for tips Alex had passed to him on some key Mafia cases.

"Not a lot, but there was one thing that may be of help. Last year, Carpen approached an antique coin dealer wanting to manufacture mass quantities of historically accurate antique coin molds. Carpen specified that he wanted these molds to produce coins that would be indistinguishable from the real thing. The coin dealer thought Carpen might have been trying to flood the market with fake coins, so he refused the job. Couldn't shake the thought that something was up, though, so he contacted us so we could investigate."

"Did you?"

"No, we had a lot more pressing cases at the time, so this got set aside. Plus, no actual crime had occurred yet. You know how that goes."

"Yeah, I do. Is that all?"

"The guy's pretty clean. Checked through the entire FBI database, and there's nothing else significant on him, or his father or grandfather. Had a couple of other hits on the name Mark Carpen, but they weren't the same guy, different social security numbers. One was a drug dealer out in California, and he's still in prison. The other was a guy from Georgia who lost his kids in a car accident. That guy's wife divorced him after the accident and he pretty much dropped off the face of the earth a little more than a year ago."

"What's the name of this coin dealer?"

"Clyde Moore. I'll email you all his pertinent info along with the case file."

"I trust you kept this under wraps like I asked?"

"Yeah, don't worry. I was discreet."

"Good. Keep it that way. Pennington will have my hide if he learns I'm investigating Carpen again."

"Well, for what it's worth, something does seem off about that coin order. My instinct would be what the dealer suspected, an attempt to make a quick buck off fake antique coins."

"But why bother if you're already worth billions? Doesn't seem worth the time."

"Don't know."

"All right, thanks Tony." They hung up.

He would be paying that coin dealer a visit in the near future.

***

Moore's shop wasn't nearly as sophisticated as Rialto had expected. It looked like a Mom & Pop jewelry shop, except the glass display cases were filled with rows of age-worn pieces of money instead of rings and bracelets. The owner sat on a stool behind the counter eying a golden coin through an eyepiece. He was about thirty pounds overweight and balding, with tufts of grey hair highlighting the sides of his head.

Alex stepped in and flipped open his wallet, displaying his credentials and ignoring the customer Moore was currently assisting.

"Clyde Moore. IRS. I need to speak with you please." His tone was commanding, indicating it was not a request.

"Uh....sure. Excuse me for a moment," he said to the customer. "Let's go to the back office."

"Sorry about the interruption." Once again, Rialto's tone implied he wasn't.

"No problem. What's this about?"

"Mark Carpen. Name ring a bell?"

"Ah. I wondered when somebody would get back to me on that. Did you find out anything?"

"That's why I'm here, actually. Carpen's name came up in another investigation and I need you to tell me everything you can remember about him."

"Okay."

"I understand he tried to place an order with you to create some antique coin molds."

"Yeah, a big order too."

"What exactly did he want?"

"He wanted me to make a bunch of coin molds so he could fabricate thousands of antique coins. Said they had to be exactly like the originals, so even an expert couldn't tell the difference."

"How many did he want?"

"Over a thousand molds. He wanted a mold for every major coin in use for the past 500 years in over 20 different countries."

"Wow."

"That's what I said. I mean, I don't know why he thought I could even do such a job. It would have required hiring a number of very skilled coin specialists to help make the molds, and even then it would have taken years to complete."

"What did he offer to pay you?"

"$4 million."

Rialto's eyebrows took a turn upward. "That's not chump change. Would that have covered your expenses?"

"Definitely, and with a ridiculous amount of profit to boot. Almost all the cost would have been in paying a couple of specialists for research and craftsmanship for several years, but I could have done that for under $500,000."

"Yet you turned it down."

"I'm a purist, Mr. Rialto, not a crook. I love antique coins. Anybody offering that kind of money for molds can't be up to any good."

"How much could he have made counterfeiting these coins?"

"Well....I don't know....assuming an average value of $500, I guess he could have made about a million dollars if he made a couple of each."

"Yet he offered you $4 million."

"I said if he made a *couple* of each. There would be no limit to how many he could make with molds."

"Wouldn't the coins he made seem too new to be taken for the real thing?"

"There are ways to make them look aged."

"What about selling them? Wouldn't it be difficult to dispense with a huge number of antique coins that the market didn't know about?"

"He'd have used intermediaries so the coins wouldn't be traced to him, but yeah, he'd still be limited by the normal rules of supply and demand. If he flooded the market with any one coin, collectors would catch on that something was up."

"So, it'd take a while for him to recoup his investment?"

"Yeah."

"What did he say he was planning to do with the molds?"

"Said he was creating a replica coin company for enthusiasts who couldn't afford the real thing. He assured me every coin he made was going to bear a stamp indicating it was a replica. I just couldn't trust that."

"Who else would have the capability of doing this work for him since you turned it down?"

"Here," Moore pulled a piece of paper from his desk drawer and began to write. "I'll make a list of people who have the expertise to do such a thing. There aren't that many. Only one other guy here in the Boston area."

Rialto took the list and thanked Moore for his time. He didn't think Carpen would be wasting his time trying to fence counterfeit antique coins. From what Moore had said, it would have taken him several years to begin to recoup his initial investment, and the profit would be minuscule compare to the billions he was already worth. When you're earning $200 million *per month* in interest on your current holdings, why would you put everything at risk with a criminal enterprise that would net you only a few million over several years? It didn't make sense. Something else was up, and Rialto intended to figure out what.

Chapter 36

October 12th, 2012, Boston, MA

"So, *what,* exactly, is it you want me to do?" Mark asked.

He studied the strong, beautiful lines of her face. Her skin looked like caramelized cream this morning, like a perfect latte. He wanted to run his finger across its softness, but regardless of how enamored he was, Mark wasn't about to check his principles at the door.

"I want you to *take care* of him," she said again.

She was referring to Dwayne Cole, her old boss, the owner of the strip club where she had worked.

"Why? What has he done that would justify it? Has he murdered anybody? Did he rape you, or any of the girls who worked with you?"

"No....not exactly."

"What do you mean 'not exactly'? He either did or he didn't."

"Then, no. No, he didn't, but he certainly made all of our lives a living hell. I've had two different girlfriends OD and die from the drugs he gave them."

"But they chose to take the drugs right? And they came to him looking for work? He wasn't holding anybody there against their will, was he?"

"I can't believe how cold-hearted you are!" She spat disgustedly.

"No! Look, I *feel* for them. I'd love to help them in any way we can. The guy sounds like pure trash, but I can't just go murder somebody because they're a filthy pig. This shifter, it's powerful. It's not to be abused. Can't you see that?"

She sighed forcefully, slowly resigning herself to the fact that she wasn't going to wear him down.

"Listen," he said, "Let me go back and investigate. I'm sure we can put him out of business without resorting to murder."

"All right, but I'm coming with you."

Mark shut his eyes, mentally kicking himself. He should have just gone back alone without saying anything. She was obviously unreasonable with regards to the guy and would only be a hindrance to him working effectively. He knew there would be no arguing with her this time.

"Fine, but this is the last time you come along on a shift without me agreeing."

"Fine."

Dwayne Cole ran a messy operation. The strip club, like all of its kind, was located in a run-down part of town. The faded pink stucco exterior, which was meant to look alluring under a plethora of bright blue neon lights at night, only looked drab, lifeless, and decaying during the day. Light had an amazing ability to reveal the truth about something.

The lights inside the "club" were kept on permanent dim, using darkness to create a mysterious ambiance. Yet, Mark was sure if those same lights were turned up, you would suddenly see what a dump the place was. Cracks and dirt and filth in all its corners. Peeling trim, scuffed paint, and deeply stained carpet. Its appeal was a lie.

Cole's back office was in fact, the only office. The only other room in the place, besides a stockroom, was the ladies' dressing room. Mark had no desire to go in there. They were just here to investigate.

Cole's office was a dingy mess. Dirty clothes, crumpled papers, and food wrappers were strewn about chaotically.

"So, what are we looking for?"

"I don't know. Let's see if we can find his stash."

"Where does he get his drugs from?"

"A local guy named Rudy."

"Did you use?"

She shot him a sidelong glance. "No, I wasn't that stupid. I knew why he was always pushing us to take them. Here it is!"

She had pulled hard enough to pop open one of the lower drawers in Cole's desk. Inside was what looked to be an enormous amount of drugs. Heroin, Cocaine, Marijuana. You name it, it was in there.

Mark grinned. "Let's flush it all. That's gotta be a tremendous amount of money he's got invested."

She returned the smile.

They dumped all of Cole's stash in the toilet, though there was so much of it, it took four flushes to drown it all.

"That oughta set him back a while," Mark said, "Let's head back. I'm gonna brainstorm. I'm sure there are some other things we can do to make this guy's life uncomfortable."

Laura laughed. "Yeah, this alone is going to make him pretty mad, let me tell you."

Over the next few days, Mark took his time shifting in and out of Dwayne Cole's business. One day, he stole his guns, the next, his money. Then, he reported him to the Health Department. He stole and flushed the guy's drugs four different times. Cole installed all kinds of security measures to try and catch the thief. He even started living in the club 24/7 for a while, but of course, Mark just shifted around him.

The pimp bought a small safe to store the drugs in, but Mark just slipped in and shifted out with the safe under his arm. After he'd blown it open, he returned it empty. Mark wished he could have seen the guy's face when he walked back into that office and saw the safe with its door blown off.

Then, Mr. Dwayne Cole started storing his stuff at home. Of course, this didn't stop Mark either. The fun finally came to an end, though. Cole eventually abandoned everything, the club, the house, and was never heard from again. Mark guessed he had gone deep in debt to some drug lords trying to keep his stash up and had to run for his life when he couldn't pay them back. His girls were jumping ship right and left since he couldn't keep them high or paid. The Health Department shutting him down for a week certainly didn't help either.

In the end, Mark was content. He felt like the guy had gotten what he deserved, and a good scare to boot. Well, maybe not everything he deserved, but it was all Mark was willing to do. He thought Laura was happy with the results too. Which was what was important.

Chapter 37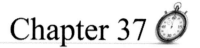

You've been searchin' from here to Singapore
Ain't it time that you noticed the girl next door baby, why not me?

"Why Not Me?"

~ The Judds

October 22nd, 2012, Boston, MA

The sun was up, bold and bright in the clear blue sky, marking a new day. A beautiful day.

Mark and Laura strolled into the office, full of smiles and laughter. They had dated for several weeks now, and Mark was overjoyed with the power of the relationship, with the way it seemed to fill a deep hole he'd born since Kelly had abandoned him. There were moments when he worried that maybe he was latching on to her too quickly, but the happiness he felt washed those concerns down the river before he could even weigh them.

He felt so good about their budding relationship, he was ready to introduce her to the rest of the crew.

"Good morning, Savannah," Mark called as they swept in.

Savannah sat gracefully behind her desk outside Mark's office working on the latest report for him on her computer. Her white cotton skirt draped daintily along the line of her legs, its hem angled so that one end revealed a bare knee while the other corner reached her ankles at the heel. A fresh, blue pastel blouse graced her shoulders, and her honey-streaked hair was wound up in a bun as usual. A pair of thin, red-rimmed glasses had slipped down toward the tip of her finely chiseled nose, but she pushed them back up as Mark and Laura waltzed in.

"Good morning, Mark," she replied.

"Savannah, this is Laura. Laura, Savannah. Savannah's been a huge help to us. She's our primary historical researcher."

Savannah blushed lightly at the compliment.

"Nice to meet you." Laura extended her hand.

They shook hands abruptly, a faint and unusual tension between them.

"C'mon, Laura," Mark said, "I'll show you the rest of the place."

Savannah watched them go, pursing her lips. She did not know the woman and had been surprised by her arrival. She was instinctively protective of Mark, and her first impression of this new woman left her feeling like Mark could do better. Something else about it made her distinctively uncomfortable, but she couldn't put her finger on it. Reluctantly, she returned her attention to editing the report.

***

Angelo Lombardi was the name of the only other coin specialist in the Boston area Clyde Moore had thought would be capable of making the molds Mark Carpen had wanted.

Alex Rialto appeared at Lombardi's shop in person, as he had Moore's, but Lombardi was much more reticent to talk. Rialto could tell the guy just wanted to get rid of him. The Italian coin dealer completely denied having ever heard of Mark Carpen, or anyone else requesting antique coin molds for that matter. Clearly, he was holding something back. A trained investigator instinctively knows when someone is lying.

It didn't take much effort to prove it. A visit to Lombardi's bank provided Rialto with copies of his account records over the past year, which revealed deposits of several large checks made out to him by a company called Historical

Enterprises. The checks totaled a little over $4 million. A little more investigation and Rialto discovered that Lombardi had not declared this as income when he'd filed his taxes. *Now,* things were getting juicy.

A visit to the Secretary of State's website and Alex found the registered agent for Historical Enterprises was none other than Mark Carpen himself. Rialto had more than enough to put Lombardi in jail for tax evasion, but the link to Carpen was still pretty weak. He had no proof that Mark had done anything illegal with those coin molds.

The next step was a hardline interrogation of Lombardi. It likely wouldn't be too difficult to get Lombardi to take an immunity deal on his failure to pay taxes in exchange for squealing on Carpen. Even if he had to encourage Lombardi to make something up, he would. Carpen was the big fish and he was up to something. As long as Rialto got him in the end, it didn't matter for what.

* * *

October 24th, 2012, Boston, MA

"Yes, Savannah?"

"There's a Mr. Lombardi on the phone for you, Mark."

"Okay. Thanks. Put him through."

Angelo Lombardi was thoroughly rattled. He told Mark about the visit he'd had from the IRS, how he'd failed to declare the payments from Mark as income, and the IRS agent's endless questions about Mark. Angelo insisted he'd denied even knowing Mark, but the guy had been relentless.

"You didn't have to deny knowing me, Angelo, or that I paid you," Mark said, "I'm not doing anything criminal."

"Well....I didn't know. I wanted to be safe....just in case."

"You were protecting your own butt is what it was. Don't worry about it. Call my attorney, and he'll take care of it for you, but you're going to have to pay back taxes plus penalties. We'll try to get the penalties waived."

"Sure, Mark."

Mark gave him the contact info for his tax attorney and hung up. Then, he picked the handset back up and paged Savannah.

"Yes, Mark?"

"Savannah, please get me Senator O'Brien on the phone right away."

***

"You wanted to see me, Sir?"

Sanford Pennington did not look happy. He motioned for Rialto to take a seat.

"Rialto, I won't beat around the bush. I just got a call from the Senate Majority Leader about you."

"About me?"

"Have you been harassing Mark Carpen again?"

"Uh....not directly. I've been investigating him."

"After I gave you a direct order to stop," Pennington affirmed.

"Well...." Rialto was caught completely off guard by this attack, though he guessed he should have expected it.

"Have you found any evidence of wrongdoing?"

"Yes. Last year, Carpen ordered some molds made so he could fabricate counterfeit antique coins in mass quantities."

"That's what the call was about all right. Rialto, you *do* realize that Carpen has some powerful friends in Congress. He's contributed to a lot of campaigns."

"No, I didn't know that, but it doesn't change anything."

"Carpen maintains the molds were to start a replica coin company which never got off the ground."

"I'm sure that's what he says."

"Do you have any evidence he's done anything else with those molds?"

"Not yet, but..."

"But? But what?! How long have you been working on this?" Pennington was getting madder.

"Uh...."

"Let me take a guess. Since I told you to stop? Is that right?"

Alex nodded.

"Okay, so, a powerful multi-billionaire has been paying this government *billions* in taxes. You, an expert investigator, can't find anything wrong with his returns that would normally launch an investigation. I order you to stop. You then disobey my *direct order*, neglecting to investigate real, known criminals, simply because you've got a feeling something's not quite right with the guy. After making me look bad in front of the President of the United States with the Santos gang screw-up, you harass Carpen's business associates until I start getting phone calls from Senators. And you still don't have anything to show for it."

"Sir, I just need more time..."

"You don't get it do you, Rialto?" Pennington slammed his fist onto the desk. "You work for me and for the government of the United States of America! You don't get to go around investigating whoever suits your fancy. I don't care how many cases you've cracked in the past. Is that clear?"

"Yes, sir. I'll drop it." He'd let it go for a few months until Pennington calmed down, then pick up the trail again.

"You'll do more than drop it. Your work's been suffering lately. I'm busting you down to customer service."

"Customer service?" Rialto burst to his feet.

"You got it. Permanently."

"Sir," he pled, "You can't be serious. I'm a good investigator."

"You've left me with no options, Rialto. You stepped on the wrong toes at the wrong time, and with nothing to show for it."

Rialto's face turned purple in silent rage. Balling his fists, he stammered, "Then, you can have my resignation!"

"I'd like that even better, actually."

Carpen!

Carpen would pay for this. He would find a way to get even with him, no matter how long it took.

Chapter 38

You always had an eye for things that glittered...

"Just to See You Smile"

~ Tim Mcgraw

"You look beautiful tonight."

"Thank you, Mark."

Candlelight glittered and danced on the gemstones adorning Laura's neck. Matching ornaments graced her earlobes and wrists. Her dress was from one of Back Bay's high end fashion shops. After spending an entire afternoon of shopping together, mainly for her, they were now enjoying a luxurious dinner at one of Boston's finest restaurants.

Maybe if I'd been able to do things like this for Kelly, we'd still be together.

He couldn't take his eyes from Laura, and his heart seemed to be following suit in hypnotic lock-step. In store after store, her magnetism had this magical way of lifting his wallet from his pocket and effortlessly placing it the hand of the shopkeeper — and he normally hated shopping.

"So, what's next, Mark? What are you planning to do with that shifter?"

"Not sure yet. Savannah's drawing me up a list of tragedies I can go back and try to fix."

"I was thinking, what if you tried to become the richest man in the world?"

Mark laughed. "Yeah, I guess I probably could, but why? We've got more than we can possibly spend as it is now."

"Just to do it, I guess. If you've got something as powerful as that thing is, you should use it."

Mark scowled.

"There are lots of good things we can do, and we *are* going to do many of them, but I don't think the endless pursuit of wealth is admirable in of itself."

It was her turn to frown. "You don't always have to be such a goodie-goodie, you know. Why can't you do those other things and still pursue wealth too? How about we buy an island? I've always wanted to have my own island."

A slight smile returned to Mark's face. "Sure, sure. No reason we can't do that. We've got all the time in world."

***

July 17th, 2027, 2:00 AM, Boston, MA

To be exact, fifteen years is what it took Alexander Rialto to find his method of revenge.

The year was now 2027. Since the day he'd quit the IRS, he had been forced to work as a menial tax preparer at various storefront operations in order to support himself. It was humiliating, but it allowed him to moonlight as a private eye. A private eye with just one case.

After fifteen years of investigation, Rialto believed he had finally discovered the secret to Mark Carpen's wealth, and he had figured it out without the use of government resources too. At first, he had refrained from soliciting the help of friends and other government contacts just because he wanted to keep a low profile. Later, as his suspicions mounted, he had decided he didn't want the government to get wise to Carpen for other reasons. No, once he figured out Carpen's secret, Rialto realized he could use it for himself. The IRS and the good ol' U.S. of A. could go jump in a lake.

Staring at his hands, he thought about how much older they looked. This morning, when standing in front of the mirror, he'd keenly noticed all the gray in his hair. He shouldn't have had to wait this long. Fifteen years of his life were gone, wasted. Which was especially ironic if Carpen's secret was what he thought it was.

He squinted to see better in the dim light offered by the street lamps. The shadowy figure, which had to be Carpen's friend, Ty Jennings, was moving along the sidewalk toward him. He was now approaching a yellowish pool of light emanating from the lamp post nearest Rialto. This large black man should have been almost 90 years old by now, but he still looked 50.

Ty didn't see Rialto as he passed. Firmly holding a silenced .38, Rialto stood from behind the bush concealing his position and extended his left hand. One short spit from the muzzle and Ty lay prone on the ground, blood welling from a hole in the back of his head.

Rialto crept toward the body, unsure of the accuracy of his shot. Sure enough, it had been dead on. Jennings was dead.

A strange whirring sounded from the part of the man's body that interested him the most, his left wrist.

The watch. That strangely futuristic, smooth, gray wristwatch that Rialto had observed on the wrists of all three men, Carpen, Jennings, and Phillips. The watch was making the whirring sound.

Its band was expanding, loosening actually, from Ty's wrist. Rialto reached down and slipped it off. He examined it carefully, looking for some key to its use. It didn't take but a few moments to figure out the significance of the numbers on the digital displays.

He slipped the watch onto his own wrist. It whirred again, tightening its band until it fit snugly. It felt good.

He used the smaller buttons to play with the numbers of one of the displays. His breathing accelerated, chest heaving in anticipation. There was only one way to be sure.

He pushed the red button.

Chapter 39

January 28th, 2013, Boston, MA

"I wouldn't go in there if I were you," Savannah warned Hardy.

Savannah had taken the brunt of Mark's tirade so far this morning. She didn't know what had brought it on, but she guessed it had something to do with that woman Laura. He'd been a mess ever since she'd broken up with him a few weeks before.

"He's in a foul mood today, and I mean *foul*," Savannah said.

"What happened?" Hardy asked. This morning, he was dressed in beige khakis, medium-toned leather loafers, a white polo shirt, and a matching navy blue sailing jacket and cap.

"Not sure yet. I've been trying to keep a low profile," she said, eyeing his odd dress. "You know it's January, right? It's only 38 degrees out."

"I'm going boating in the harbor. I'm gonna shift forward to June first though, so it'll be a little warmer."

The sound of something crashing to the floor echoed from Mark's office. The door slammed open, hard enough to cause the surrounding walls to shake. Mark filled the opening, eyes blazing.

"Where are you off to, Hardy? Going *sailing*? With who?"

"What are you talking about, Mark?"

"You know exactly what, you jerk! With Laura, right! You're going with Laura?"

Hardy's mouth snapped closed. His face turned beet red.

"You are, aren't you?" Mark pushed.

Slowly, Hardy nodded once.

"Oh boy," Savannah whispered. She ducked a bit and pushed herself back from her desk to avoid the melee she knew was coming.

"I knew it! I saw you two together last night!" Mark unconsciously swept up the lamp from Savannah's desk as he strode to Hardy. He jammed his left forearm into Hardy's throat and shoved him violently against the wall, lifting Hardy's feet a full six inches off the ground. Mark's face burned red with rage and his muscles strained and rippled under the force of it. Neither Hardy nor Savannah had ever seen him this angry. Pulsing veins bulged in his temples and neck.

Hardy choked for breath from the hold Mark had on his throat. He'd been taken by complete surprise, dumbfounded by his friend's attack, but seeing Mark raise the lamp to smash in his skull shook Hardy from the surrealism of the moment. Savannah screamed.

He chopped Mark sharply on the side of the neck with a blow that was designed to stun. Hardy never would have gotten that shot in if Mark hadn't been so blinded by fury.

Mark collapsed to the floor, uttering guttural gurgles.

"What in the world is going on here?" Ty boomed from the front door.

Hardy didn't answer. He was busy staring at Mark's prostrate form on the floor. Mark struggled to his feet, hand holding his neck, his face still twisted in anger.

"How long have you been seeing her, you scum? How long were you seeing her behind my back, *friend?*" Mark's head swayed back and forth, tears streaming down his face. Whether they were tears of fury, or simply a broken heart, even he didn't know.

"I didn't steal her from you, Mark!" Hardy rubbed his throat.

"What is this about?" Ty repeated, eyeing Savannah for help.

"I think it's about Laura," she interjected.

"You're dang right it's about Laura!" Mark yelled. "This lying Judas has been sneaking around with her on me, probably from the start. *I gave you everything, you lowlife! Everything!*"

Mark charged again, but Ty intercepted him, holding his friends apart with a hand on each of their chests.

"This is stupid! Neither one of you should be going after that tramp! She's a manipulative wench. Look what's she's doing to us!"

Mark laid a hard punch into Ty's jaw. In return, Ty sucker punched Mark in the stomach, who collapsed to the floor again, gasping for air.

"Watch it, Ty," Hardy warned softly. "Don't talk about her like that."

"What's the matter with both of you? Can't you see what she is? Get out of here, Hardy. Don't you see Mark ain't in the right mind to deal with you?" He ushered Hardy to the door. "Let's go."

"Fine, but watch what you say, Ty. I love her," Hardy whispered on the way out.

Ty shook his head in wonderment. He mouthed to Savannah '*Take care of him*', pointing to Mark. She nodded that she understood, and both the other men left.

Mark was curled up in a fetal position on the floor. His chest jerked in and out as he wept. He wasn't even trying to disguise his grief anymore, he was so lost in it. Savannah had never seen him like this.

She knelt beside him and tried to bring comfort. Cradling his head in her hands, she wiped the tears as they fell.

"No. No! Just leave me alone!" Mark leapt up and stormed into the recesses of his office, slamming the door behind him.

Savannah stood there motionless for a moment, staring after him. Then, she went back to her desk and waited in case he changed his mind or needed something. She waited all day. And she would wait even longer than that.

Chapter 40

What was I s'posed to do, standing there looking at you
Lonely boy far from home

"Maybe it was Memphis"

~ Pam Tillis

February 4th, 2010, Baltimore, MD

The sterilized lab looked like it could be part of a state-of-the-art medical facility, but it was actually in the middle of a run-down industrial park outside Baltimore, Maryland. A knowledgeable observer would have noticed right away that the equipment lining the walls and covering the stainless steel counters, while being top of the line technology, was not your standard medical equipment. This lab was much more suited for semi-conductors than an EKG monitor or a Bunsen burner.

Stanley Irvine ran this physics lab for Alexander Rialto. Irvine held a Masters from Cal Tech and a PhD from MIT, both in Physics. His doctoral thesis had been on the possibility of hyperspace and time travel using wormholes.

He looked the part of a scientist. A white lab coat reached his knees, revealing dark brown corduroys underneath. He was of slight build and his thin-rimmed glasses topped off the stereotypical image.

Stanley had been your everyday nerd throughout high school, marginalized by the other kids, but he had gained a new found confidence in college as he'd matured and found his calling in the study of physics. He was now a thorough professional, one of the top of his field, consulted by both U.S. and European companies and governments.

This was the reason Rialto had sought him out and made him an offer he couldn't refuse. For Stanley, the financial incentive had been overwhelmingly attractive, but the opportunity to work on a real life, working time machine had been simply irresistible. He would have worked on it for free, but he wasn't telling Rialto that.

Stanley had made a list of all the equipment he would need to study the device, and amazingly, Rialto had put together a completed laboratory in just two days.

He removed his glasses with his right hand and set them on the counter to his side, a gesture that meant he was interrupting his perennial reading to give someone his full attention.

"So, what have you learned?" Rialto queried.

"Quite a lot, actually."

Rialto leaned back against the counter, arms loose, eyes fixed on his employee.

"Of course, we confirmed some of your original observations, the 6 shift limit, the translateral compensation...."

"The what?"

"Translateral compensation. The device translates, or moves, your body within the 3 physical dimensions if it detects an object occupying your current physical position in your target time. Basically, it automatically calculates the shortest distance you would need to be moved so you don't pop up in the middle of an unexpected object, which I'm sure would result in your death, not to mention the violations of the Pauli Exclusion Principle which would occur. However, since the Principle can't be violated, if you did pop up within another object, it could theoretically cause you, or the matter around you, to be converted into huge amounts of released energy. The resulting explosion would be on an atomic level."

"What are the limits of this trans....lateral compensation?"

"Not sure yet. I'm working on it. It's really quite a sophisticated feature. Not only is it able to analyze and identify the limits of your body and clothing, it's able to correctly detect objects of all sizes, shapes, and materials in a different time before you arrive there. Somehow, it is able to treat time as nothing more than a 4th dimension. It can see through time just like a camera can see what's in front of it. Then, to top it all off, it is capable of effectively "teleporting" you out of the way. Not to mention it can do all this with a relatively tiny power source. According to today's science, we calculate the energy needed to do such things would be astronomical — literally. This "time machine" is way out of the realm of what anybody on Earth is currently capable of engineering. In short, it should not exist."

"Where did it come from then? Who made it? Aliens?"

"No way to know. I can't find a way to access the watch's interior to study its working parts. There's no access panel on top or underneath. I tried to x-ray it, but the metal casing blocks x-rays just as if it were made of lead."

Securing a second watch for Irvine to study had been a simple enough matter. After taking Ty Jennings' watch, Rialto had been able to move through time at ease. He'd stalked Hardy Phillips in 2027, just like he had Jennings, and now he had two watches.

The physicist had been like a kid in a candy shop receiving it and had been examining it for weeks now under an extensive barrage of tests. Rialto had issued him one clear and very strict stipulation. He was at no point to ever put the device on his wrist. Irvine had thus far obeyed.

"It's completely seamless," the scientist continued, "You said the band automatically constricted around your wrist when you put it on, and there's no apparent way to get it off that I can find. I expected there would be some kind of electric motor inside that would reel the band in when it detects the electrical field of your body. However, there are no slits where the band meets the body of the watch. That indicates to me that *the band itself* contracted. The metallic material is apparently able to contract or expand when stimulated by electricity.

"Which brings me to another oddity. I cannot identify the metal. I've tried taking shavings, but it's too hard a material for any of my blades. I even tried drilling it with a diamond-tipped bit, but no luck. Wherever it came from, this is the most advanced device I could imagine encountering. Aliens....maybe. In my opinion, it's more likely from the future. The displays operate with the English notations of AM and PM, and aliens would not use such nomenclature. That would also seem to eliminate the military. I think the future is a safe bet. It *is* a time machine after all."

"What about the display material?"

"Definitely not glass or plastic, at least not any plastic I'm familiar with. Maybe a materials engineer would recognize it."

"Did you try drilling that?"

"No, I was afraid of damaging it to the point it wouldn't be useable anymore."

"Go ahead and do what you need to. I can get more."

Stanley arched his eyebrows and cocked his head, a mixture of surprise and incredulity on his face. "You know, if you have such easy access to the future, you might consider using some physicists from then to do this research."

"Are you tired of working on it already?"

"Not at all! This is the greatest opportunity of my career. However, my job is to advise you according to what's in your best interest, not my own."

"Fine. I'll take your suggestion into consideration. What else did you learn?"

"Well, as I said, there seemed to be no apparent way to get the watch off your wrist once you put it on, but I may have figured out a way to do it."

"How?"

"I'll show you in a minute. I think you'll be more excited about my next discovery."

"Well, man, don't keep me waiting."

"I made an educated guess that whenever you shifted through time, there would be some kind of disturbance in the electro-magnetic field surrounding you as you went. That's why I had you shift in and out so much here in the lab. I set up some instruments that could detect fluctuations in the electro-magnetic field around your person. As it turns out, there *are* slight differences in the fluctuations which appear to correspond uniquely to the time to which you're traveling. When I had you shift to different years, or even hours, the fluctuations were distinct, but when you shifted to the same time over and over again, some of the fluctuations were identical."

"Yeah, well, I can tell you, it was quite unnerving to see so many versions of myself in the same room at the same time. So, what does all that mean?"

"It means that I think I can build you a device using today's technology which could remotely detect the time to which a person has shifted."

"So, if I were to shift to 1798, for example, with this other detection device, you could know that I'd gone to the year 1798 without having seen the display on my watch?"

"Not only that, I could know the hour, even the second. It would be like a radar detector, but for these shifter watches — and more exact."

Rialto was impressed. His mind was already racing with the possibilities. "How big would it be? It would only be useful to me if the device were small and portable, say the size of a cell phone."

"No problem. Detectors don't require much power. For me to develop this, though, would require a lot of funds."

"Done. So what was your solution to getting the watch off my wrist?"

"Hold on." Irvine rolled his chair back and opened a set of plastic drawers on top of his desk. He pulled out a cylindrically shaped piece of glass.

"I molded this from your other wrist. It's a glass cuff. I'm guessing the watch band constricts when it detects your body's electrical field. The fact that the watch loosens when a person dies would seem to confirm my hypothesis. From there, it was simple. Glass is a good insulator. I figure if we slip this cuff between your skin and the watch, it should no longer be able to detect your electrical field and will loosen."

"Let's try it."

Irvine clamped the cuff around Rialto's wrist and wriggled it underneath his watch band, which was not an easy feat due to the tight fit.

"Nothing's happening."

"It may be a timing issue. Perhaps it has to fail to detect your electric field for a short time before loosening."

"No, I've seen it happen before. It's always immediate."

Stanley involuntarily shuddered at the thought that Rialto might have been in a position to see such a thing happen more than once — and what that meant.

"I'll keep working on it," he said.

***

February 16th, 2013, Boston, MA

Savannah heard an odd noise coming from Mark's office. Eventually, worry overcame her reluctance to intrude. She gently pushed the door open a crack, hesitated, and then pushed it wider.

"Mark?"

He was crying. The back of his chair was all she could see, but she could hear him crying, and she knew what about. Laura.

"Just leave me alone." He sniffed, trying to hide it.

It had been several weeks since the altercation with Hardy, and more than a month since Laura had broken it off with him. She knew what Mark had gone through with the loss of his family. He always spoke of his children, but she knew wife's abandonment had hit him hard, more than even he realized. She'd always suspected his infatuation with Laura had been a subconscious desperation born of that pain. Losing Laura then had felt like he was losing Kelly all over again, made worse by the suspicion that one of his only friends in the world had betrayed him.

"Mark. You can't keep on like this."

"I'm fine."

"No, you're not, Mark. Let me help."

He swiveled his chair to face her. He was slumped low and his body looked very loose, his eyes puffy from crying. The odor of stale Whiskey filled her nose. He was drunk. He'd been drinking a lot lately.

"What would you do, Savannah? Have you ever had your heart broken before?"

His eyes were pleading. It was the weakest she'd ever seen him. Normally, Mark Carpen was a dominating, strong presence, but now, it seemed more than just his heart had been broken.

"Yes, I have." She went to him and held his head against her side, caressing his hair slowly in an effort to bring some comfort. "But Mark, you have to snap out of this. I'm afraid for you. You're spiraling down...."

"I know." He wiped at his eyes with his sleeves, pulling away from her. "You've been good to me, Savannah. You're a good friend."

She sat heavily in the chair across from him. "I haven't done anything."

"Yes, you have. You've been such a blessing....and I've just taken you for granted. How can I ever repay you?"

She blushed, but said nothing. He'd embarrassed her.

"Surely, there's something."

She whispered so softly he could barely hear it. "I just....it was nothing....you were in need."

"You stuck around when no one else did, not Ty, not...." He was going to say 'Hardy' but anger choked the name in his throat. "Surely, there's something I can do for you. Let me do something for you. It would help me feel better, I think."

"Stop drinking."

He took that like a slap, visibly hurt by how obvious his flaws had become. "Sure," he croaked, choking on emotion again. "That's a given. I'll do that. But what about you, what can I do for you?"

She looked hard and long into his beautiful, steel blue eyes. She knew what she wanted, but the fact that she couldn't have it was as obvious as the drunken tears Mark kept wiping from his face. Those tears were for Laura. Plus, what could a man like him find attractive in a mousy nobody like her.

"Nothing, I'm fine. Really. Just get better, okay?"

"Okay." He smiled for the first time in weeks. She was relieved to see that. She stood and walked out the door, back to her desk.

***

February 16th, 2013, Boston, MA

Rialto's plan was still in the rudimentary stages, but it was coming along nicely. A personal visit to his acquaintance, Tony McGuire, in the Boston FBI office provided him with a rough sketch of who the major players were in the Massachusetts mafia.

He was looking for a couple of men who were second tier leaders in that criminal enterprise. Men who were ambitiously seeking to rule, yet would never succeed due to a lack of opportunity or guts.

Stanley Graves was one such animal. He was the number two man in the Alcamo crime family. He was a very effective manager and his strategic maneuvering had increased the Alcamo family's status and position significantly. Yet, he was not a naturally charismatic leader. Men did not feel inclined to follow him, and when the current Alcamo head passed on, it was known the eldest Alcamo son would take the lead, whether he was fit or not, and not Graves. Graves not being Italian didn't help either.

Rialto had approached him delicately. Once the subject had been broached and Rialto had dissipated the man's incredulity with a demonstration, Graves had gladly signed on. He knew his future was limited with the Alcamos, and Rialto was offering him unlimited possibilities in fulfilling his avaricious ambition, and all without the inconvenience of having to get other men to follow him. The shifter would also allow Graves to leave the mafia without violent repercussions. They couldn't kill him if they couldn't find him.

Once Irvine the physicist was done studying the second watch, Rialto gave it to Graves, who would work for him for the next sixteen years until Rialto killed him. Sixteen years would pass for Graves between now and then, but Rialto didn't have to wait that long. Immediately, after giving Graves the shifter, Rialto shifted forward to the year 2029. He approached his employee at home one evening and killed him, just as he had Ty. Taking Graves' loosened shifter off his dead body, Rialto then returned to 2013.

Vincent Torino was a mercenary. Hit man would be a better term, actually, but he didn't work for any one crime family. He freelanced his services to whoever needed him, which was a neat trick in the world of the *mafiosos*. His continued existence meant he was either very successful in keeping his hits from being associated with him, or every family was so intimidated by him that they just left him alone.

Rialto guessed Torino would be excited about the opportunities a time-travel device could bring, and he was right.

Torino also accepted the shifter and professed permanent commitment to Rialto's team as part of the deal.

Rialto was establishing his primary base of operations in that industrial complex down in Baltimore where Irvine had his lab so he could always be near DC, but he was developing a secondary one here in Boston. His prime target was here, so they needed to be close.

He had asked Torino and Graves to meet him in this abandoned warehouse for an initial briefing. These men would be hard to control, not being governed by the normal ethics of most. They would be somewhat bound to him by common desires and criminal ambitions, but Rialto needed an extra assurance of their faithfulness.

"Gentlemen, I'll be brief," he said. "I am not here to control you or limit your achievement. These shifters are yours to use for your own pleasure, but when I call, you respond. We will work together on certain common endeavors."

"And if we don't?" Graves asked.

"Look over there. See that shifter?" Rialto pointed to a gray colored device on a table approximately thirty feet away. They nodded. It was actually a plastic mock up of a shifter, but it looked real enough. He'd had Irvine create it specifically for this meeting. Neither Graves nor Torino had any way of knowing it was a non-functional copy.

Rialto held up a triggering device and made a point of letting them see him depress a button in its center. An explosion immediately ripped through the table, cutting it in half and disintegrating the fake shifter.

Both men stumbled from their seats as the shock wave hit them. From that distance, it wasn't a big enough explosion to hurt anybody, but it was clear that if someone had been wearing the watch, they would be dead.

"Each of your shifters has an explosive device like that one embedded in its core," he lied. "I have the triggers."

Both men glared. They were neatly trapped in his snare and they knew it.

"And we can't get these things off, can we?" Torino growled.

"Sorry. I should also mention that my own device has an extra feature. If my body should become lifeless, my shifter automatically sends an activating signal to all other shifters, detonating them. So, it *is* in your best interest to make sure I stay alive."

They were not happy. In fact, they were seething, but they'd simmer down eventually and get used to it. He wouldn't push them too hard. He'd help them make millions, billions even. Heck, he'd just give it to them. That would make up for some of their anger. When the time was right, he'd make them work.

In the meantime, he needed to get done with this meeting so he could shift forward to 2029 and kill Torino. He was just lending them these shifters after all, even if they didn't know it yet.

Chapter 41

April 17th, 2013, Boston, MA

Mark rubbed his temples vigorously, staring at the financial statement in front of him. Something was definitely off. He'd thought his accounts were a little low last month when he'd gotten the summaries from his accountant. This time, however, there was no doubt.

His total net worth should have been somewhere around $25 billion. This month's financials showed only $21 billion. He checked the previous month's summary. It also showed around $21 billion. *Yet, he distinctly remembered $25 billion.* Somehow four billion dollars had disappeared.

Mark snatched the phone receiver from its base.

"Savannah?"

"Yes, Mark?"

"Get Ty on the phone for me, please. I need to see him right away."

***

"What's up, Mark?"

Ty sat opposite Mark in his office dressed in casual slacks and a polo shirt. He was slouched comfortably, hands laced behind his head.

"Something's wrong with my accounts."

"What do you mean 'something's wrong'?" Ty asked.

"We're missing some money."

"How much?"

"Roughly $4 billion."

Ty let out a low whistle. "That ain't chump change. Did someone steal it?"

"No....I don't think someone stole it....at least not this year."

"What do you mean?"

"I'm supposed to have around $25 billion all together. My latest statement, which just arrived, only showed a net worth of $21 billion. If it'd been stolen or embezzled, previous statements would still show the $25 billion, but they don't. They also show $21 billion."

"Maybe you're just remembering wrong."

"Could be. At least, I could be wrong if I wasn't so sure about the fact that I had $25 billion, not $21. Plus, last month, I thought the accounts were slightly lower than I expected, but it wasn't enough of a difference to be sure. This time, though, I'm sure."

Ty asked, "How do you explain the previous statements matching this month's, then?"

"For the sake of argument, let's say something happened in the past to change the outcome of one of my financial transactions, which would affect the whole of my portfolio, say to the tune of four billion dollars. Now, let's say this change happened twenty years ago. How would we perceive that change in history today?"

Ty's face lit as he suddenly grasped what Mark was saying. "Well, you would remember things as they had been, since we always seem to remember the way things were before we change them, but all the financial statements in your filing cabinets would instantly be altered to reflect the financial history they represent. Any change in the past would be virtually undetectable from documents or any other physical evidence. Your memory is the *only thing* you can rely on to know if you're supposed to have two dollars or two trillion dollars to your name.

"Exactly. Theoretically, if I'd written last month's balance on a napkin to compare with the statements later, what I'd written on the napkin would change as soon as the past changed."

"So, why aren't our memories affected this way?"

"I don't know."

They both fell quiet, processing this new set of mind-bending, time-travel hypotheses. Ty finally broke the silence.

"What are you suggesting, Mark? How can the past change by itself?"

"That's just it. It can't." He paused, preparing him for the full weight of what he was about to say. "The *only* way the past can change is if somebody with a shifter goes back and changes it."

"You don't think it was me, do you?"

"No."

"Please tell me you don't think it was Hardy."

Mark grimaced. "I guess it could have been, but no, I don't think it was Hardy."

"How could you know? You two parted company pretty steamed."

"I just know. There are things which haven't happened yet....I just know."

Ty gave him an odd look, wondering what that cryptic remark had meant.

"Then, what?"

"Somebody must have a shifter besides the three of us."

"How is that possible?"

"Same way we got ours? Maybe they found it. Who knows? Maybe whoever has the other shifter is the same person who left these shifters for me to find. There's no telling."

"You really think someone else has a shifter?"

"I don't know. It's either that or my memory has gone completely to pot."

"What if something we went back and changed happened to accidentally affect one of your past investments negatively?" Ty asked.

"Can you think of anything?"

"No..."

"I can't either."

"Then, how in the world will we figure it out?" Ty grumbled. "Do you mind if I take a look?" He motioned to the statements laying on Mark's desk. Mark nodded in assent.

Ty picked up one of the documents and studied it.

"Mark, this says $18 billion."

"What? Let me see that!" Mark snatched the statement out of Ty's hand, scanning it furiously.

"$18 billion," he whispered. "Someone else has a shifter, all right, and they're targeting us."

***

It hadn't taken Mark long to figure out which of his financial dealings had been attacked. Logically, for his net worth to drop so dramatically, some change had to have been made early in his wealth building process. Recent changes wouldn't affect the overall balances that much. It was like following a compass that was one degree off. In short distances, the error wouldn't affect your path significantly, but over a great distance, the difference would be huge.

Luckily, he remembered and was familiar with most of the early enterprises he'd entered into. To lose more than 25% of his net worth in two fell swoops, Mark took a guess that a change would have to have taken place in his accounts prior to the 1980's. So, he studied his financial summaries dating before then. Most of the stocks he remembered purchasing were still on record.

There it was. Absent from his real estate holdings were the properties he'd bought in Atlanta prior to 1970. He'd purchased a number of what would one day be prime commercial real estate in two communities he knew would experience explosive growth after 1980, Buckhead and Midtown. After 1984, he'd begun selling those properties at a tremendous profit. Whether or not those sales had been the seed for 25% of his wealth, he didn't know. He couldn't recall the original sales prices, or even how many there had been.

He was pretty sure that something else had been changed too though. His accounts had first dropped to $21 billion, and then to $18 billion. That seemed to indicate two changes to what he'd done, but for the life of him, he couldn't find the other change.

With $18 billion in the bank, it wasn't like their operation was going to start struggling any time soon, but if some mischievous person with a shifter could drop him by that much so easily, then the guy could take everything if Mark let it go unchecked. They had to do something about this and fast.

He and Ty had arranged to meet later that afternoon, so Mark waited until he got back.

"Do you want me to go with you?" Ty asked.
"Not yet. I'm just going to do some preliminary investigation work. It'll be less conspicuous if I go alone. Stick around, though, because as soon as I figure out who's doing this, I'll need your help. If somebody's got a shifter, they'll shift out as soon as they see us. We have to take them by surprise and pin their arms behind their back."

Ty nodded. "What'll we do with them then?"

"Not sure. Bring 'em back here and question them, I guess."

***

All of those real estate dealings had been done through one real estate agency in Atlanta. He'd bought up the properties between 1955 and 1970 and begun selling in 1984. None of those sales were showing up now on his financials, and tax records from Fulton County were no longer in his files.

He'd personally sat in on some of those closings and knew he'd received copies of deeds, etc. There was no doubt he'd purchased the properties. The question was why Fulton County suddenly had no record of them.

Visiting his Atlanta real estate agency, they were quickly able to provide him with records showing that as far as they knew, he had in fact purchased the lots through them. So, that part of history hadn't changed. Checking further into his own files, he'd found copies of the deeds he'd received after the closings.

Understanding dawned. Someone in the County Clerk's office had to have illegally altered the records of all his properties.

He went to the Fulton County Clerk's office and checked the deeds on file for the properties he could remember off the top of his head. Of the three properties he could easily recall, two showed they were owned by an unfamiliar corporation at the time when he should have been the owner. A third was registered to a different company, but further investigation revealed that both those corporations had the same parent company. After that, he hit a wall. The registered owner of the parent company was one John Smith.

Whoever "John Smith" was, he was the man Mark was after. This Smith had a shifter and he must have bribed one of the employees of the County Clerk's office to change the names on the deeds. Must have been a pretty big bribe too. Mark was sure altering official real estate records would carry a stiff penalty, and it was an easily detectable crime.

Research revealed a possible culprit. A young man by the name of Jeffrey Wilson had worked in the Clerk's office until 1971, and then abruptly quit. Circumstantial evidence indicated that was the year the last change had been made to Mark's property records.

If Mark was going to identify "John Smith", he was going to have to stake out Jeffrey Wilson.

Chapter 42

March 23rd, 1971, Atlanta, GA

It was a nice spring day in late March and pear trees were blossoming throughout Atlanta, though a crisp breeze made the air a bit chillier than one would hope.

"Fill me in," Ty said.

He sat next to Mark on a bench in a small park across the street from a sidewalk café in downtown Atlanta.

"That young man over there in the brown tweed jacket is Jeff Wilson. He works at the Fulton County Clerk's office. I'm pretty sure our mysterious shifter is going to meet him here for lunch and give Wilson a envelope full of cash so Wilson will falsify the deed records to some of my properties, illegally putting them in the names of other corporations. Later this afternoon, Wilson will deposit $100,000 into his checking account, which is a *lot* of money for a county clerk in 1971. Two weeks from now, the young man will flee the country and live in Mexico for the rest of his life."

"What's the plan?"

"Just in case this Smith knows our faces, we'll keep a low profile. We'll wait until he shows up for the meeting, then follow, and try to catch him by surprise."

"Do you think it's smart for us to be sitting together on this bench?"

"Why not? We're far enough away."

"Dude, a black man and a white man sitting together on a bench in Atlanta in 1971 ain't keeping a low profile."

"Ah....sorry."

"I'll shift back and get some beat up clothes. I can hang out in that alley over there and pretend to be a bum."

"All right."

After a while, John Smith showed up as they'd hoped, but somehow he must have spotted Mark. No sooner had he sat down than he glanced Mark's way and bolted, racing off down the street. Instantly, Mark was on his feet in full pursuit.

Smith turned sharply down the alleyway where Ty had been waiting, but the speed at which everything happened caught Ty off guard, which allowed Smith to momentarily slip past him.

"Ty!" Mark yelled. He was still too far away to do any good.

Ty recovered quickly and turned. He would gain on Smith in a matter of seconds. Suddenly, a short burst of static electricity crackled, and Smith disappeared before their eyes.

Mark arrived at Ty's side, stopped and rested his hands on his knees in an attempt to catch his breath. They exchanged looks.

"Looks like we were right," Mark panted, "We've got another shifter on our hands."

***

April 22nd, 2013, Boston, MA

When they arrived back at ChronoShift headquarters, Mark rechecked his financial statements. His net worth was back up to $22 Billion. They hadn't been successful in identifying Smith, but it appeared they had permanently messed up the fraudulent real estate records plan. Jeff Wilson wouldn't flee to Mexico with a hundred grand in his pocket; he'd be a clerk for the rest of his life.

"So, how do we find this guy now?" Ty asked.

"I'm still missing another $3 Billion. That means he's sabotaged me at least once more at some point in the past."

Mark breathed in deep the aroma of fresh coffee filling their office suite. Savannah had just made a fresh pot. She was using a new brewing method she called Melitta, which was basically a manual pour over, but it certainly made a delicious cup of java. He was going to need that coffee because he'd be up late tonight pouring over his various records and statements looking for something that might have been altered.

"Do have any idea where?"

"No. I already tried to figure it out once, but I didn't notice anything else amiss. I'm going to have to go through my records with a fine toothed comb. It's lucky for us this guy's acted more than once, or we wouldn't know where to find him at all now. *When* to find him, I mean."

"Why is he targeting you, Mark? Any idea?" Ty rubbed his forehead vigorously with the heel of his hand as if trying to stimulate clearer thinking.

"No. I really don't."

"Is he just trying to get our attention or is he trying to hurt us?"

"Your guess is as good as mine. We'll ask him when we find him."

"All right." Ty stood. "I'll be back."

"Where are you going? Aren't you going to help?"

"Nah. First of all, I'm hungry. Second, you're the only one who would be able to tell which investment is missing from your accounts. I've got no idea what you did or didn't do."

"True."

"You want me to bring you something?"

"Sure, get me a cheeseburger."

Late that night, Mark finally found it. It took a while to notice what was missing because it wasn't just one thing. It was a number of different stock purchases. At first, it seemed like only a couple of stocks were missing from his portfolio. Stocks he'd purchased in the 1960's. The connection between them hadn't been obvious right away.

Then, he remembered that he'd purchased both stocks from a firm called Hodges & Tomlin. That little tidbit had brought to memory a few more stocks he remembered buying through the same firm at the same time. None of those stocks showed up in his files either. He'd probably bought a total of about 15 different stocks through Hodges & Tomlin, but nothing involving that firm showed up at all now.

He decided "Smith" must have bribed someone in the stock firm to forge documents like he had at the County Clerk's office in Atlanta. Doing some rough calculations, Mark guesstimated that those stock purchases and the profits from them had resulted in about $3 Billion over the last 40 years. Thankfully, it appeared that was the extent of the damage Smith had wrought so far, but if they didn't stop the man soon, Mark would be spending all his time fixing whatever Smith undid.

The tricky part was going to be catching the guy.

"How do you wanna run it, Mark?"

"We need to figure that out. This guy obviously knows my face, but I don't know him from Adam."

"Yeah, and he ran too. That probably means he wasn't just trying to get our attention."

"That's the logical conclusion."

"And he's got a shifter." Ty leaned back in his chair.

"What are you thinking?"

"This guy's got a shifter and he's out to do you harm. He knows we're onto him, and there's nothing preventing him from setting up an ambush for us at Hodges & Tomlin. He's already caused a change there, so he knows we're going to investigate."

"But he doesn't know *when* we're going to investigate."

"True. But it wouldn't be hard for him to figure out."

"All right. So what do you propose?" Mark asked.

"Since we're not sure he knows my face, I'll go back first and do basic reconnaissance from a distance. If it's all clear, I'll come back and get you."

Mark agreed to the plan. They went back to 1967, a couple of weeks after Mark had opened his trade account with

Hodges & Tomlin. None of the stock brokers remembered Mark, however, and they had no paper record of his account. He and Ty tried again one day after the stocks should have been purchased, but there was still no record of his having done business with the firm. Same result when they tried the same day as the purchase. Not to mention, they hadn't seen hide nor hair of Smith surveilling them during any of the visits.

Frustrated, they returned to headquarters.

"Looks like we're back to square one."

Mark rubbed the back of his head.

"I don't get it. I know I bought stocks at that firm. Somehow, he must have stopped me from ever arriving there with the money."

"Where'd you get the money?" Ty asked.

Mark's face lit up. "From a bet."

"What bet?"

"A horse race. I bet $10,000 on a long shot named Willful Destiny. The odds were 30 to 1, but of course, I knew he was going to win. I used the winnings to buy the stocks at Hodges & Tomlin."

"So, maybe something changed? Something that caused a different horse to win?"

"We'll have to do some research."

"Why don't you just google it?"

"How do you know about Google?"

"I'm not such a neophyte to the good ol' 21st century anymore, man. I've learned some things."

Mark laughed and turned to his computer. In just a few minutes, he found what they were looking for.

"Bingo. Take a look at this." He swiveled the computer screen so Ty could see it. Mark had found a site where someone had posted a pdf of an old newspaper article on the race.

Racehorse Murdered!

The final race yesterday at the Fairfield Commons was tragically aborted when one of the racehorses was shot and killed in mid-stride. Willful Destiny had not been a favorite of betters, having been a longshot to win with odds of more than 30 to 1.

Within the first minute after the race began, a single bullet struck Willful Destiny in the head, killing the horse instantly. The race was brought to a halt before finishing. Police reported that the assassination of the equine appeared to be the work of a lone sniper. They currently have no leads as to his identity. All bets for the race were returned to the betters.

There was more to the article, but nothing of relevance to them.

"I guess we know what happened now, huh?"

"Yeah — and we know he's got a gun."

Ty didn't look worried. "We'll just be a little more careful is all."

Chapter 43

"Where's he at?" Mark asked.

"There and....there." Ty pointed to a roof overlooking the track's bleachers and then to a wooded hill closer to them. Mark could see the prone figure of a man in both places.

"Both those men are him?"

"Yes. He's got an ambush set up for us. He originally shot the horse from his position on the roof. After we interrupted his lunch in Atlanta, he must have realized we were on his trail and come back here to set up an ambush further away there in woods. Most likely, he's got a sniper rifle and from the woods, he's planning to let loose on anyone who makes a move on his rooftop position before his previous self kills the horse. He's essentially providing his earlier self with cover.

"Well, let's not keep him waiting."

Mark and Ty's special forces training had taught both of them to move silently through brush and forest, so they had no trouble sneaking up on Smith from behind. Both carried assault rifles and holstered pistols.

They were twenty yards away when a startled quail suddenly burst up in a flurry of wings. Smith whirled at the noise and turned to face them. Whipping up his rifle, Ty drew a bead on Smith and yelled "Freeze!" Mark rushed the man at a dead run.

But it was too late. Smith was gone. He'd had no desire to duke it out with Mark and Ty on fair terms, so he had shifted out as soon as he'd seen them, and there was no way to chase him. Apparently, the guy wasn't going to risk a confrontation where he didn't have the element of surprise. Mark didn't blame him.

Nabbing a fellow time shifter was going to be a very difficult....and a very *dangerous* task. Unfortunately, they had the disadvantage. Smith knew where and when to find them, but they had no idea how to find him.

***

April 24th, 2013, Boston, MA

"How can you eat that stuff, man?" Ty grimaced.

They were sitting at a local McDonald's and Mark was stuffing his face with fries. Ty had already finished his salad.

"This is how." Mark smiled and lifted another bunch of fries to his mouth.

Ty laughed, and then the conversation took a lull. After a minute Ty asked, "Mark, are you ever gonna forgive Hardy?"

Mark's face darkened at the mention of his name.

"No," he growled. "How can I? Even if I could, I don't want to. And I certainly can't ever trust him again."

"You can't hold a grudge forever, you know. We were a team. I hate to see that broken up over a girl."

Mark glared. "We aren't a team now, and that's all there is to it."

"Yeah, but Hardy's the only other guy we know that has a shifter. We could use his help to...."

Ty didn't finish his sentence.

After a couple of seconds, Mark looked up to see why, but Ty was gone. His first thought was that Ty was playing games and had shifted out, but Ty's tray and empty salad bowl were missing. He could have taken them with him, but this was a pretty stupid joke if it was one.

Alarmed, Mark jumped to his feet. Where *did* Ty go? He realized he hadn't heard the customary static pop that always accompanies a shift.

Frantically, Mark checked the bathroom and the parking lot. Ty wasn't the only thing missing. Mark's car was gone too.

Come to think of it, Mark felt kind of odd himself. Looking down, he didn't recognize the clothes he was wearing. His outfit was outlandish, right out of the 1970's. It certainly wasn't what he'd put on this morning. He dropped his hands to his pockets and to his dismay discovered that both his wallet and keys were missing. He still had his shifter though. That, at least, lowered his growing panic back down a notch.

A worn backpack sat on the bench where he'd been. It suspiciously looked like his old backpack, the one he'd carried into the mountains. He unzipped its side. Therein lay two shifters. Two *unused* shifters.

***

Mark was beyond annoyed. He was jaws-clenched, temples-throbbing angry. Smith had gone too far this time. Somehow he'd traced Mark's history far enough back that he'd been able to undo everything Mark had done since coming out of the Georgia mountains.

The two shifters in Mark's backpack meant that the history where he'd sought out Hardy and Ty to be a part of his team had been undone. Ty was dead in Vietnam. Hardy was.....well, Hardy was still in Delta back in the 1980's.

The fact that his wallet was gone could only mean that so was the wealth he'd accumulated. All of it. The loss of all that money didn't bother him that much; he could earn it back.

What really got him steaming was the work it represented. It had taken months and months to get everything set up the way he wanted. Now, he'd have to go back and redo everything. He'd have to rehire Hardy & Ty, relive all the conversations he'd had with them. He'd have to rehire Savannah, have all those costumes remade along with everything else. The first time it had been fun, now it would just be annoying.

Mark guessed what Smith had done. There was only one thing he *could* have done to erase it all in one fell swoop. Somehow, Smith must have interfered with Mark's first purchase of Wal-Mart stock. The sale of that stock had singlehandedly launched Mark out of poverty and into financial independence. That was the only thing Smith could have messed with that would have affected absolutely everything else Mark had built.

He had to get back to Georgia. He pulled his pockets inside out. Penniless, again. At least he'd just eaten.

Nope, a sharp hunger pain canceled that thought. *Great.* He'd had no wallet, so there had been no lunch with Ty.

No car, no house, not one thing outside of whatever he'd originally had in that dad-blamed backpack and he'd eaten the last beef jerky he'd had in there right about the time he'd found the shifters. He would have to hitchhike and find other creative means to support himself until he could get to Lawrenceville.

He wasn't going to redo everything from scratch. Instead, he would find a way to undo the undoing Smith had wrought. And this time, he'd make sure Smith didn't mess with him again.

***

A little begging, a lot of thumbs stuck out on two-lane highways, and a few creative time-travel, money-making schemes, and Mark made it back in Lawrenceville. He figured out what had happened pretty fast. Smith had robbed Brand Bank one night after hours, and the employees of the bank had found him locked in the vault the next morning. Which puzzled Mark. Why hadn't Smith just shifted out of the vault?

Of course, the police didn't find any money on him and were baffled by how he could have gotten inside in the first place. The only thing Smith wanted, however, were the Wal-Mart shares in Mark's safe deposit box.

The newspaper account reported that Smith had escaped from police custody immediately after being arrested, so finding him outside the bank wasn't an option.

Mark could remove the shares from the box before Smith got to them, but he wanted to catch the man red-handed. He wasn't about to let him slip away again and repeat his frustrating meddling.

Most likely, Smith didn't "break in" to the bank's vault as much as he had shifted in. So, Mark did the same.

It was midnight, and the scene was a bit confusing. The bank's power had been cut, and the entire building was shrouded in pitch black darkness. Inside the vault, Smith sat cross-legged in a corner, illuminated by the weak glow of a flashlight. Mark had his own flashlight, which he swiftly brought to bear on Smith in synchronized movement with his pistol.

Smith looked to be of Italian descent. He had a strong, angular nose and thick, dark eyebrows which matched the almost black sheen of his coarse hair. Charred fragments of paper littered the floor at his feet. The smell of recent smoke filled Mark's nostrils.

"You didn't!" Mark cried. He knew those fragments could only be the shares he was seeking.

"I did," Smith replied dryly, glaring.

"The newspaper didn't mention anything about you burning my shares!"

Smith shrugged. He didn't seem especially riled or surprised by Mark's appearance. Which made Mark even madder.

"You...." Mark was ready to spit. "What's you real name?" he demanded.

Smith grinned cockily. "Wouldn't you like to know."

Mark steadied his pistol and took aim. He needed to be careful. He was so angry he might lose control, kill the guy, and then he wouldn't learn anything. Not to mention the guy technically hadn't done anything worthy of being shot....yet.

"Where's your shifter?" The guy's wrists were bare of any device. "How'd you get in here if you didn't shift?"

"I did shift." He squirmed, finally looking a bit uncomfortable.

"Then, where'd it go? I haven't found a way to get mine off."

"It was an unforeseen consequence of me burning your shares."

"Huh?"

"You want your shares back?"

"Yes."

"Shift back to 9:43 PM. Have your pistol ready and threaten me with it when I try to burn your shares."

"Are you crazy?"

"9:43 PM."

Mark's jaw trembled. It could be a trick, but if it was, he could just return to this time and catch the guy again. He reset his watch and shifted.

Smith was standing now, Mark's shares in one hand, a lighter already flaming in the other, ready to ignite them at any second.

"Drop the lighter! Now!"

This time, Smith was seriously startled by the sudden appearance of an armed man screaming at him. He dropped the lighter and it self-extinguished. Smith recovered from the surprise and reached for his shifter.

"Oh no, you don't!" Mark leapt onto him, and in one swift motion they were wrestling for control of Smith's arm. The guy had more wiry strength than it appeared. He kneed Mark in the groin, and during the momentary lapse in concentration the pain caused, Smith freed his wrist and shifted out of the vault to an unknown time.

Mark scooped up the discarded shares from the floor, happy that at least he'd just returned his life to normal with minimal effort.

Slowly, realization of the opportunity he'd just missed crept into his mind.

What an idiot.

He wanted to slap himself. It didn't matter if the shares had been burned. Mark could have always scrounged up a little money to buy some more and redone that work.

The shares were nothing compared to stopping Smith. He'd just had Smith in his sights, trapped, unarmed, and *without a shifter!*

Somehow, the burning of the shares had caused Smith's shifter to disappear from off his wrist. By preventing their fiery destruction, Mark had inadvertently allowed Smith to keep his shifting capabilities and get away. He should have let him rot in jail without a shifter and just bought more shares. That would have ended it. Now, he was back to square one in trying to find the guy.

He patted his back pocket and was relieved to feel his wallet had returned. Ty was probably back at headquarters in Boston now. At least everything was back to normal for the time being.

He was about to leave by shifting out of the vault when he noticed a scrap of paper on the floor. Realizing it had likely fallen from Smith's pocket, he picked it up. Its scribblings were cryptic. He needed to get back to the office and see what they could make of it. It might be a worthwhile clue.

Chapter 44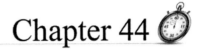

IN finite
terlock

L-04-14-65 L.H.O.
K-11-22-63 J.W.B.

"Do you have *any* idea what it means?"

"Not a clue," Ty answered.

They'd been studying the thing for hours with no breakthroughs. The best guess so far was that it was some kind of technical specs for something. Maybe for the shifters? Was Infinite Interlock the name of the company that made the shifters? Was Smith affiliated with them? Was he now trying to eliminate Mark because Mark was never supposed to have gotten a hold of a shifter in the first place?

"We need to take a break, get a fresh perspective," Mark said.

Just then, Savannah came in with a couple of cups of steaming coffee.

"Savannah, your timing is impeccable, as always. Some coffee would help a lot right now," he paused, "Hey, would you take a look at this? We can't make heads or tails of it."

Coming closer, she pulled a delicate pair of glasses from her pocket.

"Hey, I thought you'd gone to contacts."

"Uh....yeah, but not today." She scrutinized the paper on the desk. "Seems pretty straight forward to me."

"What do you mean?"

"It's the Lincoln and Kennedy assassinations, but the assassins are mixed up."

"Huh?"

"The L-04-14-65. That's short for 'Lincoln - April 14, 1865'. But the initials following it are for Lee Harvey Oswald, Kennedy's assassin. The second line is 'Kennedy - Nov. 22, 1963' followed by the initials of Lincoln's killer, John Wilkes Booth."

Dates! By now, Mark should be an expert at spotting dates in unusual formats, yet somehow he hadn't seen it.

"You're right. There's nothing else it could be."

She beamed.

"So what's the Infinite Interlock mean?"

"Not sure. Maybe it's a reference to all the historical coincidences between Lincoln and Kennedy."

"What coincidences?"

"Well, some people have identified all kinds of 'connections' between the lives of Lincoln and Kennedy, especially with regard to their assassinations. Some of the connections are kind of silly, like both of their names having seven letters.

"But there's other things, like the fact Lincoln was first elected to the House of Representatives in 1846, Kennedy in 1946. Lincoln was elected President in 1860, Kennedy in 1960. Their parties' conventions those years were both held in Chicago.

"They both had Vice-Presidents named Johnson. Both were concerned about Civil Rights. Both lost a child while in the White House. Kennedy had an advisor named Lincoln who warned him not participate in the motorcade. Lincoln supposedly had an advisor named Kennedy who warned him not to go to the theater, though there isn't much evidence of that. Both Presidents were shot in the head, on a Friday, in the presence of their wives.

"Both assassins were southerners and killed before going to trial. Booth killed Lincoln at a theater and was caught in a warehouse. Oswald killed Kennedy from a warehouse and was caught in front of a theater. Oh, and both assassins also have fifteen letters in their names."

Ty whistled. "Whew. Ask a question, get a mouthful."

Savannah blushed. "It's kind of a fun trivia type thing among historians."

"I think I remember reading something about that in middle school. What do you think all those coincidences mean?" Mark asked.

"I don't know. I've always just thought it was some funny quirk of history. Never treated it very seriously myself."

"Okay, thanks, Savannah."

"You're welcome." She dipped in a mock curtsy and left the office.

"Sure helps having an expert historian on the payroll, huh?" Ty said.

"Yeah, especially in our business."

"So....Smith dropped a scrap of paper containing cryptic info about two presidential assassinations. What is he planning, and what do we do about it?"

"We split up. One of us goes back to 1963, the other to 1865. We take a look around and see if we see Smith anywhere nearby."

"Sounds good. Which year do you want?"

"I think I'd have an easier time than you right after the Civil War. How about you take Kennedy, I'll take Lincoln," Mark offered.

"Done."

***

November 22nd, 1963, Dallas, TX

Investigating in Dallas in 1963 without arousing suspicion wasn't exactly an easy thing to do with Ty's skin color being what it was. Still, if you played it right, it could actually work to your advantage.

There was no way he would get close to the President. Security would be too tight. If there was need for a more in depth investigation, he would come back with Mark and have him pose as a secret service agent.

When was Mark going to forgive Hardy anyway? The three of them had made a pretty good team until Hardy had messed around with Laura. Ty had never liked the woman personally. He'd seen right through her from the start. He'd grown up with women like that. They were only after one thing: money.

It was all moot anyway. Hardy was with her now. Both his friends were blind to what she was, and neither would listen to him. Mark just needed to get over it for the sake of the company, for the sake of their friendship.

Ty decided the best way to begin would be to study the Kennedy motorcade as it passed by. He would observe the crowd and see if he could spot Smith anywhere.

He had to admit, though, it was exciting to think he was about to witness such an historic event firsthand. He'd only been nineteen when the assassination originally took place. He could still vividly remember the black and white images that had played over and over on small television screens around the world. Who could have imagined he would ever have the opportunity to rewind the years and see it up close like this? He would likely see it a number of times before he was done.

The presidential motorcade was now turning the corner from Houston Street onto Elm, where it would soon pass in front of the Book Depository and the Grassy Knoll. Ty's main task was to find Smith, so he kept the motorcade in the corner of his eye as he scanned the crowd.

Abruptly, his visual search came to a halt as his eyes fastened on a figure standing in the doorway of the Book Depository. The man wore an orangish-brownish shirt which was unbuttoned halfway, revealing a white T-shirt underneath.

His angular face looked *oddly* familiar. In fact, the man looked just like Oswald.

The cracks of rifle shots shattered the afternoon. Ty didn't think to look around and see where they were coming from, he was so fascinated by the Oswald look-alike. If that was Lee Harvey Oswald, then there was no way he had killed Kennedy. What if he'd really been a patsy like he'd claimed?

"Hello, Ty."

The voice was as unexpected as the gun in the man's hand. It wasn't Smith. Nor was it anyone else he knew, but somehow this man knew him.

Two other men grabbed Ty's shoulders from behind and pinned his arms. Where had they come from?

"Do *not* let him get either hand free, not even for a second." The gunman tossed some cable ties to the men.

"Cuff him. Then, take him into that building and down to the basement. Outside the utility entrance, there's a vehicle waiting. Give the driver this address." He reached around Ty to hand a slip of paper to one of the men. Ty used the opportunity to try and head butt the guy. If he could break free from the others' grip for a just moment, he would be able to shift out of trouble.

However, the gunman sensed the move and deftly dodged it. He reared back and slapped Ty across the face with the back of his hand. As he swung, his jacket cuff pulled up on his arm, and Ty caught a brief glimpse of dull pewter on his wrist. He had a shifter.

Ty felt a trickle of blood dribbling down his chin. "Who are you?" he growled.

The man ignored him. "You know what? Why take any chances?" He slammed the butt of his pistol down on the back of Ty's neck and knocked him out cold.

He must have been out for hours. The sun was much lower in the sky now — it was probably late afternoon. Ty was sitting on the cold floor of an abandoned warehouse. The plastic cable ties on his wrists were gone, replaced by a two pairs of metal handcuffs. The other ends of each were cuffed to two separate iron rails embedded above his head in the concrete wall at his back. The rails were about four feet apart, so there was no way for him to get either hand loose to shift.

"Well, there you are, Sleeping Beauty," a slimy, sing-songy voice cooed.

It was the same man who'd knocked him out. His thick hair was jet black, except for a single odd tuft of gray right above the brow.

Ty tried to respond with something coherent, but all he could manage was a low moan.

"Yeah, it'll probably take you a minute to recover. When you're ready, I'd love to fill you in on what we're going to do to you."

"Who are you?" Ty croaked.

"You asked me that before."

"I saw your shifter."

The man raised a hand to cover his mouth in mock surprise. "Oh no! You saw my shifter. How else do you think I would know who you are, idiot?"

Ty said no more.

"Ah, cat got your tongue now? No worry. It'll be over soon. You're too late to save the President anyway, if you were concerned about that.

"Don't hope for one of your friends to save you either. They may be able to jump through time like temporal kangaroos, but they can't save you if they don't know where you are.

"Tomorrow's newspapers are going to be filled with the tragic news of the assassination of John F. Kennedy, and no one will have time to worry about some black man showing up dead in an abandoned warehouse on the other side of town. Just to be safe though, we're going to make sure your body's never found.

"I've got some guys digging a trench outside right now. As soon as they finish, we're going to shoot you in the head and dump your body in the hole. Then, we're going to fill it back in with concrete. Ain't nobody gonna be the wiser, and your friends will never track down your whereabouts. How's that sound?" He smiled wickedly.

Ty grumbled unintelligibly.

"What was that?"

Ty spat at the man's feet.

"That's better."

Chapter 45

April 14th, 1865, Washington, D.C.

"Yes?"

"I have an appointment with the President."

"You must be Kennedy from the Department of the Interior?" The secretary was dressed sharply in striped gray pants and a black frock coat which ended just above the back of his knees. His vest and tie were a slightly darker gray. He spoke with a slight accent which sounded German.

"Er....Yes." Mark had bribed an official in the Department of the Interior to set this appointment up, but he hadn't known the man was going to choose the name Kennedy for him.

Sweat dripped from his palms and butterflies were doing somersaults in his stomach. With everything Mark had been through in his short life, it was hard to faze him, but today he was outdoing himself. He was about to meet the President of the United States. He was about to meet Abraham Lincoln.

He followed the male secretary down a series of halls that looked amazingly similar to the halls of the White House of his day. Most noticeably different was the absolute lack of any modern touches. No telephones, light switches, or exit signs. The light level in general was dimmer since the only source available was sunlight streaming through the window panes. Candles were positioned throughout the home, ready to be lit once evening neared.

They arrived at a large paneled door, and the secretary knocked. Another clerk inside the Oval Office opened it.

"Mr. Thomas Kennedy from the Department of the Interior to see the President."

"Thank you, John. Please show him in."

Gaunt was the best word Mark could come up with to describe Lincoln. He was tall and gangly, and sunken-in cheeks and eyes gave him an almost sickly appearance. The stress of the war was clearly visible in his visage. Yet, his eyes were bright and engaging. His physical presence was magnificently compensated for by his powerful personality.

His voice was a little higher than Mark had expected.

"Welcome, Mr. Kennedy. I don't believe we've met before." Lincoln extended his hand.

Mark shook it, still unbelieving that he was actually standing in the Oval Office shaking hands with Abraham Lincoln. "No, sir, we haven't."

"I understand they sent you over to speak with me about my reconstruction program for our southern neighbors."

"Yes, sir."

"Tell me, is there much support over at Interior for my plan?"

"I support it, sir."

"Those words are refreshing, I assure you. I've received such little support of late, truthfully, for the last five years, but I suppose one grows accustomed to opposition. Do your superiors support the plan?"

"It's doubtful, sir."

"That's more what I expected. The Radicals have extended their unsavory influence into all areas of the government it would seem. I can understand it. We've lost near half a million men fighting this bloody war. Most want to exact a terrible vengeance on our southern brothers for it."

"Yes, sir."

"The South has already paid a heavy enough price, as much as we have, more even. We must now heal and restore if we are to hope for the future of this Union."

"I think future historians will agree with you, sir."

A knock interrupted their conversation. The clerk opened the door, and the same male secretary poked his head in.

"Sir, sorry to interrupt, but Senator Sumner is here to see you on urgent business."

"Yes, I'll be right with him."

"Also, General Grant has sent his regrets that he will not be able to join you tonight at the theater."

"Fine." The secretary closed the door again. "Mr. Kennedy, I hope you'll forgive me for cutting our meeting short, but I have some things I must attend to before the evening."

He took Mark's hand and shook it.

"Mr. President, please do not go to the theater tonight."

Lincoln's smile froze. He gripped Mark's hand more firmly.

"That is an odd thing to say, young man."

"Please, sir. Don't go."

Lincoln looked Mark straight in the eye, holding his gaze without wavering for a full minute, searching for the meaning behind Mark's words. At last, he spoke.

"What will be, my son....*will be.*"

Then he was gone, down the hallway to meet the senator.

***

Mark wondered if the Lincoln assassination would be a "protected" event like the death of his own children. Something unable to be changed. He guessed it would be. If he were able to prevent Abraham Lincoln from being assassinated, it would theoretically change the entirety of American history which followed. Still, he wanted to try.

Whatever forces of the universe ruled such events proved his guess correct. The best and easiest way to stop the assassination was obviously to shift directly into Lincoln's box right before Booth burst in and fired the fatal shot. Mark tried numerous times to shift directly into the box, but his shifter wouldn't perform. Then, he tried right outside the box. When that didn't work, he tried immediately prior to the shooting, then several minutes before, then fifteen minutes before, but nothing worked. He couldn't get anywhere near Lincoln's box, anywhere close to the time of his death.

The shifter wasn't flashing red or anything. He could shift to other moments sufficiently distanced from the time of the shooting. The shifter just would not allow him anywhere near the vicinity of Lincoln or Booth in a way that he could prevent the shot.

Echoing through Mark's mind were Lincoln's last words to him. *"What will be, my son, will be."*

Mark waited for the fated event on the lower level of the theater. The play that night was *Our American Cousin*.

At 10:15, a shot rang out from the balcony level.

So hollow the sound of a great man's death.

The high-pitched screams of several women followed. The pandemonium was just beginning, most not having yet realized what that loud pop signified.

"Sic semper tyrannis!"

The shadowy figure of John Wilkes Booth leapt from Lincoln's box to the stage, catching what appeared to be his heel on one of the flags draping the box. More cries and shouts were heard now. Booth landed hard on the wooden stage, and stumbled. Mark knew from history books that Booth had just broken his leg.

For a moment, he considered pursuing Booth. He knew where Booth was headed. In fact, he could shift to right outside the door where Booth would escape and capture him. But why should he?

Booth wasn't much longer for this world anyway. In a short time, he would be cornered in a barn by a mob and killed. What would Mark's meddling gain?

No, if he couldn't stop the Lincoln assassination, he had only one purpose here, to find Smith. There was something Smith was planning around both the Lincoln and Kennedy assassinations. His only hope for figuring it out was to hang around and see if he spotted Smith anywhere and try to capture him.

Suddenly, a hand gripped Mark's wrist firmly, covering his shifter and preventing access to it. Mark instantly reacted to remove the man's hand, but the grip was like steel.

"You struggle and I'll start yelling you're part of this bloody conspiracy. You won't get your hands free before you're killed."

The speaker was dressed in the uniform of a theater usher. A glint of gray metal peeked from under his sleeve. He had a shifter, but he wasn't Smith. Someone else.

If glares could burn, the man's eyes would have been scalded from his head under Mark's stare. As it was, the usher didn't even blink.

"There's another man behind you, pointing a gun at your back. If your right hand moves anywhere near your left, he will put a bullet in your head long before you can shift out. Got it?"

Mark nodded.

"Good. Walk with me. We have a carriage waiting."

They pushed their way through the frantic and growing crowd to the exterior of the theater. A black carriage was parked curbside. The door opened from the inside as they approached. Mark stepped up to it and something slammed down hard on the back of his neck. Dark swirls swam before his eyes and then he blacked out.

He came to in a barn. At least, he figured it was a barn with the hay and other, more malodorous indicators laying around.

His head throbbed like a thumb that's just been pounded by hammer swung at full force. Struggling, he finally managed to sit up. Both his hands were tied with thick rope to opposite sides of a horse's stall. Smith sat on a stool in front of him about twenty feet away, a malicious glee illuminating his eyes. He was flanked by two strongmen. One of them was the usher from the theater — the one with the shifter. Mark couldn't tell if the third man had one or not.

"You were out pretty good there, Carpen. I was getting tired of waiting."

"*Smith!*" Mark hissed.

Smith threw his head back and laughed. "Yeah, I guess that's how you'd know me isn't it? I was never important enough to catch your attention before, was I?"

That was a cryptic comment.

"What is your real name then?"

"Rialto. That's all you really need to know. That and the fact that Ty Jennings is getting whacked right as we speak. Well, I guess he's actually getting whacked a hundred years or so from now. Time travel certainly twists one's concept of sequence of events, doesn't it?"

"You'll never get away with it. We'll see to that."

"I've *already* gotten away with it, don't you see? In a few minutes, you'll be dead. Ty's being taken care of too. Who else would stop us, or undo what we do here today? Hardy Phillips? Not likely. We've taken great lengths to make sure no one can find either of you. Even if he could, we'll get to him long before he figures out where to find you. It's a done deal."

Mark shook with rage.

"By the way, how'd you like our little trap? Did you honestly think that piece of paper fell from my pocket by accident? No, the whole bank thing was a lure. I knew you could simply shift around and undo it, or just go buy more shares, but I also knew you would want to try and find me.

"My shifter disappearing off my wrist was a glitch I hadn't foreseen. I'd originally intended to just leave the paper on the floor for you to find, but I was stuck once I'd burned the shares."

Mark had wondered about that before. "Why is that? — Smith, Rialto, or whatever your name is — Why did burning my shares cause your shifter to disappear?"

Something flashed behind Rialto's eyes.

He continued as if Mark hadn't spoken. "Anyway, it's a good thing for me you're so stupid. If I hadn't goaded you into shifting back and stopping me before I burned them, I would have been at your mercy. That was your one chance to get me, Carpen, and you missed it. *I* won't miss. That, I promise."

Mark glared, but Rialto ignored him, confident in his victory.

Rialto turned and instructed Mr. Usher. "Once I've gone, shoot him. Make sure it's in the head."

"What do you want me to do with the body?"

"Bury it in the woods. Do it far from here and deep in the ground. We don't want any animals digging him up. As long as the body is never found, no one can ever come back and save him. Oh, and don't forget to get his shifter once he's dead. We don't want to bury that."

End of Book 1
Chronoshift Trilogy

Want a peek at a Secret Chapter?

The author has installed a secret chapter on ChronoShift's website that can only be viewed there.

1. Go to www.Chrono-Shift.com
2. Use the same login give earlier in this book and click on "Search Archives".
3. Enter a search for "Chapter X".
4. Follow the instructions.

Don't forget to look for the next installment of the ChronoShift Trilogy

Chase

Coming Soon - 2012

CPSIA information can be obtained at www.ICGtesting.com
Printed in the USA
LVOW08s2004030114

367758LV00002B/5/P